Special thanks to the following without whose help this book would have not been possible:

The Judge, my Mentor, for giving me the courage to write; My husband Bobby who read, re-read, had confidence in me and loved me; and my new friend Rande whose artwork has wrapped this book in its proper package.

Louisanna and The Lopsided Kingdom

Myra F. Dingle

WestBow
PRESS
A DIVISION OF THOMAS NELSON

WestBow Press books may be ordered through booksellers or by contacting:

WestBow Press
A Division of Thomas Nelson
1663 Liberty Drive
Bloomington, IN 47403
www.westbowpress.com
1-(866) 928-1240

Cover Artwork © Rande Hanson.

All images used with permission © Paperwhimsy.com

ISBN: 978-1-4497-5216-3 (sc)
ISBN: 978-1-4497-5218-7 (hc)
ISBN: 978-1-4497-5217-0 (e)

Library of Congress Control Number: 2012909168

Printed in the United States of America

WestBow Press rev. date: 07/27/2012

Just because it comes in dreams and visions doesn't mean it isn't real.

1

My given name is Mary Margaret Louisanna Broadclothe, but I have always been called Louisa except by my grandmamma, who always calls me Louisanna because that was her mother's name, and it is very important to my grandmamma. Nimee is what I call Grandmamma simply because it is easier to say, and that is what I have always called her.

I wonder why I have so many names that I am never called. My mother would tell me if I could ask her, but she is not here. Neither is my father. My father died in a war. He was an honorable, high-ranking soldier, or so I have been told. Like so many other women, my mother had a hard birth with me and only lived until I was three months old.

Asking Nimee why no one calls me by Mary or Margaret would do no good. I have asked her and I get a new sensational reason every time. The older she gets the more thrilling and unbelievable the stories are. Some people say Nimee is eccentric, and others say she is a little off her rocker. Nimee is very different from other grandmas I have met—I can tell you that! She lives as she pleases, does what she wants to do, and often sees and hears things others cannot. Cerena says Nimee has a gift of seeing between this world and the next and that the gift runs in our family.

Cerena is not your normal sort of nanny. For one thing, she knows more about the solutions to any problem than any person should, and has the largest heart in the entire world. Her brown skin is so soft you could believe it is chocolate mousse, she always tells the truth, she never breaks her promises, and the only thing that makes her sad is that she truly misses Africa. All of her family is still there except her husband, Eli, and me, of course. I know Cerena considers me her own family because she calls me *babo,* which means "baby" or "my child" in her language.

Eli manages the men and their wives who tend the grounds of Nimee's house. The grounds are more like a huge, fancy garden than a yard. The annual plants as well as the seasonal beds have to be flowering all year round. Eli sculpts and trims the live figurines himself. My favorites are the hedgehogs I stumble over when I am not paying attention. Without a doubt, the largest and most important sculpture is the personification of the angel Michael, which stands in the middle of the grand garden. Eli learned to be a plant sculptor when he was a young boy in Africa, where he lived and worked with his family on a plantation. To the best of my understanding, a plantation is the biggest farm in the world.

Nimee tells everyone that Eli has done a fine job of getting the grounds back in order since we arrived here from New Delhi early this spring. We have lived all over the world because Nimee will just pick up and move us to her next favorite place to visit, and we will stay there for several months or sometimes years. Our last home was in New Delhi, India.

In New Delhi, our house was much smaller, but in spite of that, we came here with so many trunks that you would not believe it! Of course, Nimee wears only the best clothes and she changes for every meal, including tea. She never puts the same dress on two days in a row or two *weeks* in a row, as far as I can tell.

Our house here on the island is so big that you could get lost in it. There are many halls, stairways, floors, and rooms. Nimee and others on our island believe that our house is inhabited by spirits. I asked Cerena if that meant it was haunted, but she did not know how to answer that.

My room is really four rooms all put together. I really love my room in this house, especially the window seat where I can read and look out at the morning sun. My bed is much like the one I had in my room in New Delhi. It is very high off the floor. Nimee describes me as petite. I need a stool to get into my bed, but what's wrong with that? Once I'm in, I feel safe, all cuddled up and like a fairy princess. Cerena says the angels watch over me when I sleep. I am glad she says that, and hope it is true, because my dreams are full of all sorts of creatures that are not angels! The dreams come more often since we arrived here and I've begun to wonder why.

2

One thing my Nimee likes to do—and has enough room and help to do—is to host parties. Our house has two very large dining rooms, three drawing rooms, two conservatories, and a ballroom. We have two kitchens as well—one for everyday cooking and the other for preparing meals for special occasions, like dinner parties and dances.

Sometimes I wonder where all the people who come to our parties live. I have never seen many of them anywhere, though I have met a few at church. There are no houses within miles of ours, unless you count the lopsided house on the green hill.

Although my Nimee has no husband, she is an independent woman who does not mind—and might in fact prefer—socializing in perfect taste on her own. She is known as a gracious hostess wherever she goes, despite her eccentricities. Nimee expects me to act like a lady at all times, even if she is a little off-kilter herself.

It was on the first of these many occasions—the night of Nimee's first party, —which was a dinner and dance celebrating Nimee's return to the island, that I visited the Lopsided Kingdom and the house on the green hill.

Now when my Nimee has a party, it takes the effort of every house helper—even Cerena and Eli—to make things go exactly the way Nimee intends. The entire house has to be cleaned, including the rugs, which have to be taken outside and shaken out. There is one particular carpet of Nimee's that tells a story all on its own. I love when it is cleaned because then I can see the story on it again. It is the oldest carpet in the world. Anyone could figure this out because of who Nimee allows to clean it: only Eli. Not only is it old, but it is also so big that you can only see the story it tells by crawling on your hands and knees around and around on it, over and over again in smaller and smaller circles until you get to the middle.

On the rug, there are warriors in helmets, mail, and breastplates with belts and long, double-edged swords. Some of them are being led by others on black-and-white horses with ornate red, blue, and purple saddle clothes and plumed headgear. The horses are prancing as if they hear music.

Behind the warriors are both men and women on horses and others are walking. Some carry children, and some of the horses have bags lying across their saddles. All among the warriors, horses, and those walking are many different breeds of dogs: spaniels, retrievers, hunting hounds, and little furry whelps. In the very front of the line, one of the warriors on a horse carries a gold cross that seems to say for whom they are traveling. Once you get to the middle of the rug there is a huge tree with many roots and branches stretching out in all directions. Cerena once told me it depicts the Tree of Life.

Nimee expected me to make an appearance at the ball, but only while her guests were arriving. I suppose she can remember being young herself. I had to dress in my finest party clothes, but soon after, I would be excused to my room on the third floor.

This was my first party since we moved here, so I did as I was told. I met the guests, ate some of my favorite finger foods (mostly cheeses with curry and sweets from the silver trays), and asked to be excused. Nimee excused me, and I was free for the entire evening to do whatever I pleased!

3

Once I was in my room, I hopped on my bed, looked around at the interior decorating, and decided it was time to make this room my own. I needed some treasures to perk the place up and give it a taste of Louisa! This evening, I would have the opportunity. Our island is on the very northeastern coast of the Atlantic Ocean, and the wind blows all the time. It was light until nearly ten o'clock in the evening at this time of year, and since it was early June, it was still cool in the evening. I decided to wear hiking clothes: short boots and a jacket with a big pocket and hood.

I was not usually a dishonest person, but sometimes my willfulness got the best of me. I knew if I asked to go out, I would certainly be told no—that it was not safe for a girl my age to go walking off the property alone—so I didn't ask permission. Instead, I made my plan.

There were three sets of stairs in our house. One was squarely at the front door. That was a definite *no*. Another was on the third floor, and it descended into the conservatory. On that night, it might have been sort of risky because guests might be there with their drinks, admiring the plants and stained glass from Belgium. My last and only choice was the stairway from the second floor down to the servants' quarters, which was very near the kitchen.

I knew Nimee would be occupied with her guests. It was hard to tell if dinner had begun or whether the drinks were still flowing and people were still milling around. I thought of a dozen different scenarios of how I might get caught making my escape. After all the *what's* and *ifs*, I decided

I could *what if* myself out of time. I finally went down the stairs to the servants' quarters, out the back door, through the back gate, and down the hill, and I was gone! Whew! I made it.

By the time I looked back at our house, I could see that every light was on, and the music began to fade in the distance. The windows glittered like stars. I was happy Nimee was enjoying her friends, her favorite foods, the music, and her home.

As for me, I looked up at the sky, and the moon was already shining directly over the round, green hill where I was headed. As I walked, I tried to skip because I loved to, but there were more little crags, rocks, and small streams between our house and the green hill than I could see. I was glad I decided to wear boots. Otherwise, my feet would have been both scraped up and very wet and cold. My curly hair was getting curlier by the minute because of the moisture in the evening air, even though I had my hood on.

After stumbling over rocks and stones, jumping over streams, and clumsily missing and splashing cold water all over myself, I actually began to climb the round, green hill. As I looked up, the hill no longer appeared to be round. It looked very steep and more like a mountain, so much that I could no longer see the top at all. I saw no way to climb it. There was nothing to hold onto to help pull myself up. The hill was just thick green grass—the thickest grass in the world.

I was just about to give up and go back when something zipped by my head. I thought it was a bug, but it was too big. Here it came again. This time it was zipping back and forth and back again. This time it zipped and hovered near me. I turned this way and that trying to see what it was as it bobbled up and down and zipped back and forth, making a sweet whirring sound.

In the sound, it said to me, "Take one step further." With that, it was gone! This was so strange and happened so quickly that I hardly had a chance to think about it at all. Had whatever it was actually spoken to me? Yes, it had. It told me to take one step more, but why should I? It was hopeless. Or was it? If a flying, bobbling, zipping, whirring, beautiful thing actually was there, why shouldn't I believe what it said to me? I took one step further, and then another and another. This was impossible! I was walking, not climbing! It seemed as if the side of the hill was flattening out as I went.

I looked up, only to see huge, high steepness. I was only a little winded, so I kept going and going. I guessed I was almost halfway up. I turned to look back at our house and kept my balance long enough to see it fading in the distance, the lights still glimmering. And then down I fell! It was more of a roll than a fall and not all the way down. I was stopped by a large, moss-covered rock that I was positive was not there on my way up.

It seemed to have been somewhat hardened on the outside but had a softer middle to be able to stop a person's downhill roll but not to allow me to sink into it altogether. It also had wonderful, soft green moss growing all over it so my head didn't clunk on it when I hit.

After I landed, I was a bit discouraged, mostly because I wanted to get to the top of the hill and over it to find treasures before it got dark. After all, I had to trudge all the way back home and sneak to my room and into bed before Cerena noticed the lump of pillows was not me.

All right—this was surprisingly soft for a rock, and I was comfortable. I pushed on it, trying to figure it out, and was very thankful it was there when I needed it, but I really did need to get started again.

Up I jumped, and off I began, remembering what the whirring voice had said. I was about three quarters of the way to the top and was thinking about looking toward our house when the bobbling, zipping, and whirring came again.

This time it stopped by the right side of my face, but not so close as to scare me, and bobbled right there. I stood perfectly still because I had never seen anything like this creature in my life! It was the size of the smallest hummingbird you have ever seen, and could have been the tiniest angel or fairy. It had the smallest wings in the world, hair you could see straight through and clothes that no one can describe the colors of because they are not in our color spectrum. This time it said, "Louisa, do not look back," as it looked me straight in the eyes. Then it was gone. This tiny messenger was trustworthy before, so I did what it told me to do. I was so amazed that it had spoken to me in that beautiful, whirring voice that I completely missed that it had called me by name.

All during the time the zipping thing had been bobbling around my face, I had not noticed that up ahead the sounds were not so pleasant. Where we live, we have thunderstorms now and then and sometimes lightning, but never earthquakes, floods, or tsunamis. The rumblings that began could have been all of these things combined coming towards me, and were not far away.

I kept going and looked up as a steep ridge appeared above me. At the same time, darkness closed in so fast that it was upon me before I knew it. I remembered, "Take one step further. Do not look back." I kept going. By now I was really afraid of what was happening and what might come at me next!

There was no way around the ridge that I could see and I wondered how I could leap high enough to grasp the edge of it to possibly climb over. I took one step with my eyes closed, afraid of the sounds and the darkness closing in around me. Slowly I could tell behind my closed lids that it was getting brighter! Opening my eyes, I saw steps of stone twisting and turning up, to where I could not tell. They were all I could see because the brightness covered everything except them. I realized I was trembling inside and out and that I was saying words that I did not understand!

A voice out of the blinding light answered me. "Do not be afraid. Put your right foot on the step and come." As quick as a flash, I did it, and then my left and up I went, around and up, around and up, the thundering noises and the blinding light never stopping. There was no railing to hold on to, but I kept going.

I could feel a gentle force behind me keeping me in motion and stable on the steep, uneven stone steps. Slowly the sounds began to fade away. The light became less blinding. I realized my feet were on flat, soft, solid ground. As my eyes adjusted to the changing light and my ears to the sound, I could hear rushing water from every direction. I looked around, saw that I was safe on the grass at the top the green hill, and that I was surrounded by waterfalls.

4

My brain began to clear from the noises and the unusually strange happenings along the way up the hill. I realized my jacket, hood and boots were making me too warm. The breeze was wonderful. The grass was so deep and soft that my feet sunk down further. I was a little tired so I just laid flat down with my arms and legs stretched out as if I were making a snow angel. I looked up at the sky and took a big deep breath! Neither the sun nor the moon had moved an inch as far as I could tell. How could that be? It should have been getting dark by now! I reasoned to myself that maybe it was because I was up on the hill and because we lived on a sort of half-island, I could see the sun both coming up and going down.

When my wits returned I remembered that the reason I had come up here in the first place was to find treasures for my room, so I sat up. About five feet away stood the trunk of a huge tree which I was certain had not been there before. How curious is this? I thought. The tree trunk towered up and up into the clouds and the branches spread out to cover at least a ten to fifteen feet in circumference. It would have been impossible to have missed seeing this gigantic tree under any circumstances. Well, as far as I was concerned the tree was there and that was all there was to it. How I missed it before was no matter but examining it was the next thing!

As I was crawling around the tree on my hands and knees, I discovered a perfectly shaped hollow at the base of the gnarled roots that caught my attention at once. A first-rate hollow in the trunk of a tree is hard to find! As everyone knows, these are some of the most enchanted places in the world. I had come up the green hill to look for treasures but to my way of thinking, finding a hollow in a tree trunk was an elusive treasure I would be a complete fool to pass by for any reason!

My hands were getting damp and covered with moss from the tree roots and as I looked down to brush them off, I noticed something on the ground. At first glance, I took them for miniature flowers. On a closer examination, I saw they were hundreds of tiny toadstools scattered in groupings around the outside of the opening in the trunk of the tree amongst the roots and moss. "How sweet," I said aloud. "It looks like a fairy city."

I followed the groupings, crawling on all fours toward the hollow and peered in as far as I could. It was a deep and empty hole, sure enough! Sadly, my head was too big to go all the way in. "Oh pooh! I wish I were smaller so I could fit inside. I am sure fairies must live there!" I said again, to myself.

As I looked, glowing light from inside the hollow appeared before my eyes. It flew toward me and soon I saw that the light itself was a tiny creature. It looked warm and charming, so I held my hand out to it. The tiny thing lit on the palm of my hand. Her body was that of a young woman with small transparent wings. Her auburn hair fell from the top of her head in soft curls around her long, graceful neck, and her skin was milk white. As she flew, soft bits of shimmering stardust surrounded her.

"Hello, my name is Dulci," she said to me. "If you would like to come all the way in, just wiggle your nose three times with your eyes closed and say *please.* Then you shall have your wish."

"Really?" I asked in wonder.

"Hurry," she said, "for we must have you inside quickly!"

"All right," I said, and I closed my eyes and wiggled my nose. Before I could get the word *please* off my tongue, I felt a small swish and was inside the tree surrounded by many tiny shimmering fairies.

"Goodness gracious! We are so thankful you have made it inside the Faylinn! We can never be sure who might come along and swoop someone up. Isn't that right?" the tiny figure asked those around and about us.

"Yes!" and "Absolutely!" they all agreed.

Dulci went on, "Oh, goodness gracious! I haven't properly introduced everyone! These are all my lifelong friends and companions of the Faylinn." Then she introduced me to many of them by name. There were so many that I could not tell you because I do not have that much memory in my head! "We are fairies," Dulci said. "Oh, and good ones, we must assure you!"

"Thank you so very much for saving me from whoever might have swooped me up," I said. "My name is Louisa. I came up the green hill and saw the lopsided house and was hoping to find treasures to take back home with me."

"Oops," Dulci said. "It seems we have gotten the wrong impression. It was our understanding by what you said that you wished to visit our Faylinn."

"Oh, but I did! I did very much! And now that I am here, I can do both—visit with real fairies and then go to the lopsided house."

Dulci looked at me with a questionable expression and turned to her friends. A few of them huddled together to talk about what seemed to be something to ponder about. With them so close I noticed how small I had become! I was not by any means the size of a fairy! However, Dulci could sit on my knee and was about the size of a new taper candle now as opposed to being weightless in the palm of my hand as she was before.

"Dulci, I am sorry to interrupt," I said, "but how did I get to be this size?"

"You wished it. Do you not remember?"

I thought and answered, "I did? No. Really, I do not actually remember wishing it before you gave me the instructions."

Dulci turned back the others and said to the group, "You see. I told you so! Oh goodness gracious! What have I done and what will the queen say this time? I listened to Louisa, heard her words and granted her wish. I am such a foolish and thoughtless fairy!" Then she looked as if she would cry right there on the spot!

"Dulci, Dulci, it's all right." I said. "Come here and sit on my knee."

Not only did Dulci come, but they nearly all did. I had a lap-full of fairies. All were shimmering except for Dulci, whose shimmer had become dimmer by far. I took that to mean she was really feeling badly about whatever it was she thought she had done that was so awful.

Dulci was weeping now, so I asked for help. Another lovely fairy whose name was Elva explained, "Dulci has had permission to use her graces for a short time and she dearly loves to use them. She heard you speaking outside the Faylinn that you wished to be small enough to fit into the hole, so Dulci granted your wish."

"Well, I am very happy that she did and I see not one thing wrong with it as far as I can tell. May I ask one more thing, Elva? What does Faylinn mean?"

At this Dulci began to not only weep but wail!

"Oh no! What did I say to upset her now?" I asked in distress, thinking this had to be the most hysterical fairy in the known world! Elva explained as best she could, "Dulci now knows because you asked what Faylinn means that you know nothing at all about fairies or graces."

"Well," I answered, "I can be told, and I can learn if you help me. Can't I?"

As I said this, Dulci lifted her head, sat up, looked at me and smiled. She said through her sobs and tears, "Oh goodness gracious. I never thought of that! I suppose a girl without wings can learn as quickly as I can!"

I thought I heard someone from behind me whisper sarcastically, "I would surely hope so." I agreed totally.

Another older fairy whose name was Tania was appointed by the group to teach me the secrets and stories of the Faylinn whatever it was, when someone came from farther back in the hole and made this announcement: "Her Highness has learned we have company and requests her presence at once."

At these words, all the fairies got to their wings, formed a group around me and ushered me forward down a hallway inside the tree trunk. On either side I saw roots and branches that had been made into columns, shelves, small tables, chairs and sconces with shimmering lights so one could see one's way. Portraits of lovely female fairies hung framed along both sides of this long hallway. There were small openings made into oval and rounded double doors with golden hinges and handles in the shape of ivy leaves, fish, infinity signs and alpha and omega symbols in gold along the hall beneath the portraits. On the floor were hand-loomed rugs of silk and linen of the most glorious colors. These colors do not exist in our world as far as I can tell. I wanted to stop and look at everything, feel it and touch it, but the others kept me moving forward.

The area ahead opened into a much-larger space, both in height and breadth. It was well lighted up to the top and down to the ground with the shimmering candles and fairy dustings. As I looked up and around, hundreds of fairies were lit on the walls, shimmering and fluttering their multicolored wings. Dark green moss covered the floor and wound around giant oak roots and smooth stones. Groupings of the tiny toadstools were scattered hither and yon, and the vibrating and pounding sounds of rushing water grew louder the further in we drew.

I saw a reflecting pool in the center of the room and the stream running into it from the upper right. The stream seemed to run straight from the tree. Water that was as clear as any water in the world washed into the bottomless pool.

I was so overcome with the enchantment that I did not hear that someone was calling my name. Tania said to me as Dulci and Elva gave me nudges, "Louisa, Her Highness has called for you! There she is!"

"Really, her highness! Where?" I asked.

Dulci pointed shyly, and I looked up to see a throne set upon a high bridge spanning the pool. It was accessible by a half-circular stairway made of white stone. All around the fairy queen was a dancing glimmer as bright as the sun.

"Dulci, bring our guest to me," the queen said. Dulci, Elva, and Tania flew me up to the bridge, and I found myself in front of the throne of a Fairy Queen. She said to me, "Welcome to my kingdom and to our Faylinn, my child. They tell me your name is Louisa. I am Orla, queen of the Rose Dianna Grace Faylinn."

I stood there and looked at her in stunned wonder. I had met a queen only once before when I was five years old. She was the queen of England. All I remember about meeting her was that I had to learn how to curtsey for her and was frightened to death at the sight of her.

She was so important looking! This queen was nothing like the one in England!

Queen Orla's hair was so light it could have been liquid silver flowing down to her shoulders. On her head, she wore a platinum crown with the sign of infinity in the middle of her forehead. She was clothed all in white satin from shoulders to her feet, except for her, arms which were laced roses and ivy intertwined. She wore single diamond earrings that caught the light and gave off colors in our spectrum and many other colors unknown to us if she turned her head even slightly.

Around her neck was a pendant of platinum and pure nard in the shape of an ivy leaf, which gave off the scent of every lovely herb there is in the world. On her right middle finger, she wore a ring of whitest ivory cut into a perfect rose blossom, which was also platinum. Her wings were shimmering so brightly it was difficult to look at her for any length of time. She was aware of this and apologized by allowing her shimmer to wane in deference to my eyes. Queen Orla stood in front of her throne.

"Oh, my dear, if only I could grace you with your wish," Orla said.

"What wish?" I asked.

"That you could stay with us forever and become one of us," she answered.

"Did I say that aloud?" I asked.

"Yes, my dear. You did. You say many things aloud to yourself. Are you not aware of that?"

"I guess I wasn't," I replied. "You see, I am an only child and have no friends to play with, and since I have landed here, well, everything has been so amazing and wonderful."

Orla answered, "Would you like to know more about our Faylinn and the particular kind of fairies we are, Louisa?"

"Oh yes! I would like to know everything there is to know about everything!" I answered.

Orla told me there were many things I did not know about fairies. In fact, I knew hardly anything at all. I had never thought about where fairies came from. I just thought they *were*.

Orla taught me that a fairy is a sprite, which means a tiny being with half a spirit. Unfortunately, eons ago when there was the big war in heaven and God threw Satan and his companions from heaven like lightning, the fairies were thrown down with them because they had so little spirit. It was true that most fairies were evil, and the Most High did the right thing, as He always does. However, over time and once in the state of being as they were between heaven and hell, and in a world dominated by Satan, many fairies chose not be his servants. They chose instead to wait, to watch and to form families or groups called Faylinns. Faylinns are generally of male or female fairies only. Among the evil fairies, some cohabit, and because of interbreeding with other bloodlines, they often produce mutant, rebellious offspring. The greatest thing is that the fairies made a choice.

Orla went on to tell me that each Faylinn has a unique giftedness. Some used for good and some are used for evil. "Our Faylinn has chosen to use our giftedness which is Grace to grant the true and pure wishes of others. We are known as the Faylinn Graces or as Graceful fairies."

"Louisa, I must warn you," she continued.

"What is it Queen Orla?" I asked.

"There are fairies that have chosen Satan as their master. They appear much the same as Graceful fairies, but they are filled with evil. They live and breathe to inflict pain, sorrow, hopelessness and chaos on anyone or any situation. They have a queen as well. She is the most evil of them all. Satan allows them to draw all their evil from her. Her Faylinn is to the north where there is never light, always dark, damp and often freezing temperatures. It is only the pure evil running through their veins that keeps them alive in that tremendously dark and unfriendly climate. I warn you, Louisa, for in time and if you remain in our kingdom, she will come to know of your presence here and she will seek you out."

Thinking this was the most frightening story about fairies anyone had ever heard in her life, I asked, "Orla, what is this queen's name, just in case I stumble near her?"

"Her name is Le Annis. She is known as Le Annis the Banshee."

"I believe I know what a banshee is," I said to Orla. "I have read about them in books. Banshees are horrid and angry women who dislike men in particular and everyone in general and have huge rages of temper, usually involving throwing fire and speaking wildly."

"Yes, you do know. You have described Le Annis to the tee, Louisa. Le Annis has both female and male fairies among her followers, many have inbred. The bloodlines crossing have produced mutant fairies, angry at who they are. The evil queen has them at her full command. These beings will even kill for her.

"There is another group that we do not call fairies ourselves, for we do not want to be associated with them in any way. They are called hogules. They are evil fairies who inbred with the Nephilim when the world was new and before the great flood. These creatures as well as the Nephilim, live to please Satan and will kill for him if commanded. The Hogules live in the northern areas called the Banelands. The Nephilim, or what is left of them, live there as well.

"As for Le Annis, she feeds off of her pent-up rage which stands behind powerful evil. She is a comrade to the leaders of the hogules and Nephilim. I hope this helps you understand my concern for you."

I listened to all Orla told me about Le Annis and the hogules, hoping never to encounter this fairy queen or any of them!

Orla said to me, "Louisa, we know nothing of human beings with full life and complete spirits because we are not allowed to cross over to the land of the living. You must forgive Dulci if she has so quickly granted your wish to come into our Faylinn and off your path. We surely meant to cause you no harm or inconvenience!"

I told Orla that it had been my utmost honor and privilege to visit their Faylinn, and that meeting fairies and their queen was a human girl's dream come true! Orla asked me if there was anything or any wish she could grant for me. "Thank you!" I said. "Your Majesty, the only thing I can think of is to get me safely to the lopsided house and that we all meet again someday!"

"Your wish is my command, Louisa. Go in peace and safety!" As Orla said these words, I felt a swish and was standing outside the lopsided house!

5

Christmastime, Nimee always puts a Gingerbread house under the tree for me. Looking at the lopsided house gave me the same magic feeling in my tummy. The front yard sloped down toward the other side of the green hill, and from where I was at the top, I had a glimpse of the sea in the distance, with rolling hills in between down to the cragged cliffs at the edge. As I looked around in every direction, I could see that every waterfall ran down and down and down into the great ocean itself. In some of the waterfalls there were rainbows forming in the mists and huge white-winged birds flying in and out through the bows. My eyes were filled with the most beautiful colors in the world, and my ears did not understand the sounds they were hearing all at the same time. It was like music no one has ever heard before in the whole world as far as I could tell.

The back porch of the house was a normal porch. There were a few steps up to the blue-screened door. There were flowers blooming all around the back porch—sunflowers that were bright yellow with dark orange centers, giant ferns, towering hydrangeas, tropical hibiscus as high as trees, both golden and ruby red. There were lilies of the valley in colors that lilies should not be—blue, red, dark purple, lizard green, white, silver, baby pink with blue edges, and baby yellow with pink edges. There were many flowers no one has ever seen in the world and cannot name. All of these were very tastefully planted and well-tended daily as far as I could tell, even at first sight.

Good manners dictate that you that you do not go onto someone's porch unless you have been invited and are expected, so I moved on around toward the side of the house where a rose vine was growing. As I drew closer, I could see ivy growing thickly among the roses. Around and under the vines lay a carpet of multicolored rose petals that were untouched. The roses and ivy ran around most of the house and produced a halo effect, which added a touch of magic to the little house itself. The air was full of butterflies—so many no one could possibly count them! There were so many butterflies of different sizes and species that no one could ever tell about all of them. I put my hand out just to see, and sure enough, one landed on my arm! I wondered what I should do. I put out my other hand, and another lit right on my finger! Then one landed on my head and another on my shoulder right by my ear. It fluttered against my cheek softly, making me afraid to move. I closed my eyes because I enjoyed the feeling. I heard a musical voice say, "Look, she is the One, isn't she?" Thinking it was the zipping, bobbling thing again or even one of the butterflies speaking, I didn't answer, but opened my eyes to find out.

Near the front door of the house was a window standing open. The panes were dusty blue and diamond shaped. I could hear three voices conversing in the most beautiful language I had ever heard! Not able to help myself, I peeped in to see them. They had been having a gracious meal, but now, to my amazement, they were looking out at me! Inside were a woman, a man and the strangest-looking little creature I have ever seen, all smiling happily.

"Hello," I said. "My name is Louisa. I came up the round green hill to look for treasures for my room and found the lopsided house. It is yours, I suppose? I am very sorry if I have disturbed your dinner."

They looked at one another and then at me, and the woman said, "Louisa dear, you have not disturbed us in the least! I am Anna, and this is Sol, my husband."

The man who was Sol said, "As a matter of fact, we have been expecting you for quite some time. Let us introduce you to Jepetto, our adopted son."

The little creature, whose name was Jepetto, began to dance around, pirouetting with glee. He said, "Oh my yes! Yes we are glad, glad to see you, that is true!"

I did not know what to say about this, so I just said thank you to them and nothing else. Anna and Sol asked me no more questions but said they were certain I must be hungry after my climb. They said it was silly of them to be carrying on a conversation through the window and invited me inside where there were cucumber, shrimp, and cheese sandwiches and fruits of a kind I had never seen, but they were delicious. There was iced chamomile for Jepetto and me and wine for Anna and Sol. After sandwiches and cheese, there were lemon chess tarts and truffles with dandelion centers for desert. I was so full I would have unbuttoned the top button of my trousers if I had not been brought up to know better! My tummy had a warm feeling, and my head, ears and eyes began to feel a bit strange as well. It was a very pleasant sensation and not overwhelming, so I sat, listened and enjoyed every bit of it.

All the time I was eating I had not said a word, neither had my three dinner companions—at least not to me. Sol and Anna had been talking between themselves, and although I could hear every word, I could not make out much of anything they said. Most of their conversation was like music and humming.

As far as I could tell, Jepetto was hopping around on a stool that apparently was his and smiling his goofy, crooked smile as he looked at me. I returned the smile, but kept from hopping or any dancing because I was feeling a bit giddy. I don't think Jepetto's feelings were hurt in the least. I was beginning to see that he thought of himself as quite a toe dancer, even for a boy! Actually, given the unusual build of his body and the shape of his feet, he could perform miracles on them!

Jepetto stood about four feet tall and had ears and feet much too large for his body. His ears drooped nearly to the ground, and his strange flat feet were as long as his legs. He had wide round eyes that seemed to pop too far out of his head, a long thin nose and a wide mouth that covered his face from ear to ear when he grinned. He grinned nearly all the time, even when there seemed nothing worthwhile to grin about. His only clothes were short red trousers, brown suspenders and a green five-pointed hat with tassels hanging from each point, all of different colors and shapes. I understood that he had a multicolored dress hat with bells that he wore for festivals and other special occasions.

It seemed a burden for Jepetto to sit still. He was hopping up and down on his stool and gesticulating to the three of us furiously most all the time. Anna would say to him something like, "Not yet. Be patient. We understand how you feel. We are excited as well," or things of that order, apparently to calm Jepetto's hopping and gesticulating, to no avail. It was hard language for me to understand because it was so musical and I was feeling a little mellow from the tea.

"Anna and I have lived in the lopsided house for so many years we cannot count them," Sol said, "along with our friend here, Jepetto. He has been with us for many years now and is just like a son to us."

All the while little Jepetto was hopping up and down and dancing around on his stool, and Anna was shushing him to no avail. Sol continued, "We know you have wished for some of the things on our back porch and there are things there for you. Darkness will be upon us soon and we would not want your family to be worried about you."

"Oh yes, treasures, treasures, good, good, let's go, let's go," said Jepetto. He was dancing and twirling around again.

Sol stood up and said, "Now to the blue porch. There you may choose from all the treasures what you like."

It was beginning to get dark and somehow I knew what they said was for my good even though I wanted more than anything to stay. I loved the room we were in with the light green walls of painted wood stenciled with pink and yellow roses, rustic old pine floors stained darker than dark at the board joints from age, and clocks on every table and wall, all telling a different time and ticking in their own rhythms.

Sol's books were piled high everywhere—on the floor in neat sideways stacks, on chairs not in use and of course on the shelves made for them which covered one entire wall of the room. I noticed that almost every book was leather bound and very old. Many of them were nearly tomes and were equipped with multicolored satin page markers that were faded and frayed badly on the ends.

Anna's embroidery loom stood in one corner with a piece that was almost finished of sixteen vestal virgins from a Greek play. Each girl's hair was a different color, ranging from black as black to true red. Their clothing was flowing and loose. The dresses were held together with large jewels of opulent colors from deep purple to tender rose and also the garnet spectrum from deepest raven to lightest dainty fern green. Anna promised that she would one day tell me the story of the vestal virgins herself, but that now we should go on to the back porch. I agreed reluctantly.

The lopsided house was much larger than it looked from the outside. In fact, I found it to be an entryway into a larger world. It was a passageway to other places entirely. The passage continued out to the place called the Arielian Plains, the Truthlands and onward into the whole of the Lopsided Kingdom.

Between the room in which we had eaten our supper and the blue porch, we encountered many small and strange passageways. I asked where they went, but was told, "Later, my dear."

A door stood before us. It was a plain, everyday door made of wood and painted brick red. Around the door, the wood was bright yellow. The knob on the door was very small—so small in fact, it was hard to see. I nearly missed it and asked, "How do you open this door? It has no knob."

"Look again, my dear," answered Sol. "Are you quite sure you do not see the knob?"

At this, Jepetto began hopping up and down as happily as he could and pirouetting as well. Around and around on his flat toes he went, repeating, "The knob, the knob!"

I looked again after gazing at Jepetto's little dance and sure enough, there it was! It had appeared there in seconds. "How did …?" I started to ask.

Anna took my hand and said, "The knob will only appear to those whose hearts are pure and true—to those who have a real desire to enter. Beyond the door is a passage."

"A passage to where?" I asked excitedly.

"Take the knob, open the door and we shall see," was Anna's answer.

It was the most beautiful brass knob I had ever seen. It was in the shape of an infinity symbol so one could grasp it on either side to use it to open or close the red door. How curious, I thought. I had just seen this symbol somewhere; was it at home or in the other room? I could not remember.

Sol said to me, "Louisa, in order for you to enter, you must open the door yourself. Simply turn the knob."

"All right," I replied.

Reaching out both hands and placing one on each oval, I turned the knob to the right. Nothing happened. The door would not open. "What have I not done?" I asked.

"There are two circles. You have two hands on the door," Sol replied with eyebrows raised, looking at me. With both hands firmly on the two ovals, I turned the knob first to the left and then to the right. At this, a puff of wind came from beneath the door and it began to creak rather loudly. "Well, give it a pull!" Sol exclaimed.

I did as he said and pulled as hard as I could. The door came slowly open toward us. What I saw before my eyes was impossible, yet it was there. All laws of size and dimension were broken inside the vastness we entered beyond the door. Through it we stood on a stairway that was most certainly hundreds of feet in the air. This stairway descended to the right and left in half circles, meeting way down at the bottom and forming yet another stairway which ascended into the air, on the opposite side of the space we were in. Where this stairway met at the bottom of the expanse, it again formed concentric circles, which eventually broke off into the distance ahead and went on as far as we could see.

The entire area was devoid of anything domestic. This was no living area. I could tell this was a place used only for traveling. It was not a scary place so to speak, but neither did it give you a warm and happy feeling or make you wish to remain there. There was a smell, touch and insight I felt that made me know it was an important place.

In the place where we stood on the stairway, there was a blue door to our left. Sol opened it without any magic, pomp or circumstance, and then we were on the blue porch. I spied a rattan chair and immediately sat down with my head in my hands. "What is it, child? Are you ill?" Anna asked sweetly.

"Not really." I said. "I suppose I am just not accustomed to all of this wonderful magic; the red door, passageways that go on forever, and fairies and Faylinns all in one day. I am very tired."

"Of course you are, my dear." Anna said. "Sol, let's go at once to the porch so that this child may get home. She is too tired for anymore today."

So to the back porch we went, me between them hand in hand. Inside the porch, the blue-screened door opened to the outside. The air was cool and fragrant, I supposed from all the wonderful flowers on the lawn.

I could tell as I drew nearer to the ledges that all sorts of lovely and exotic bouquets were inside the pottery and vases! I looked at the couple, who had taken seats on a rattan sofa. I cast a quizzical look at them and Anna answered my question before I asked. "Yes my dear, you may touch them. They will not break, child. Choose one container, either pottery or of glass. It must be an empty one and you may take it for your own."

After trying to make up my mind between two, I chose a very small one that looked like fairy glass. "She has excellent taste, does she not, my dear?" asked Sol.

"Oh yes!" was Anna's reply.

As I was examining my delicate vase and pondering the fact that I had to leave, Sol said, "You may choose one more yet. Take it from the open-lidded jars and you must make haste, for it is getting quite late. Do not worry, for your choice will be certain."

For a reason I did not consciously comprehend, I knew he spoke the truth.

My eyes had been on one of the jars of keys. It was the tallest jar with the widest neck, and it held large and ancient keys mostly made of copper and brass. I stood on tiptoes and put my entire arm into the jar. One of the keys jumped into my hand!

As quickly as that, Sol and Anna were patting me on the head, Jepetto was smiling at me, and hand in hand the three were leading me out the door, down the steps and to the down slope of the round green hill.

"It has been a pleasure, my child," they said. "Go safely home, do not forget us, and we will see one another again as soon as you know in your heart the 'Time is the Time.'"

"Well, thank you very much for everything!" I said and started down the hill, waving good-bye, still in somewhat of a daze.

~~~~~~~~~~~~~~~~~~~~~~

The green hill was much easier to get down than it had been to climb. The view from the top was equally as steep, but as I put my right foot out and took one step at a time the ground seemed to flatten out as before and the steps down from the ridge were more familiar and less frightening. Once I reached the smushy clay rock, I stopped and looked at our house. The party was still in full swing. All the downstairs lights were on, as well as the ones in the second- and third-floor halls. I could faintly hear the music from the ballroom. Time had surely stopped somehow! It felt like I had been away for hours because of all that had transpired on my outing.

As I walked on at a quick pace, I was planning how to best get back into the house and up to my rooms unnoticed. The servant's entrance was still the way to go, but at this point, food preparation would be over. Cleaning up and putting away would be the order of business.

All the household helpers, as far as I could figure would still be serving and fetching in and out of the butler's pantry, which would cause me no trouble, as far as I could tell. That was my plan. I would enter by the servant's entrance, go up the stairway to the third floor into my rooms and pop into my bed before anyone could have missed me. At the back door, I stood on my toes and looked in through the glass. There were two cooks moving around in the big kitchen. I ducked back down. Because of the dance music, I could not hear what they were saying or even if they were talking. I wondered where Eli was and whether he was outside seeing to the cars or inside with the butler. After looking in the window once more and seeing no one, I quietly opened and closed the door and up the stairs, I flew.

On the second-floor landing as I was looking behind me, I bumped squarely into Cerena! It nearly scared the breath out of me! It seemed to me that Cerena was in as much of a hurry as I was, and she started to go on about her business, but then she stopped. She turned around and saw how I was dressed with my jacket tied around my waist and no shoes on and she said, "Louisanna, where are you going, or better yet, where have you been?"

I do not lie if I can absolutely keep from it, so I said, "I'm not going anywhere. Where are you going in such a hurry? Is Eli waiting on you to bring him something? I'm sorry I bumped into you. I guess I wasn't looking where I was going. You know how I am. Ha! Ha!"

"What do you have tied up in your jacket, Louisanna?" Cerena asked me with a funny look on her face and her head cocked to one side.

"Oh, nothing really. Just some silly little nonsensical things for my room. I'm on my way up there to bed now. I'm so sleepy." I pretended a big yawn.

Cerena looked suspiciously at me but said, "I want you to do that right now. I have a good many things still to do. Say your prayers and sleep tight." Then she kissed me on the top of my head.

Once I was in my rooms with the door closed, I let out one big sigh of relief and said a thankful prayer that I had not had to tell a lie.

6

I had no earthly idea of the time I felt Cerena's gentle hand on my face. Once I sat up in bed rubbing my eyes, Cerena took a good hard look at me and asked, "Louisanna, did you have your bath last night? Your hair is a messy noggin! I will get your tub ready. We will not be going out to church today. Eli will be leading Morning Prayer in an hour, and your grandmamma expects you down. We will have breakfast afterward. All you need is a morning shift." Still feeling a bit tired and smiling sheepishly, I dressed and joined the rest of the household downstairs.

Cerena always looks beautiful, but on Sunday she wears the clothes of her culture. Her dress is a wrapped one that she made herself of cloth of deep purples, blues, greens and yellows that we do not have in this country. In Africa where Cerena was born and grew up this cloth is called *madras*, and the color in it comes from plants that grow in that region. Cerena and Natlie tell me each piece of this cloth is one of a kind, with no pattern ever being alike. Cerena had her hair wrapped in a green cloth, which I thought went nicely with her dress and eyes. On a normal Sunday we attend the Church of All Souls, South Newfoundland. Today Nimee decided we would worship at home because everyone was tired from the previous night's party.

When we have worship at home, Eli leads us in Morning Prayer and gives a short kind of sermon. Nimee calls it a homily. On this morning, Eli read from the Bible, first from the Old Testament in Isaiah 6. I know because we read along in our own Bibles. It was about Isaiah's vision of finding himself in God's throne room and realizing he was a sinner and lived in a whole world full of sinners. Isaiah believed when he saw God that he would surely die! He was then burned on his lips with angel tongs and his sin was taken away. After he had seen God, God asked Isaiah who would go for them (the Trinity), and Isaiah said, "Send me!" All the hosts of heaven sang a new song to the Lord!

In his homily, Eli said Isaiah was just a person like you or me and that this meant that, like Isaiah, if we choose by free will to be God's servants, He gives us the ability through His spiritual gifts to do for Him whatever He chooses for us. Eli is a very wise man. I think he would make a good preacher in a real church.

Eli is like a father, teacher and grandfather to me all rolled into one. Eli has been in our family as long as I can remember. He is a tall very dark-skinned man from Africa. He has a long broad nose, high cheekbones and a large, happy smile that shows his bright white teeth. Eli always dresses in black trousers and a khaki shirt that he buttons at the neck. Over his shirt, he wears a dark brown leather vest, buttoned up all the way. On his feet, he wears well-polished riding boots. Eli speaks perfect English as does Cerena. Sometimes I hear them speaking to one another in Rwandan which is their native language.

I learned all about the planets, the stars and the heavens from Eli. When I was very young, he and I would lie on the warm grass and look up at the stars on clear nights. Eli pointed out each constellation to me and told me the wonderful stories behind each one. Eli was also my Bible teacher. When we lived in places between schools as Nimee often had us do, Eli taught me to read from the Bible and not just the easy stories! He believed in interpretation as part of the lessons. Somehow he always made my lessons fun and the stories come to life for me. Knowing that Eli is a part of our family makes me feel very safe and secure.

A prayer is read in our church every Sunday, and Eli read it as he preached, "Listen to these comfortable words: 'We have an advocate, Jesus Christ the righteous, and He is the propitiation for our sin and not for ours only, but for the sins of the whole world.' Now just try to wrap your mind around that! Sometimes I think about it all day long. It's a big, big thing to think about. As for me, it is like lying on your back and trying to count the stars on one of those clear black nights.

All during our morning prayer, I was thinking about this prayer and about when we to go to the altar rail for the Eucharist which is when we take the Lord's body and blood in thanksgiving and remembrance for Him giving up His life for everyone. This is one of my favorite parts of church, if not my favorite. We kneel and hold our hands palms up for the bread from the priest. The bread must go right in our mouths. Then the priest passes the silver chalice that holds the wine. I always have to stand up to be able to drink from it. The church wine is terribly sweet, but it burns going down. As far as I can tell, if you are drinking what means the blood of Jesus, it should burn—like fire!

7

A bird is on the wing and you do not know why.
You can make the mountains ring or make the heavens cry.
The key unlocks them both. It's at your
command. You hold the hope of love and
truth in your trembling hand.

I wanted so much to have someone to tell all about my night up the round green hill, the amazing things that went on—the bobbling, zipping thing, the voices in the whirring, the lopsided house, the man and woman and the treasures I had been given. Oh pooh! What were the chances of anyone believing it at all? Would I believe a story like that? Probably not. After all, the treasures were mostly in my head and heart at this point. The only ones I had to show were the tiny fairy vase and the huge, ancient key. Anyone could say that an aunt had given me the vase, and I could have found the key in our own house. I closed my bedroom doors and lay down on my window seat after we had cold soup and hot bread for brunch in the garden.

Sunday afternoons are quiet because it is everyone's day off and the whole house is napping. I just love Sunday afternoons. I held both the vase and the key in front of my face and stared at them for a long time. My mind drifted to the words Eli had said this morning … the host of heaven … tongs from the altar on my lips … forgiveness of sin … we have an advocate … a propitiation … the lopsided house … climbing … zipping … words like music … glowing light …

I must have napped myself, because the next thing I knew Cerena was whispering through my partially opened door, asking if I wanted to come down for tea and an early supper or if she could bring up something for me a little later. I rubbed my eyes and asked her what the time was. "Three quarters past four, Babo. You must have been tired from growing. You have been asleep for nearly three hours."

"Cerena," I said. "I love you." Then I ran and hugged her tight.

"I love you too, my sweet."

"Will you bring up some of those same sandwiches, some crackers, and lemonade, if there is any, when I pull the bell? I won't keep you up late, I promise."

"Of course I will. You seem to be thinking exceptionally hard on something. I am always here if you would like to talk."

"I know," I said. "You are my best listener, but I need more time on this one."

"Very well, Babo, let me know when you are hungry." She kissed me on the top of my head and closed the door quietly as she left.

As soon as Cerena closed the door, I went to the bookshelf and began to write in my journal about all that had happened the night before. I wrote about, "We have an advocate, the propitiation for our sin," Isaiah and the tongs, and my dream. I had to go to the big Webster to find the meaning of propitiation and I still needed to ask Eli exactly what it meant.

I had dreamed about the zipping, bobbling, whirring voice helping me when I was terrified of something, but I don't know what exactly. You know how dreams are; everything is all tangled and muddled. In my dream, I heard myself answering the voice, saying to it, "I am not afraid of you." I was speaking to a large creature that was half-human and half-bird. It was mostly white with shimmering wings. I could not tell if the human half was male or female, but it was a very beautiful creature whichever it was. In my dream, its beauty consumed me, but I woke up afraid and trembling.

8

It began to rain early Monday morning. Nimee said it was not unusual for it to rain and blow for at least three days at this time of year. It is referred to as a nor'easter. Nimee grew up on this island and knows the patterns of the weather. In New Delhi, our climate was tropical and the rains came in the afternoons with great force and were gone just as quickly, leaving everything green and steamy. According to Nimee and Eli, we were about to have a spring storm, and it could hang on a few days. That meant I would have to find a way to amuse myself inside.

Ever since we had arrived I hadn't been able to do any scouting out of the creepy old parts of this big house because it was being cleaned. Ernestine, our head housekeeper, had gone over it two or three times to make sure things were in order to suit Nimee if she ever had an occasion to walk into any room in the house. This seemed silly to me because I had never seen Nimee set foot on the fourth floor. I also knew quite well she would send up to the attic for what she needed since there was no elevator and she was one of the people who thought the house had spirits.

Since the big party, all cleaning was finished and at least the third and fourth floors were clear for snooping. I knew no one lived in any of the rooms on the fourth floor because Cerena told me. I didn't know what was up there and this was a good time to find out!

By the time I was back upstairs after breakfast, the rain was pouring so hard it sounded like hammers on the roof. My rooms are corner rooms and my bedroom has windows on the front and left sides of the house.

My window seat is in the left window, which means that if I want to look toward the round green hill, I have to look through the window in the front of the house. There are draperies, shutters and all sorts of things like that making it hard for me to see out and for others to see in, which I suppose was the purpose—to give me privacy.

All I could think about was going back to the lopsided house to see Sol, Anna and Jepetto and of course the fairies! If I could not go, at least I wanted to be able to look that way to make it more real. Since there were other windows on the front of the house like mine, I decided today was as good a day as any to find them.

The way to get to those rooms was to go around the stairway and down the opposite hall toward the front. I passed three doors on that hall and by reason knew that the last door—the one opposite mine—was the one. The door was a double one like mine with intricate carvings, inlay, two large crystal-and-ivory knobs and huge brass hinges. It towered over my head as I looked up at the top of it. It took both my hands to turn the knob, but the door was locked. I looked at the keyhole and ran to my room to fetch my treasure key. After I placed it in the lock and turned the knob, the door opened!

A thrill of excitement started at the back of my neck and rippled down my spine. I closed the door behind me quietly. Then I began to look around. The room was not as dark as I suspected, with a little light coming through the open shutters and sheer curtains. The layout was similar to mine. It was a suite of rooms including a large bedroom, a dressing room with a closet, sitting area, and a bathroom even larger than mine. I moved on toward the front window and as I neared the dressing table, I had to stop dead still.

I thought I heard the doorknob turning. Was someone coming in? Thankfully, it was simply the door creaking or my guilty conscience for being where I did not belong. That did nothing to stop me.

I sat down on the stool at the dressing table, put my hands in my lap, sat up straight with my shoulders back in good posture, looked at myself in the mirror and smiled. The mirror was large and oval-shaped. As I was admiring myself, I saw in the reflection a dark blue velvet chest on the side of the dressing table in front of me. It was about twelve inches square with a small silver hook and latch on the doors. I was taught not to go into things that were not mine, but this had no lock that I could see. I nearly put my hand out but stopped. I took one more look in the mirror, pretended to puff up my hair, and went to the front window for the reason I'd come here in the first place.

I pulled the curtains aside and was so happy to see the outside shutters were open! The rain was falling steadily now, but not in torrents, so I had a good view of the round, green hill. After pulling the dresser stool over, I sat down and pressed my head as close to the window as I could and leaned my elbows on the sill.

Everything was growing very green and fresh from the rain and the sound of it tap, tap, tapping as I peered toward the distance put me into a sleepy stupid-ness. I did not stay that way for long.

Over the very top of the round green hill a faint glow began. I thought it was my imagination playing tricks on me, but it grew to a brightness and size of a burning, glowing tennis ball. The glow completely consumed my view, as it had on my way up the hill. As I looked, a tiny speck appeared and began to move toward me from inside the glow. Once it reached the window, I could see it was the zipping, bobbling, whirring thing, and it was dancing around outside in the rain! Then there was another one and now another! The three of them zipped, bobbled and danced around each other in front of me and were having so much fun that I was hopping up and down myself!

It finally dawned on me that this was probably not a social call. I thought they must have come with another advocate, a helping word, so I should pay attention. I moved very close into the window again, and so did they. The whirring began very close to the window, and in my heart I heard, "Louisanna, in this room is a pearl of great price but also a danger to your heart." They bobbled up and down and zipped away into the glow.

As I watched them go, the glow faded as it had come to a small, faint light on top of the hill until it had gone completely out. I just sat for I do not know how long to see if the light would come back. I wished that it would. That light was the most wonderful thing in the world as far as I was concerned. I would have rather been in that light than have one hundred bowls of chocolate ice cream and sugar cookies! It is so wonderful there are not words in the world to describe it that I know of.

I thought to myself that these encounters so far had conveyed important messages about something that frightened me or that I needed help with, so it might be a good idea to take a few minutes to think about what had happened during and prior to them. This was especially true now that I was pretty sure they were helping words and a person could put their trust in them. I should add to that any things that might happen to put me in danger or fear in the future.

Surely this message was important because three of them, not just one, came all the way to my house to deliver it! The other times they had come bobbling to me, I was afraid. This time that was not the case. What had I been doing before they came with this message? Oh yes—I was thinking about opening the velvet chest. I had come into this room and was looking around. I was sort of afraid of opening the blue chest because it was not mine. Is that what I was not to be afraid of? What was this they said that was a pearl of great price in the room? But what could be a danger to my heart? It couldn't be both at once to my way of thinking. How can something be both good and bad for you at the same time?

With that, I reasoned myself into deciding not to listen to the warning because it made no sense to me. I went to the dresser, loosened the latch of the chest, and opened the doors. Lying in the blue velvet box were three tiny vases snuggled down inside tight holders that fit their shape exactly, each one having a different shape but very close in size. One vase was missing. Each was very fragile and thin and looked as if it could have been made by fairies and … what? The shape of the missing one looked so familiar! How could that be? I knew that shape. I had picked it myself from the ledge at the lopsided house! One of my treasures! *Compose yourself,* I thought. *Go back to your room. Look at it again. Bring it and see if it fits. What is the meaning of all this if it fits? Maybe I should have listened to the warning.*

~~~~~~~~~~~~~~~~~~~~~~~~

Back in my room, I was gazing at the tiny vase, still trying to sort it all out. Something inside me was missing, just like the missing vase, as if there were a hole right in the middle of my chest. It even ached. This was a new feeling I had not experienced before. I did not have a chance to think more about it then or to go back to try the vase for a fit. It seemed I had been in the bedroom only a little while but to my surprise Cerena came to the top of the stairs and told me lunch was ready and I should come down right away.

The conversation at lunch had turned to my antics of the morning. Apparently it was no secret that I had been nosing around and had gotten into the bedroom . Nimee had given me a surprisingly stern rebuke that the front bedroom was not my playground. She told me to find other places to explore and she hoped she would not have to scold me on the issue a second time. Scolding's by Nimee are not bothersome to me, as she loves me dearly, means what she says at the time, but forgets right away because her heart is golden, soft as butter and as nutty as they come.

My emptiness inside was coming from another source entirely. Alone or not, the warning about danger to my heart put aside, to my way of thinking, the way to get rid of it was to find out if the vase fit. Somehow that would solve the puzzle.

It was too soon to go back to the bedroom that afternoon. Cerena knows me very well and is not easily fooled. I knew she would be upstairs in the next hour or so to see what I was up to. I was sure of it. Since she knew I had been in the room, I was half-tempted to ask her about how something could be both good and bad together. I finally decided against it because if I asked her about that, I would have to tell her everything. It was not time for that—not yet.

9

Dinner came and went without incident. We had salmon with caper sauce and cucumber soup. They are two of my favorites, and I overate a bit—not to mention cinnamon bread pudding for dessert! Cerena said prayers with me and tucked me in. I never intended to doze off, but I did. Something—I have no idea what—woke me wide awake! I jumped out of bed, nearly tumbling over my stool, feeling extremely clumsy and hoping no one had heard. I was glad I had not slept the entire night and thankful for whatever had awakened me. I lost no time by dressing and went directly out my door and to the opposite bedroom in my bare feet with the tiny vase.

The hallway was not completely dark because Eli leaves small lights burning at night in case anyone needs to move about. I had the key in my dressing gown and my vase tucked away in a pocket. I had tiptoed down and around the opposite end of the hall and was standing at the huge door to the forbidden room. Everyone in the house was quiet and sleeping. As I stood there rummaging for the key, out from under the door came a burst of cold air, chilling me to the bone! *What was that?* I thought. I had to put my hand over my mouth, for I nearly screamed and gave myself away. I was quite scared of one of the alleged ghosts or spirits, but then I reasoned, *There are no ghosts, Louisa. It is the bad whatever that does not want you to get your pearl of great price. Do not be afraid of cold air. You have come this far. The zipping, bobbling things are always there to help you. Open the door and go in!*

This self-talk did the trick, and I placed the key in the lock, turned the knob, opened the great door, and walked in. Once inside the forbidden bedroom however all was darkness and shadows. There was just enough light from the hallway to search for a match to light one of the big candles nearby. I squinted my eyes closed and put my hands over them to let my eyes become accustomed to the dark. As I turned to the nearest table, I found matches in the drawer, lit a candle in a large silver candlestick and went directly to the velvet chest.

After opening the latch, I unwrapped my vase and was about to place it into the empty space, but suddenly the space itself began to shrink and grow! I sat in utter amazement watching it grow smaller and larger, over and over as if the space itself were alive, had a mind of its own and did not want to allow me a chance to fit my vase into it. The vase was acting in the same odd way. After a few confusing and infuriating moments of this, I wrapped the vase back up and began thinking what to do next. *How terribly odd*, I thought. *It is the middle of the night, and I am half asleep. The light is very dim in this room. Surely, I imagined that!* I began to unwrap the vase once more when a rush of air came at me from behind, blowing the candle out leaving me chilled through.

As I turned around to trace the source off the gush of air, my eyes caught in the half-light a shadow form or were there two? There were two. One was a figure in flowing robes pressing against or in front of another figure behind it. All I could make out of the one behind were red eyes and only for a second. The first figure's hair covered everything. Suddenly, the forms were gone.

The gushing air stopped. My neck settled down, but I was shivering. Still stupefied by vases that change size, candles that blow themselves out, shadows with red eyes and being still half-asleep, I scurried back to my bed and pulled up the covers as fast as my legs would carry me! As I ran, I heard the huge door to the forbidden bedroom squeak as it gently closed behind me.

10

In the morning Cerena knocked lightly at my door and looked in. When she saw I was awake, she came in and opened my curtains which made me cover my face from the light. "Cerena, please come over and sit on my bed. I have something to ask you about, or to tell you, really. I cannot tell you which it is, but I need you to listen."

She came and sat beside me as I remained laying down. "What is it, Babo? I am right here. Has something upset you? You have worry marks that are not healthy or pretty on your forehead, and your eyes look quite sad and a little red. Are you not feeling well?" she asked, putting the back of her hand against my forehead.

"I am not ill in the least. In fact I feel fine and have lots of energy. This is it, Cerena. I have been having the most curious dreams and the strangest things happening to me. I have met quite the most unimaginable people and creatures in the past few days that am beginning to think I have gone completely crazy! Can you tell a difference in me this morning or yesterday? Do I seem myself to you or quite insane?"

By this time I was sitting up, propped up on my pillows where Cerena moved over close, put her arm around me and asked quietly, "Do you remember when you were very small, about five years old and you had dreams that you described to me as full of fairies and birds and billowing curtains and jars of secrets?"

"Not this minute," I said as I looked into her eyes.

"Well, you did have such dreams and shared them with me and your grandmamma. Your Nimee dismissed them as your creative imagination and too many fairytales before bed, but she knew better. I, on the other hand, came to believe you either actually saw these things in real life or your dreams were so vivid that it made no difference. They were all real as far as you were concerned. Now why don't you start by telling me about these new dreams, and we will go from there?"

I listened closely to what Cerena had said and answered her. "Cerena, I knew you would really listen because I am sure some of them were not dreams at all. I believe as well that others were. Everything is getting all mixed up and tumbled together," I told her.

"Babo, start where you can remember and tell me as if it were a story," Cerena said calmly.

I started from the beginning—the past Saturday evening when I had planned my escape up to the round green hill. I told her about everything—everyone and thing I had met, what I had been told, the dreams in between, the two visits to the forbidden bedroom, all about the vase, the changing shapes and the shadowy figures. I recounted everything in minute detail. "Oh, Cerena, I know you think I'm crazy for sure!" I said in desperation.

She had been listening to my every word with a never-changing expression that I did not understand. She sat up, looked me in the eye and said, "Louisanna, I do not believe you are crazy in the least and if you are, I say all the better for it. I cannot tell you whether these things are real or not, whether they happened to you in a dream or in reality. There is a very fine line between the physical world and the spiritual one. Some people are born with the gift of being close to the door between those two worlds. People of that sort are curious, creative, visionary, imaginative and of uncommon sensitivity. Your Nimee has this about her in every way, and such a delightful, wondrous human being she is. It seems true enough that she has passed this part of herself on to you.

"Listen to me, Louisa. Your gifts are treasures but also a responsibility and you must learn to use them with wisdom and only for good. Do you understand, Louisanna, for that is all that I know how to explain?"

I had more than a thousand questions, but Cerena only put up her hand, which I knew was the sign that she simply would not or could not answer. She did not know. I was quite relieved to find out that I had not gone mad, but that I had these strange gifts and to hear about the line between physical and spiritual world. That could explain a good bit of what had been happening in my case. In the spirit of imagination, sensitivity and vision, I decided to approach my next visit to the lopsided house with creativity.

I wrote a bit in my journal that night:

Remember to ask Eli about how to use my gifts only for good. Find more about these gifts. Who should I ask about the shadow people I saw? I am quite sure the first shadow was there to protect me from the one behind … I was quite suspicious of that one … Maybe that's what the message of both good and bad was all about … Who knows? (I should have a talk with Eli very soon …)

Little did I know how all these questions would be answered and not only by Eli.

II

___

The next morning, I dressed hurriedly, not forgetting to put the key and the tiny vase, wrapped securely in my pocket. I went down in time to ask Cerena for a quick breakfast in the kitchen because I had planned to play outside in the nice sunshine today. She agreed and told me not to go far. She explained that she would be extra busy today, but she expected me for lunch. I asked her where Grandmamma was today. "She has gone to town with Eli and Ernestine for a bit of shopping."

"Well," I asked, "how about a late lunch then?"

"Oh, all right, Louisanna. Just see to it you stay dry. The yard and paths are in puddles." As I answered she added, "Stay out of trouble."

"I will," I said as I tumbled out the back door.

Not wanting to take the chance of anyone who might be about in the front of the house catching me going toward the hill, I ventured way off to the left of the house down a pathway of underbrush, got myself sopping wet, went up through the tree line and cut across the field. I trudged through the muck from the rain until I was nearly one-fourth of the way up the slope of the hill, with the mushy rock in sight. Taking off as fast as I could, I ran toward the rock. The landing was not at all what I expected. I stumbled twice along the way, nearly falling, and once I reached out for the rock and landed on it, I hit hard. My hands and arms were screaming in pain and I felt as if I had fallen out of a tree, for all the breath had been knocked from my lungs. On top of this, my friend the rock was no longer mushy. It was hard as any piece of stone could ever be!

As I nursed my wounds and recovered my breath, I tried to reconstruct what had just taken place. Was this the same rock? It was exactly the same shape and in the same general area as far as I could tell. Maybe it was indeed made of clay and had hardened. That would not make sense because we had just had at least a day and a half of hard rain. If anything, it should, by logic, have dripped and melted, at least a bit. Well, it was no good wasting time on matters that cannot be understood or helped. I would have to lick my wounds and move on, not depending on that rock for cushioning in future.

Suddenly I felt the rock beginning to move! Turning around I heard a low voice speaking to me very slowly.

"Ouch," it said. "My shell is tough, but you hit me rather hard and I'm afraid you woke me up." Staring me in the face was a giant tortoise—the biggest one in the whole world. He looked older than the world itself and was covered with moss just like the rock. "Well, I'm very sorry!" I said to the tortoise in great surprise. "I didn't know you were there!"

He replied, "Don't worry. It is a common mistake. I am often taken for a part of this rock and in a way I suppose I am. What is your name, if you don't mind me asking?"

"I don't mind at all. My name is Mary Margaret Louisanna Broadcloathe, but you may call me Louisa."

"Thank you so much," said the tortoise, "because I don't have enough breath to say all those pretty names at once."

I had never met a speaking tortoise or one this old, strange and big! He was sort of funny-looking too. He had huge pink eyes with green dots that hung in his head like a hound dog's eyes. His mouth was very pointed and quite green. The sound of his voice was like the ringing of a gigantic brass bell. Bong! Bong!

"What is your name, if you don't mind?" I asked.

"My name is a long one similar to yours, so please call me Mel," answered the tortoise.

"I am pleased to meet you, Mel," I said.

Mel took his time and spoke just as a tortoise moves—very slowly. I liked him immediately! "Well," I said, "it has been so nice meeting you, but I suppose I'd better be on my way. I'm in sort of a hurry."

"I can see that," he answered. "Do you mind if I ask where you are going?"

"I'm going to the top of the hill. I met some new friends there and want to see them again. Have you ever been to the top? It is very, very beautiful country with waterfalls, fairies and all sorts of treasures."

Mel answered, "I've been most everywhere in my life and since you have been there before you know the way, Louisa?" he asked with his tortoise head cocked to one side and a worried look on his brow.

"I know the way. Don't worry about me," I said with total security in my voice.

As I walked away, I waved and said, "I hope to see you again, Mel!"

"I'm sure you will, Louisa. I am sure you will. Take care and Godspeed," he answered.

Bruised, limping and wet, I continued uphill. I climbed and climbed and climbed, stopping three or four times just to catch my breath and rest my legs and arms. I was on all fours going up because the ground did not lay down and out as it had for me before. Several times I wondered where the bobbling, zipping its were to help me, but they were nowhere to be found.

I was so angry at that rock for turning hard and bruising me all up and at the its for not coming to my aid that I said to myself, "I can do this on my own. I don't need anyone to lead the way or some old rock to fall down on. I've been up there before, and I can go again!"

About this time I reached the rim of the top of the hill. It overhung looming large and treacherous. The sky was growing dark as the clouds began to swirl and the thunderous noises were all around me. I closed my eyes and reached up for the rim of the overhang when out of the darkness a large hand took hold of mine and lifted me as though I was a feather up, up and out of the storm.

The being that stood before me was entirely beautiful. I had expected Sol and Anna would be there waiting for me, but at the sight of this creature, all thoughts of either of them or their little funny-looking friend left me. I have no idea how long I stood gazing upon this man-like being. He towered above me and could have been over seven feet in height. His body was covered with feathers of shimmering shades of velvet blues and dark almost black violet all the way down his arms and legs, but his feet were that of a human and very strong. At the top of each shoulder, there were tips of what were quite certainly wings of the same colors with silver threads running through. His skin was a dark chestnut and smooth and his hair was long black and braided down to his shoulders straight back from his face with silver stars woven into each row of braids and at the end. He stood with his hand down at his sides, open-palmed. He smiled and rays of sun radiated from his smile. His eyes were the brightest and darkest blue in the world and as he looked at me, fire shot out from them in all directions and yet straight into mine.

I did not know what to say or do in the presence of this being, as I was wondering if this might very well be God himself! He certainly looked important enough to worship.

"Louisa," he asked, "do your scrapes and bruises hurt? Did you have no help up the hill? What has happened to your little friends?" His voice was that of rushing water and cello music blended together.

Still dumbstruck, I answered, "Well, I suppose they hurt a little, and no, I didn't have help. I don't know what has happened to the its who helped me. I suppose they are angry with me or don't care about me anymore."

"Well, you no longer have to worry about them, for I am here to help you now, and I have much more power than they," he answered.

"Who are you?" I asked.

"I am the Son of the Morning since ancient times. But now that we are friends, you may call me Apollyon. Here, let me," and he kneeled down and placed his hands on my shoulders very lightly and my bruises and scrapes were gone!

"You certainly do have power!" I said.

Wanting this being to know I had other friends with special powers, I said, "I have some friends here who live in the lopsided house that I would like to introduce you to!"

Apollyon responded quite sharply, "You've been to that little house, have you? And did you find anything there that captured your attention or imagination? I can show you worlds and treasures beyond your wildest dreams that could never be contained in such a lopsided little house as that!"

I thought about Anna, Sol and Jepetto and how much fun and how light-hearted they had been. I thought about how kind they were to me and how they fed me a banquet under the billowing canopy. I remembered how magical the jars were and how much I loved my vase. I remembered where it had led me and how the key had all but leapt into my hand from inside the jar. I was confused by Apollyon's demeaning attitude about the little house, but I kept my feelings to myself.

I looked around to see where all the butterflies were, but there were none to be seen. Although I could hear the rushing of the waterfalls, I could not see them or much of anything else through the dark clouds and haze that was surrounding us on all sides.

"You are looking for your friends or others to play with? If it is more company that you wish for," Apollyon said, "you have only to ask!" He turned slightly to the left and motioned with his winged arm to a group of animals slowly making their way through the cloudy haze a distance away. "Come, my comrades, and meet our new traveling companion," he said to the group of animals. In his company were a pair of hyenas, one huge horse, four goats, a half-dozen wolves, and seven extremely large, severe-looking ravens. Between the horses' legs slivered a serpent-like lizard that had a plume and horn.

The horse came and stood beside his master proudly and as he did, the lizard wound itself up and around Apollyon's right leg and arm. As it did so, its small legs it had walked upon withdrew inside itself, and it rested its head on Apollyon's shoulder. I could not take my eyes off the horn. It looked as if it could have been made of wood and so old that termites had nested in it over centuries. It coiled out and around and was hollow at the end. I did not like this creature from the time I saw it appear from a distance, but it was by far Apollyon's favorite.

The remainder of the company grouped themselves around Apollyon and the horse like a sheepish entourage. Their master waved his hand over them and smiled, showing his glimmering white teeth and said, "Louisa, meet my friends and faithful followers. My comrades, this is she—the child for whose arrival I have been waiting."

At these words, every animal turned its gaze upon me with the same look in its eyes that Apollyon had. It was a look that I could not pull myself away from and yet it made me feel uncomfortable in my stomach and made the hairs on the back of my neck stand up. I thought to myself, *I am in for a real adventure this time!*

"Hello!" I said cheerfully. "Yes, my name is Louisa and it is good to meet you all. I hope to get to know each of you and learn your names soon." I looked at each creature and smiled my best how-do-you-do smile. I continued speaking to the group, "My new friend Apollyon told me that we might be friends."

The group of animals had been staring at me with dead expressions up until now. At my inference of being friends, their eyes turned to Apollyon and then to one another with expressions as if they understood nothing I had said. The only members of this group who seemed at all alert were the serpent and the terrible, fierce-looking wolves.

Since I had gotten no response from his comrades, as he referred to them, I addressed Apollyon. "Excuse me," I said. "I hate to interrupt," I said because he was having a conversation with the serpent, "but we are all gathered here in a group and it seems that you are preparing to travel somewhere. Is that right?"

"Well, and you are a quick study, Louisa," Apollyon answered me.

"Where are all of you going? Is it going to be an exciting journey with elves, dragons, fairies, damsels in distress and such? If that is the kind of fairy tale adventure you're planning, I would really like to go with you."

"Ah-ha, and do you like the idea of such an adventure? I see! Well, you shall have one for that is exactly the journey for which we leave. I would stress the dragons and the damsel in distress are the main players in our plan."

To this I replied, "Oh, how exciting! When do we leave?"

Apollyon answered, "There is no better time than the present!"

12

"Shall we then go?" Apollyon asked.

To my surprise, all of the company answered at once, "We shall go for you!"

These regular, everyday animals can speak! I thought to myself. *What else may I expect today?*

The company lined up with the horse out in front with his master on his back. I was told to walk beside Apollyon and the horse to his right. Behind the horse were the goats and then the hyenas. The ravens flew just above us except for one that sat upon the master's left shoulder and the snake remained coiled around his leg and arm and rested its terrible horned head on Apollyon's right hand. Once all of us were in order and to my greater and greater surprise and growing uncertainty if I was in the right company, the raven on Apollyon's shoulder gave the order, "Now we begin our journey!" and all the company gave a loud shout and hailed, "Let us depart, yea!" The horse lifted his front legs high in the air and pounded his hooves and we were off.

"Where are we going?" I looked up at our leader and asked.

The ancient one, the Son of the Morning, looking straight ahead and replied, "You will find out as we go, and soon enough. My inner kingdom is not far but will seem so to you, so there will be no need to for questions or complaining. There will be enough to see of that which your eyes have never feasted upon to keep indifference from creeping into your mind, Louisa." He answered in a tone that told me I should not ask more.

I would have in fact turned around and gone the opposite way to find my real friends, but the snake was hovering above me with its terrible horn. As I did not want to bring its attention to myself, I said nothing and walked on with the others with no idea where I was being lead or how I would get out of the situation in which I so quickly found myself.

13

All the time I had spent carelessly with Apollyon and his bedraggled companions, Anna and Sol were very concerned about my whereabouts and safety. The two were seers or prophets in the sense that they are able to see things that are happening now in their world—the world of the Lopsided Kingdom. I had met them only once, but I seemed to have known them all my life. Sol's and Anna's names are from ancient times but not as ancient as Apollyon. He has been ruler of the Lopsided Kingdom since the very beginning of time. That had been prophesied to change somehow through me.

Sol and Anna knew the Time was the Time for me to return to their kingdom and they had been waiting for me. When I did not come up the hill and over it at the exact place as I had before which was the place ordained for me to come up, they knew I was in some sort of trouble.

Anna said to Sol for the third time, "Oh husband, I do hope with all that is in me the child did not come up and enter the wrong way."

"I do wish as you do, my dear. There is only one way to enter, and by entering the wrong way, if that is what happened, she has surely been snatched up by the evil one."

Anna continued, nearly in tears, "We know too well that the prophecy will fall on the child. For hundreds of years now he has ruled, kept the truth buried and the great nymphs, priests and prophets imprisoned. The Banelands flourish while the people of the Truthlands live in fear. They bear no children or hide them. The horses and other four-hoofed animals have fled to the Elysian Fields and still he taunts them, keeping them imprisoned with his wolves. Our lopsided house which is the only entryway to the Arielian Plains is the one remaining stronghold hidden from him and his minions."

I did not know until the first night of my journey that I had the gift of prophecy myself, though I always suspected it with all that had happened at home. This gift that in the end saved my very life!

〜〜〜〜〜〜〜〜〜〜〜〜〜〜〜〜〜〜〜〜

I do not know how to tell how exhausted I was by the time Apollyon allowed us to stop for the night. He did not allow us to slow down or rest for one minute. He was riding and the remainder of us walked for hours until the sun had been long set and I could see the moon through the haze of clouds which never moved or were blown away.

We reached a body of water that seemed to come upon us out of nowhere. Surrounded by mountains that were high and steep, we could see looming darkness and fog rising from the water. This must have been a regular stopping place for travelers for there was a deep well surrounded by stones and an elegant tent such as I have seen in books. It was made of silk cloths of dark purples and blues and trimmed in gold leaf, fit for *Arabian Nights*. There was also a trough for water and animal food but no covered place for animals to bed down that I could see. Most of the grass was around the large tent and beyond there was only sand or stone.

The animals went right to eating and drinking from the troughs. I had no idea what was to become of me for the night. One of the goats had been quite friendly to me compared to the others, so I approached him and asked, "Sir, have you an idea where I am supposed to eat or sleep tonight?"

"Oh, yes. The master will have you with him. And well you will be fed and in comfort will you sleep, for you are …"

One of the hyenas poked him and said, "Enough, Johann. Quiet, for you know what is good for you!"

As I was listening, the goat whose ribs were showing from misuse and hunger gave me as crooked a smile as a goat can give and went back to his eating. At this, I heard Apollyon's voice behind me, "Conversing with the lower company will get you nowhere, Louisanna. Come. It is time to dine."

Apollyon led me into his elegant tent. He offered beautiful clean clothes laid out for me and sent me away with a young dark-skinned woman who took me to a smaller tent in back. There I bathed and put on the clean clothes. I had no idea what became of my clothes, but the new clothes were beautiful! I now wore a silk petticoat that was golden yellow and a linen and silk pinafore of dark green, both tea length, my blouse was cotton and silk, also yellow, with gathered, ruffled sleeves to my wrists. I wore white stockings and the loveliest slippers made of calfskin that were crimson and purple with golden stars. The young dark-skinned woman braided my curls and wove little moons and stars into the braids, both gold and silver. She had no mirror, but a large, polished bowl where I could see my reflection. I didn't look anything like myself, I thought, but I looked pretty in an odd sort of way.

She led me back through the night to Apollyon's tent. Several lanterns were burning brightly on each side of the entrance and inside the tent. I was glad for that because I was not looking forward to being with him in the tent. Apollyon was lounging on one of the many huge pillows in a circle in the second room, which I supposed was the room for eating.

In the center was a large wooden bowl of fruit, nuts and cheese, and beside it was bread that I had never before seen. This bread was flat and brown in color and enough to feed an army. "Come, sit and feast yourself here beside me." My host beckoned to me with his fingers, which were strangely free of feathers in the light of the tent.

I did not want to sit close to him or his snake, so I said politely, "Thank you, but this pillow right here looks very comfortable and just my size." I sat right down about three quarters of the way across the circle from him.

"Oh my, a very independent one she is and quite of her own mind," Apollyon said to the snake and the several young women who had come into the room and were hovering around him like a harem.

"Eat!" he said to me commandingly, until I began to take a few bites of bread. After this, he said to the snake, "Little Horn, sleep by the entrance to our tent tonight so that no one comes nor goes until I awake." As he said this, the snake, whose name I now knew, slithered past me and coiled up at my only possible way of escape. Apollyon looked at me with smiling eyes full of pure evil.

14

Footfalls echo in the memory
Down the passage we did not take
Towards the door we never opened
Into the rose-garden
—T. S. Eliot

At about the same time I laid my head down, one of the women dimmed the lanterns in our tent. I was unsuccessfully doing my best to keep my eyes closed hoping to go to sleep and wake up and find out this had all been a horrible nightmare. Meanwhile, my real friends, Sol, Anna and Jepetto were, unbeknownst to me, planning my rescue.

Inside the Lopsided House, Sol and Anna were calling upon many more friends I did not know I had in this kingdom to gather on that very night. They were arriving in groups. Among them were leopards, several fine toads, a pair of great white Pyrenees dogs, one very old owl, several large house cats and an ancient plumed falcon.

Inside the lopsided house, Anna repeated ancient words that had not been put to use in centuries:

Time is the Time.
The Passage many is compelled to hold.
For adjoining journeys come to unfold in
Time. To thus encompass in arena all,

Unseal your sides old house,
Or entirety falls.

Anna finished these words and the walls of the lopsided house began to stretch and widen. The house became the exact size necessary for the number of Sol and Anna's friends who arrived that night! Everyone had a seat, and no one even had to bump elbows as they ate together. As they arrived, Anna and Jepetto served everyone the foods of their liking. The food that appeared on the table expanded the same as the house did.

Once they had eaten and gathered around Sol, he told them, "We all knew the child would come and she did, as we expected. She chose her treasures perfectly, as we knew she would and arrived home safely the same night." All eyes were fixed upon Sol. Jepetto was nodding his head in agreement and jumping up and down on his stool, yet trying as hard as he could to contain himself, for he was excited for all the company and because there was a mission to be done.

Sol went on, "This child as we all know, has to come to us for the purpose of the journey to Eden. It was our responsibility and it was the prophecy that she go but not with him! For a reason we cannot clearly see, something set her off course when she started up the green hill the second time. She came up the wrong way!"

After a brief moment of whispering and gasping, an echoing hush fell over the group. Some looked up wringing their paws and wings. Others bowed their heads as if they were praying, but no one said a word.

Finally one of the toads spoke up. He raised his bright green head and said, "But there is only one way to enter the kingdom."

"Ah," Sol answered, "there is only one way to enter the kingdom of God, but many try to enter by other means. This is nothing new. People have tried it this way since ancient times, the same way Louisanna did, I imagine—by clawing and clutching her way up on her own without help. It is no good. It leads only to destruction."

The old owl said, "It seems clear to me—(hiccup!) do excuse me—that our enemy saw her coming this way and drew her up out of the storm. I am sure of it. I have seen this before." His voice was that of an old brass horn and many years in a British university library. He apologized again, saying to Anna that her bread pudding was exceptional and he had overeaten much to his chagrin.

Anna said, "No matter worrying over spilled milk or a hiccup, Huckabee. The child is our responsibility as well as reversing this wrongful turn in the fulfillment of the prophecy. We have no choice in what we must do! I have seen that they have arrived at the River Styx and will be crossing over into our enemy's inner territory first thing tomorrow. We must set out tonight!"

The old owl spoke up once more. "I say, do we need to call upon a champion for the child?"

The falcon said to Sol, "I am prepared to fly."

"And I to run with him," said Borneo the panther, "in order to cover both the ground and the air from his watchers and we may very well need her by the time we cross that terrible river."

The male Pyrenees said, "Do not underestimate our power. Our legs are strong and swift. We are able to climb with much nimbleness, and as gentle as we seem, for righteousness' sake, we are able to tear the throat out of any enemy!"

The housecats began to step forward. "Do not forget that we are chameleons and able to grow into lions or become as small as sand flies as the need arises, for we have been given the gift." Sol and Anna looked around at their company of fine friends.

"Not yet. We do not know who her champion will be. We will know when the time comes for that, for one of us will be given the sign." Anna continued, "I have been given the knowing and Sol as well that we are to go ahead with our journey through the Passage. Traveling across country is much too dangerous. Satan has his minion spies out and about. This is the very reason for the Passage. Why risk it any other way?"

Sol was rubbing his chin as he did when thinking and added, "Not to put a pun on it, but to be the devil's advocate here, we must remember our seeing gifts are cut off once we go a certain depth into the Passage. I agree that they come and go, but it is hard to tell when they are available to us. To me, that is a drawback. What say you all, those with the seeing and those without?"

After a long discussion, including Jepetto hopping up and down, gesticulating and pirouetting in hand with a few of the toads, when his vote was called for, it was decided that the panther and the falcon would go by countryside. This way the falcon could fly like the wind back and forth with news to them and from the panther, who could run just as fast and was a worthy opponent to any of the evil one's minions.

The remainder of the company would indeed go by way of the Passage, with Sol and Anna in the lead.

I nodded off to sleep despite my hyper-vigilance over the snake and had no idea how long I slept before the dreams began. They were filled with images of Sol, Anna, Jepetto, many speaking animals and me tumbling and falling over, up and down the green hill in the storm and darkness, the horrible snake at my heels. I woke myself up calling out for help and was sweating and crying. I sat up suddenly terrified that anyone in the tent might have heard my cries . I looked around and all was dark and quiet. I was panting. The lanterns had burned themselves out. I must have been asleep for quite a while. As my eyes adjusted, I could tell dawn was nearing and that I was in the tent alone.

Outside I could hear voices and scuffling about. As I was about to get up, the woman appeared who had helped me with my clothes the night before. She took me to a small tent to wash, fed me a bit of food and told me to wait inside the tent.

I tried to remember my dreams—Sol and Anna, the horrible snake— and I remembered what Cerena told me about the gift of having a foot in both this world and the next and what a thin line there was between them. Cerena had cautioned me to use my gifts for good. Maybe if I tried—really tried—to use them, I could somehow bridge that line now and get some help from someone on this side of the world! If I was here, then Sol and Anna surely had to be close by.

I closed my eyes very tightly and thought only of the beam of light I had seen shining and consuming everything from the window of the spare bedroom. I don't know why I thought to do this, but little by little I began to hear music-like sounds and the rushing of waterfalls. Out of those sounds came a vision of Sol and Anna. They were convening a group including Jepetto and seemed to be readying themselves for a journey. Within the music, I could make out a theme of what their conversation was about: finding someone who was being imprisoned by a dark and evil presence. I was about to see more and was coming to wonder if this could be me when I was suddenly yanked from my half-dream by the arm of one of the women who served Apollyon.

15

Outside in front of the tents everyone gathered in a loose line and was complaining that they had not had enough to eat. Apollyon's voice rang out as he came out of the dimness on his horse with the snake already coiled around his arm.

He laughed at us and said, "Ha, ha! You will have more to snivel about than your bellies unless you are very careful to do exactly as I say while crossing the river. Most of you have made this crossing before and only live to make it again because I accompanied you and well you know it! The rest of you take heed and know that from the time we enter the boat until you again see the sun, a fate worse even than death may overtake you if you attempt to leave my guard. Do you now understand my words?" Not one of us answered. He shouted at us again, "I will not waste my voice on you! We go! The woman will lead. Follow her. Louisa, you will ride behind me on the new steed. Mount, with the woman's help."

I turned in the direction he pointed and there was a smaller horse, much like his own, barebacked, with only bit and reins. Even as terrified as I was and shaking in my very shoes, I was able to get on the horse and settle onto her back quite easily. The woman turned her head up to me and with a look of fear and sorrow in her eyes she led us to stand behind Apollyon and took her place at the front of the line beside the river.

We were upon the edge of the water and I could see in the distance that the entire river was blanketed in thick mist that was coming upward from the water or so it seemed. Out of the mist there came the sound of a hollow echoing bong, interspersed with wailing cries. I would say on a scale of one to ten, it was a ten of the most sorrowful sounds in the world. Coming out of the mist was a vessel of a kind I have never seen, with a wide deck and sharp up-turned sides. A hooded figure was standing and steering the boat. As it drew closer I could see that the long staff he used to steer was topped with a human skull. How could I escape? If I got onto that boat, I was sure I would never see this side of the river or home again!

Once the boat was set upon the bank, the morbid sounds grew less frequent and much softer. The figure in the boat said, "Your Ferryman is here. All with the courage to cross come. The master knows the weight of my load. I have no need to put my aged and sorrowful breath to the test today. Beware all who enter."

At this Apollyon stopped him. "That is enough! Do you not think they know what they do? With whom do you see them? You have but one use to me! Do your work, old man!"

The stooped figure looked up long enough for me to see part of his horrible face—nearly a skull itself! He quickly pulled his hood down with one of his skeletal hands and I saw long, yellow fingernails. The ferryman made his way to the back of the boat and we began to board.

The woman, my horse and me, Apollyon and his horse, Little Horn, the head raven, one of the hyenas and the male wolf crossed together. The ferry seemed to fit itself to accommodate the number and weight as was necessary. The crossing was nearly unbearable. The bonging and horrible cries grew louder and the mist was now certainly coming not only off the water but from all around us and the stench made it hard to breathe.

To make things worse, the hyena, the wolf and Apollyon joined in with their cries and howls with the wailing as if they were part of some hideous choir. As for me, I hung onto my horse's mane for dear life for fear of falling into the wretched water.

I felt my horse trembling under me and bent my head down to her ear. "Are you afraid?" I asked. She gently shook her head yes. "Can you talk?" I whispered again. Yes again. "Are you a good horse?" I asked once more. Once more, her answer was a gentle yes. *Thank goodness,* I thought! *Maybe, just maybe, I have a friend!* I gave her a soft pat on the side of her head.

After what seemed like a million years, I felt the boat hit land with a sudden thump and we were thrown forward. We were led from the ferry and out of the mist onto land, soft, boggy and smelling of death. The woman turned to look at me with pitiful eyes but quickly looked away and straight ahead. The wolf came around and herded us into line behind Apollyon and on we went without a word. I turned only to see the Ferryman disappearing into the mist of the river wondering again if I would ever see the other side.

16

Sol, Anna, Jepetto and friends had set out a number of hours ago, the panther running ahead with one of the falcons to spy out my exact whereabouts. The two made it to the river just in time to see us board the ferry. The falcon returned to the group to bring the news. Borneo was awaiting his orders at the camp we had left at the river but was getting anxious.

The falcon reported to Sol's group, "Yes, we saw her board with him, but not all his company went. Only one hyena, one wolf, the two horses, a woman, one enemy raven and the horned serpent entered the ferry. It seemed to us the remainder of his group was ready to cut loose and run. They were grumbling in dissention as I left."

"This is good news and bad news," said Sol.

"We have prayed that among them there may be one who is a true believer who has gone undetected." said Anna. "Now that she is under his control, it may be her only hope until we can reach her ourselves."

"This second horse we did not see. Are you certain there were two who boarded?" Sol asked the falcon.

"I am quite sure. There was a small steed, a blonde mare," the falcon answered.

Sol's company was now deep into the Passage and still heading toward the Truthlands. They had crossed the concentric circles and managed, with Sol's and the old owl's ability to do mathematical calculations and Anna's memory of celestial navigation to find the exact stair to step off onto the

Truthlands pass itself. The roads changed without warning even as you looked at them and often stairs are very deceiving inside the lopsided house. Thus far Sol and Anna had proven to be excellent in their leadership.

There had been steep ups, downs, and sharp twists and turns up until now. At one juncture several of the toads nearly lost their lives to the depths with all their hopping and playing with Jepetto and paying no attention to what was ahead. Happily the housecats and the great Pyrenees leapt to their rescue. Mimi the female Pyrenees, came back with three green toads hopping out of her great soft mouth, smiling from ear to ear! As for the toads, they were only glad to be alive and were wildly wiping dog slobber off their fine clothes and muttering under their breath!

Tobias, the elder toad, scolded the young ones for their behavior and nearly losing their lives as they furiously attempted to catch up with Anna and Sol. Jepetto was at their heels listening to Tobias' every word and wishing he had been such a hero as the toads!

The area of the Passage they were now approaching was a resting place. The road was wide and spacious here and sunlight came in from high above. Hundreds of feet above this place there was once an ancient castle, now abandoned. Parts of the outer waterworks and the drainage system of the huge drawbridge of the castle provided the light. In a season such as this there was a gracious amount of light and everything was dry. There were even some mossy plants and roots growing hither and yon. Problems in crossing at this place came in the times of rain when huge amounts of runoff would gush down the sides and sometimes straight down the opening, flooding the passage beneath.

The travelers were fortunate to be here just long enough after a rain that there were plants and some animal life, but they did not have be feet deep in mud or sludge with nowhere to sit and rest. Although Anna had food and the ability here to call for more with her gifts, the toads, Jepetto, and the cats and dogs set out at once to forage. Soon Anna had a pot of her most savory stew of potatoes, underground parsnips and onions, garlic, and mushrooms on the fire. Sol and the others made beds and other resting places for the night for everyone and settled down with his pipe and flagon. Anna soon joined him and was nodding away on Sol's shoulder. It was good to be comfortable.

In no longer than fifteen minutes Jepetto and all the green toads were hopping up and down frantically, Jepetto pulling on Sol's sleeve and the toads nearly under Anna's skirts. They knew their place and they knew they were not to speak until they were called upon at a time like this. "What is it, Jepetto and is something wrong with you toads? You are all about to throw Anna down with this hopping!"

At this, one of the largest and greenest toads came forward and bowed before Anna and Sol, which was his custom. "If I may, we and our friend and confidant Jepetto have been in consultations since last evening and we have—"

Anna interrupted him, "Tobias, thank you for your beautiful manners, but please, if you have good news, tell us simply!"

Tobias continued, "We thought it a good idea, and so we sent three of the chameleon cats in the form of eagles ahead to the Elysian Fields to secure a spy and companion for the child. There they found a herd of horses that had been acquainted with some women who served in our enemy's tent near the river. One of the women among those who were serving the child who was also a prisoner took a certain young Elysian mare to carry the child on her journey."

"Jepetto and his friends did well, didn't we, didn't we?" Jepetto chimed in, all the time still hopping up and down and twirling around.

"Oh yes, Jepetto, you did, you did indeed!" Sol and Anna answered, patting his head as best they could, as he was still in frantic motion.

"Well, this is an answer to prayer, and before we move another step, we will give thanks," Sol said. All the company circled in together as before and this time, Sol sang an ancient song of praise that rang up to the wire opening and throughout this deserted land.

As Sol's voice rang out, his song was heard far away from the spot where he stood. Up above the mountains and waterfalls, through the rainbows and tall trees, clinging to the hilltops, down into the deep lush green valleys and up again onto the very Elysian Fields themselves, blanketed with masses of wildflowers blowing in the gentle breeze, up and up into the very throne room of the King of Kings, the song rang out.

Alleluia, He is worthy, alleluia, alleluia. He is
worthy, alleluia, alleluia, amen.

Sol, Anna, and their friends had no idea that the whole host of heaving itself was singing with them . They sang in unison as one body and it was indescribable. Sol and company did however have faith, and their praises were heard and had not gone unmerited, for as they began to travel once again the next morning, a powerful helper was on the move—a helper sent from highest heaven!

17

It had taken at least a day of traveling with this evil creature that held me captive to reach what he called his inner realm, as far as I could tell. I was very hungry, thirsty and tired. Whether it was day or night, I couldn't tell. The only light seemed to come from below rather than above. It was a gloomy, glowing, flickering, muted, and shadowed source of light, the likes of which I would never have imagined existed. There were no stars or planets or any clouds in the sky. In fact, I could see no sky that I could describe at all.

The air was thick and smelled old, making it very hard to breathe. Apollyon came around to my horse and me, smiling broadly. He held in his hand a silver flask with a jeweled top. He reached up, set me down on the ground beside him and said, "It is time for some nourishment for you, my lady. This will quench your thirst for many hours. Now drink." He put the flask to my lips. I took a sip reluctantly, but the drink was sweet and I was hungry so I drank it right down. "Very good," he said. "And now, the best is still to come!"

He took a box of pure onyx from the woman behind him. The box was bright with clear blue gemstones in the shapes of tiny stars. "Go ahead, take it," he said, and he put the box in my hand.

My hand began to feel heat coming from the box and as I looked up at him, he said, "The box holds power. Eat from it!" Inside the box were squares of bite-sized candies. Once I tasted them, I ate as fast as I could until they were gone. They were the best things I had ever tasted in the whole world!

I could not bear the heat of the box another second and dropped it. "Oh, I'm so sorry I dropped your beautiful box. I hope it's not broken!" Then I stooped to pick it up. As I did, I looked up and Apollyon's face was changing before my eyes! His eyes glowed fluid red and his mouth became a gaping hole full of two rows of sharp and uneven teeth. I was so terrified that I covered my eyes, but not in time to keep from seeing a pair horns emerging from between his braids. A deep growl came from the very pit of his body but then all was quiet as I heard his footsteps walking away.

I stood trembling with my hands still covering my eyes for quite a while, afraid to move or speak. I felt a gentle nudge against my shoulder and could tell by the smell that it was my horse. "My lady, I will bend down. Mount while no one is looking, for in a short while you will not have your wits about you. It was the food and drink. You must trust me."

The horse was already down and as I got firmly onto her back I whispered, "Yes, I will trust you. What is your name?"

"Aprion," she answered.

"Aprion," I whispered to myself, and all my senses took flight.

18

Arboreal

The company of Sol and Anna had reached the part of the Passage near the banks of the Styx. Here the passage ran close to the ground itself before it dropped off completely to go under the terrible river. Craggy rock and sand fell from the walls and pools of mud were easy to step in. The stench of the river was faint here but tolerable. Those who had traveled this way before, like Sol and Anna, knew how to set up a safe and dry camp for one night at least, even though there was little light.

Borneo, the panther who had been sent ahead, was there awaiting them at our deserted camp by the river. Sol sent Mistletoe one of the housecats, outside by way of an old tree root hole in the side of the Passage to show Borneo their exact location. Once outside, Mistletoe knew this hole would never do for a panther. It had been a tight squeeze for her. The two cats had to go back a half mile to secure an opening large enough.

Once he was safely inside and fed, Borneo reported, "Once I reached the river and saw the evil one and the child gone across, the remainder of his minions ran at the sight of me. They are traitors and cowards without him to drive them like slaves. I saw no signs of loyalty from that group."

Sol thanked the great panther for his report and went on to inform the assembled group, "The horrible body of water that is the entrance into the center of evil stands before us. Beyond is only hopelessness and death. We have no power there or to go on in his realm outside the Passage. Therefore, we will continue here until Anna or I receive further instructions. If memory serves I believe we will reach a place where we may see, or we can double back to such an area if need be."

Anna spoke up now. "I have seen that the child has crossed over. She has been seduced in some way that I am not sure of, but this seduction makes her unable to see across the lines of the living and the dead, of good and evil. Our hope is that Aprion, her horse, will keep her safe by her goodness until a helper can break through. For now, we wait and pray."

The company had many questions for which there were no answers. They soon quieted and gathered in small groups and prayed. Anna grasped Sol's hand and told him so no one else could hear, "Sol, I know that the child has seen the true face of the enemy."

"Yes, I know this as well. We have only to pray that in the end she will not remember."

Sol and Anna drew all together for prayers for the child, their journey, thanksgiving for their safety and bringing Borneo back, and for a safe and good night's rest. When sleep overtook them, each one dreamed. During different times of the night, each member of the company was visited with this message:

Arise. Do not fear.
Time is the Time.
Darkness flees.
Your hope comes on eagles' wings.
Lift up your heads. See with seeing eyes.
Praise.

As dawn drew near and the sun did its best to show itself inside the covered passage, a wind began to blow out of nowhere. One by one each awoke—Anna, Sol and Jepetto, rubbing his eyes, and all the others as the wind blew, rushing, rushing around them. They stood up and looked around.

A being drew near and stood before them. She was as bright and clear as any waterfall ever seen. Her hair was blowing around her lovely face in all the colors of the spectrum and her clothing was wraps of snow white and gold. She hovered just above the ground but did not fly. Her entire countenance spoke of power and peace. She said, "Do not be afraid. Your chameleons are speedy and creative! They wasted no time! I have come as a messenger to tell you that your prophet is at this moment on his way to the child. There will be a battle as there always has been. The war is ancient, but the child is of now.

"This battle is not yours. Yours is to pray and praise. Continue. The prophet will join you soon. Elijah who was and is now will be the child's human champion. He has always loved the child and will do what is needed. Trust him.

"You all are to go, by way of the hills, to the Elysian Fields. Others are now gathering. From there the imprisoned water nymphs of old will hear good news. The priests and prophets will be called forth. There will be feasting and praise together after Elijah comes from the heavens to free the child, if hopes and help remain strong. The bird is on the wing!" She smiled at the company and was gone.

"Was that who I think it was?" asked one of the smallest toads who was peeking out from under Sol's long robes.

"Yes, it was the great and ancient messenger angel, Arboreal. In latter Scriptures she is called Gabriel, the one and the same messenger who bore the news to the Virgin that she would be the mother of our Emmanuel. She has come to us and we must heed her words for she speaks only truth," replied the old owl.

All eyes were upon him as the wizened old bird spoke these words. Only Sol and Anna were on their knees in an attitude of prayer, whispering in unknown tongues.

Eli's Calling

Mere seconds after Arboreal delivered her message to Sol's company and as Sol and Anna's prayers were being heard, Eli was awakened from a deep sleep in his bed in Nimee's house with Cerena beside him. It was my own Eli, who trusted in his Lord and had led prayer for us two days before.

Eli had had fitful sleep. It was the dream again, but this time he knew to get out of bed and listen. Eli's ability to have a foot in both worlds had been nearly smothered out of him by his mother when he was a child. African men in New Delhi were doubted and feared by the British colonists enough as it was, his mother taught him. To be able to make anything of himself his mother brought him up to blend in, not be in any way special, use only the gifts your employer finds to his advantage and be loyal and honest.

Eli had therefore buried his ability to do things such as speak out the meaning of prophecies spoken in different tongues during worship. He would refrain from coming forth to put his hands on those who were sick, but he prayed for them silently. Outside of worship and within his community and culture, Eli was able to discern an evil or oppressive spirit within a building or in a person. He had been unable to smother these dreams. Now he would listen.

He rose from his bed, careful not to awaken Cerena. Knowing somehow to dress himself, he also gathered his coat, hat and boots but tiptoed out in his stocking feet upstairs to the spare bedroom opposite mine.

As he rounded the top of the stairs at the end of the hall there she was—Arboreal, shimmering in light. "Do not be afraid, Eli. You are right to have come. The child is in danger. When she is again in the light she will need to see you. Are you ready to go for her?"

Eli replied, "Is she not here? No one has missed her?"

The great angel answered him, "In this world she is here. In the next, she is not. It is there that her very soul is in peril for our ancient enemy has her and is on his way to use her as his pawn in his continuous game to tempt the mortal soul and make himself god over all heaven and earth. He and his minions make for Eden itself!" "But how and why Louisa?" Eli asked her.

The angel then told Eli about how the second time I attempted to climb into the next world, I entered the wrong way and Satan himself had seen his opportunity and snatched me up, pretended to be my friend, and impressed me with his beauty, powers, and gifts until I was totally without escape.

"He neither knows nor does nothing new," Arboreal said. "He is the great imitator, the great liar and the father of lies. She has friends of the true King in that Lopsided Kingdom. Her friends have powers with limits that do not compare to his. They are now deep in prayer."

Eli asked, "Lopsided Kingdom? What does the name mean?"

She told him, "Those from other times and places who have entered and returned have given it that name. On earth, it is nearly impossible to see with the human eye, unless you have true spiritual eyes that the ruler of the world is the evil one. Yes, our God has him on a leash, it is true, and may rein him in at his whim. That would take away the free will that the true King has given each person to choose good over evil. In the Lopsided Kingdom, one cannot but see, except in the very few places where truth and righteousness abide, that the enemy rules all.

"The deceiver has so overtaken the souls of people and even the beasts that all live in fear. Chaos reigns, and love is of the past. So long gone is truth that the word has no meaning but in a few places. The beasts no longer live in freedom and they fear him and believe they cannot live or be fed without him. They follow him for their every need.

"Many men and women have fled and died, while others have given in. Many others have eaten poison. The prophets are silent and no one hears truth. Their great protectors the water nymphs are in prisons in the caves and caverns, awaiting Elijah the true prophet to call them forth in the name of the one true God.

"He continually stands by the gates into the kingdom, waiting for this child who is the prophesied one to come as his next victim to do with as he pleases. The evil one has now taken this child very expertly and we must not tarry. Do you understand, dear Eli?"

"I do. Tell me, what is it that I must do—anything!" Eli's eyes were streaming with tears as he answered, but his back was straight and he felt stronger than he had since he was a boy of seventeen.

After the angel and Eli had spoken and Eli was on his way out to the hill, he was thinking over all she had told him. He understood that he must climb up the hill and enter the other side on his own. The angel could not help him. Everyone must do that on his or her own.

Eli was terribly concerned about what the heavenly messenger told him the evil one was planning to do with me once we arrived at his destination. The place he was taking me was Eden itself. The reason he needed me was I was a living person who had free will. I had free will to choose God or to choose him as my master. Could it be that he planned some sort of reenactment of the sin of man itself and this time he planned to win for eternity so that the kingdom would no longer be lopsided, but solely his—completely under his domination? No longer would anyone or anything have even free will, but total dependence on Satan? I knew nothing of this as I rode semiconscious because of the food and drink Apollyon gave me twice a day. This blocking of my senses and being inside Apollyon's territory had altered my ability to see things, even in dreams. Aprion and the woman who had charge over me kept me quiet. When I looked around all I could see was darkness. I heard sounds like people crying out for help and no one listened to them. Once, when my senses were less dull, I caught glimpses of terrible, frail-looking bald-headed humans in masses reaching up to us out of a massive ditch beside the path, desperate for help. Apollyon did nothing to soothe these suffering souls at all. As for me, I had the feeling it was his fault they were there and in that state to begin with.

All the time we were getting closer and closer to what Apollyon called the "light." I could tell because up ahead there was a glimpse of an opening, a cone into another sort of landscape. The air grew less dense and easier to breathe. The smell of death was mixing with fresh air, but we could see that the sun was setting even as we reached the light realm. I lay my head down against Aprion's soft mane and she whispered, "Sleep, my lady, for by dawn we will be at the very gates of paradise."

I looked ahead and saw Apollyon laughing. The snake sitting high on his shoulder, bellowing from his horrible horn over the cries of the souls we left behind. I was too tired and confused to understand anything. I fell asleep. I dreamed of home and Eli calling my name.

19

Sol, Anna, and company heard the message from the angel with both fear and thankfulness. The falcon went on ahead to find out just how deep underground the passage went under the River Styx and whether crossing would be safe. He returned with news that the passage itself was sound but infested with mupamoles.

"I was afraid of that," Sol said. "I have seen them before. They are, for their size the nastiest creatures alive. They have never seen the light of day so they are albino and completely blind. They make up for this with their keen sense of hearing."

"What sort of creature are they and do they pose any danger to us?" Anna asked.

Sol answered, "They are a prehistoric rodent—small but fiercely combative. Once they hear a sound, they strike, usually hitting the target around the feet and legs. Once they have a hold, they will not let go."

"What defense do we have against these mupamoles?" Anna asked.

Sol said, "The housecats are probably our best bet. They are fast and the right size. I will talk with them now." Sol called Mistletoe and the other cats, some whom had dealt with mupamoles before and a plan of action was made for crossing that part of the passage.

As they talked of a plan, Sol told Anna that never had anyone in the kingdom expected a crisis so deep in the prophecy for a child to actually be brought into the evil one's plan to reclaim Eden and the human race as his own. In the past, for centuries, for eons even, it had all been a game—a game only. Now this event that might happen in the garden could hold the fate of the world in the balance if Apollyon had his way.

Arboreal had also given good news about Elijah who loved the child, an Elijah who was to come to this kingdom and be their helper and the child's champion.

Sol and Anna spoke together as they began to move on from the night's camp. "This Elijah, we should give all thanks for his coming! Yes, for the power of the Most High that is in him will overthrow the evil. He may be the one to call our prophets out from their hiding places! We have been so long alone and with no one to teach us!" They held hands tightly and gave thanks.

Sol felt a tug on his robe and could clearly see dust being stirred up along their path. He looked at his wife and without looking down, he asked, "Anna my dear, have you noticed a disturbance of any kind along about the area of your feet or near the hem of your skirt?"

Anna responded, "Why do you ask, husband? What do you mean?"

All the time the two of them were having this conversation Jepetto was hopping up and down and as high and fast as he could, trying to get them to listen to what he was saying. Sol and Anna pretended not to see or hear him. This was a little game they often played with Jepetto just to tease him in love and because Jepetto especially liked it.

Seeing Jepetto having so much hopping fun, the frogs soon joined in and there was quite a show! By the time the game reached its peak, Jepetto was pirouetting on the back of one of the Pyrenees, several toads were doing a jig on the other one and the rest of them were doing toad swing circles around Sol, Anna and the rest of the company. Everyone was very happy and laughing as they traveled up through the Passage toward the hills to meet up with their other companions, many of whom they had not had direct contact with in hundreds of years. Little did they know that Apollyon's spies were listening closely and watching their every move.

Wormfly

Apollyon had many minions who so craved his approval that they were willing to stoop from the beautiful creatures they were created to be into ghastly forms and shapes to do his bidding. Wormfly was such a creature. Created a magnificent monarch butterfly he had freedom to soar on the winds, see above waterfalls, live among the loveliest of the flowers, dine upon nectar to his heart's desire and die when his Creator's time for him came. Wormfly traded all this for an eternal life of another sort altogether.

He was so enthralled by Apollyon's beauty, charm, power and promises that he was now an ash-colored moth. His body was the size of a pin. As for legs, he had four much too long for his body but just as thin. His wings that were once the color of peacock feathers were now ash and blotched; just large enough for him to struggle to get his pin-like body off the ground. Apollyon named him Wormfly because of his ability to blend into any environment. When he was not of practical use to Apollyon, he could roll himself up into a cocoon so thin that it looked like a tiny worm. He was one of Apollyon's most effective spies but the most depraved and hated by all the followers of Apollyon because of his ugliness and because Apollyon used and treated him so shamelessly.

Wormfly was with Sol, Anna, and company as they were traveling, talking and finally having their game together with Jepetto and the toads. He had been on the top of Sol's head where he overheard and saw everything. Wormfly was to report all he had found to Apollyon as he always did.

Wormfly was having second thoughts and these thoughts were frightening to him. About the time the travelers reached the area of the lopsided house, masses of butterflies had joined them. Butterflies of every species, size and color were flying around free in the air and among them were monarchs, such as he once was, many hundreds of years ago. Wormfly had forgotten what he had been, but at the sight of the butterflies, hearing their lighthearted voices and the sight of the monarchs, something rang out inside his dried-up, pin-like insides. He had known only pain, fear and shame for it seemed always, but now there was something bittersweet about these creatures that lured him. He wanted to want to know what they were. They gave him a feeling of —was it life?

Wormfly wanted to leave the top of Sol's head, take flight and join the butterflies in the air to be free to fly with them. He was about to try his pitiful wings when he remembered how he looked in resemblance to them. If he could even manage to get himself up and stay up as high as they were, these beautiful flying things would see his ugliness and only laugh at him and go as far from him as they could and well he knew it. This was his lot in life every day since he had become what he was—since he had chosen Apollyon over freedom. In the world in which he lived there was no mercy, no kindness and no love.

Wormfly had listened carefully, hidden down in Sol's hood, to everything about this child, the danger she was in and that Apollyon already had her within his inner kingdom. This he knew to be true. Now he knew what his plans were for the child. Unlike him, this child might have her own free will to choose. That was not certain and apparently would not be until the exact time came.

Wormfly was having second thoughts. Yes, he was. Wormfly could continue to be a spy, a Wormfly, or could he—could he—help the child? Could he help these good people find a way to give the child a better chance to choose? Wormfly would die, but as he said aloud to himself, "I am dead as I live."

20

As I dozed on Aprion's soft neck, half asleep and half aware, a vision came to me—the first one that had been this vivid. Little did I know that I was the only seer whose visions were coming clearly and steadily even inside Apollyon's inner realm and that the visions were happening as I saw them.

In my vision, I saw Eli more than halfway up the green hill and struggling. He was winded and defeated by the impossibility of the vertical climb. Just as the angel had told him that I had taken both paths up and the consequences of that decision, he finally remembered what he had known so well all his life and cried out, "My Emmanuel, I trust in You with all my soul! Help me now, for the sake of the child and to do Your will!" Eli had not finished his prayer before he was encompassed with the same bright light as I had been. Bypassing the terrible thunder, darkness and fear, the stone steps appeared before him and I saw him climb up and over the ridge to safety upon the soft green grass on the green hill.

A moment before my vision began to fade, Eli was standing up and looking around. I saw Jepetto, the toads, the pair of Pyrenees, and the rest of Sol and his company running and jumping toward him with open arms. Eli's arms were open too! Sol, Anna and all were crying, "Welcome! Welcome!"

As for me, I drifted off to sleep again with a smile on my lips and with the comfort of knowing Eli was coming for me.

I woke up with a fit and a start, and I found I had been secured with leather straps to Aprion's back at the waist. I sat up and saw that we had arrived at dawn to a clearing in the forest. Awaiting us was a camp of sorts with a stone fire pit for cooking, a makeshift tent of heavy velvets and a nearby well. This was a resting place used regularly only by Apollyon. As for me, I was simply relieved to be off my horse's back, out of the binding straps, and able to walk around. It was also nice not to be in that awful stupor! I stretched and began walking toward the well, where I heard rushing water.

I was stopped suddenly by Apollyon's voice. "Louisa, where are you going?"

I turned sharply to see him looking down at me with those piercing eyes and I said or tried to say, "I was just uh, I was, uh going to the uh …," and he interrupted me asking, "Is there something you need? For I will have it brought to you right away." With that he gestured me back to the tent, where I was put back in the charge of one of the women.

As he was standing there looking at me with his hands on his hips, I drew a deep breath of courage and said, "I heard rushing water and was going to see if there was a waterfall. I really like them and was hoping to see another one. That's all I was going to do."

"Well," he answered wryly, "if it's waterfalls you wish to see, do not worry your little self, for where we are going and will soon be there are more waterfalls and the most beautiful ones in all of creation! Now, is there anything else you like in nature—animals, plants, flowers, trees, fruits of a special kind? For if there also is anything that your heart may desire, and you may have it all! It is all for you, Louisanna! I have saved it all for you. Think about these things and later we will talk more about this, yes?"

He smiled condescendingly as he told me these things. I was so hungry and tired that I just stared at him and thought to myself, *I could eat every kind of berry or fruit or even a leaf right now!* But I kept quiet and just smiled back at him and replied, "Yes, sir. That would be quite nice. Thank you, sir," just as I was taught.

"Well then," he replied, "now we will rest, eat, drink and be again on our way, for the morning is high, and time is a precious thing."

After the food and water or whatever it was in the containers went down my throat, I began to feel better. I was also allowed one bite of bread and cheese and he gave me no more of the fancy candies. The fresh well water was the best thing I had ever tasted in my life! It was cool, crisp and fresh as a cucumber. Heavenly water!

Apollyon soon told us it was time to go. The woman and I whispered to one another that we wished we had been given a little of the crispy roasted meat Apollyon had from the pit, but he did not offer to share it with any of us and we knew not to ask.

Aprion was in good spirits and ready for me to mount again. I gave her a firm but gentle pat and she in response, quietly shook her lovely mane in the breeze. *Maybe she was lucky enough to have been given some of the leftovers,* I thought to myself. Off we went, this time to my despair and great apprehension, without any of the women. There were now only that evil man, his horse, his awful horned pet, Aprion and me.

My beautiful clothes were filthy and ragged, at least the outer parts, so I was only in my under-dress, picked and messy looking, stockings and slippers. There were some of the braids left in my hair and one of the women attempted to help me wash and pull my hair back up, but Apollyon would have none of it and rushed us on. His moods seemed to change like the wind. These mood swings were so unpredictable that they were beginning to scare me.

As for me, I tried my best to pay him no attention and used my imagination as if I were in another place entirely. It was not hard to do because all around me it seemed as if we were entering a gateway to a place like paradise, which is at least on one side of our path; and the other? It was very strange! I had never seen a landscape with such opposite sides to it in my entire life! I could not believe there was another place like it in the world.

If someone had asked me to describe the difference in them in two words, I would have said paradise and purgatory. I do not say heaven and hell because there was no presence of angels or the face of God Himself. I felt nothing that gave me the sense of being separated from God, yet uneasy in my heart and stomach. Eli says that is where a person's soul lives, in the heart and in the stomach. Eli! I thought, *Cerena and Eli, I miss them! Where must they think I am? I've been here for nearly two days.*

My homesick thoughts were brutally interrupted by the crashing sounds of huge boulders falling from the mountainside to my left! Aprion was so startled that she rose up on her back legs, nearly throwing me off her back!

From out of nowhere came scurrying, flying and slithering, horrible creatures of all kinds, the like of which are never to be seen in the world! There were horrible flies screeching in tiny, incoherent words and rat-like mammals with rotted backs and tails as long as a full-grown garden snake and ears like bats. I caught a glimpse of what appeared to be half-worm, half-wasp creatures. Their heads were at least twice as large as rest of their bodies. The rat-like creatures were both fleeing and attacking the worm-wasps at once in retaliation it seemed, as the screeching flies bore down upon the rats.

Out of yet another nowhere appeared the terrible head of a flying serpent so huge that its body cast a shadow across the entire clearing. Its wings and tail arose from behind the mountains. It flew over our heads, wailing strange unknown words. To these words, both Apollyon and Little Horn cried out answers in hideous and bizarre sounds. My fear was that this flying lizard would come to swoop me up with its dreadful claws and eat me alive!

Apollyon must have known this was my fear because he yelled to me, "Oh no, and well your so-called champion will not come for you. Not yet! For you, Louisanna, are mine still!" And he let out a terrifying laugh. This gave me shivers down my spine and I closed my eyes. I kept my head down and held on to Aprion's neck as tightly as I could, crying into her mane.

Many other creatures too terrible to describe were among those exposed out of their dark nesting places at the boulder slide. The echoing, ear-piercing sounds they made were at least as pitiful and horrible as the hordes of souls we had passed the day before. Total chaos reigned! I looked up ahead; little horn was echoing cries from his vile pipe and Apollyon to my disgust, was lifting his hands as if in praise and laughing. For the first time since I left home, I was absolutely terrified.

21

Eli and Sol

We as aimless souls in ever issuing carriers of time, or do we believe it only to be the lovely remains, Through glowing spirals of intense, pulsing universe, seeking, searching to restore or yet to reclaim that, for which as until he fell prostrate Augustine strained, in our restless and heated selves cannot find. When at our conception should blink, a sole interval of faith, grasp within the hole, that which our yearning and painful consciousness seek, turns its very Shekinah glory back, is found, to our effervescing gladness, even close of all hearts' compulsion to striving, to be the very object, receiver and ere more, the exactness, verity and Truth. Moreover, its selfsame Fulfillment and Font, both Alpha and Omega.

Eli was now in the company of Sol and Anna, and they were making straight their way toward Apollyon's destination by a route in the Passage that would take them through the Elysian Fields. Eli and Sol, both being men, had many things in common, such as the ability to see, hear and know spiritual things and their meaning. Both men were steeped in the knowledge of their cultures, Eli in the South African and East Indian and Sol in that of ancient Israel and his present kingdom. The most important thing they had in common was they were men of furious faith. They immediately bonded and talked of all things they shared as they traveled. Anna listened and was glad by hearing the deep sharing of these two powerful men of faith and courage. She also loved to hear them laugh, holding their sides, nearly doubling over. It had been so long since Sol had this kind of comradeship and Anna was glad for him.

Jepetto, along with the toads did their best to get the attention of the two, but to no avail. Jepetto finally stumbled over his own huge flat feet while trying his best to pirouette and fell on several of the green toads who were following much too close behind and in front of him.

Sol looked down at Jepetto and asked, "Are you all right, my fine boy?"

At this, Jepetto straightened up, brushed his large, long ears off, pulled and straightened his trousers and answered still moving up and down on his large toes, "Yes, Sol. Jepetto is just fine, just fine. The toads wish to know if we will be going through the Elysian Fields on our way. Jepetto and the toads like the Passage, but sunlight and grass would be nice, too!"

"Ah! So that is it, is it? The toads have the question?" asked Sol with a chuckle in his voice.

Jepetto looked up at Sol with his head propped to one side and hands akimbo, yet still walking and answered, "Well, we all want to know, but chiefly the toads." Sol looked at Eli and they smiled broadly at one another.

Sol answered Jepetto and patted him on the head as he did so, "We shall, dear one. Toads, you too may know that we will see the Elysian Fields by the end of this day!" At this statement, the toads and Jepetto began to hop and skip and pirouette and hop all over the other animals, telling them the news!

The Truthlands and its people had its center in the Elysian Fields. If anyone asked another in this kingdom where to find a people who believed in and still worshipped the true God, they would be directed to the Elysian Fields. Not only was it attractive for that reason, but it was also by far the loveliest expanse of rolling hills in the kingdom. Wildflowers bloomed year round, because the climate there was mild and humid from winds off the sea.

There were still many birds and flying insects as well as hundreds of thousands of ladybugs to pollinate the flowers, trees and grasses. The wild horses lived there in peace and were very populous and beautifully bred.

The most appealing things by far about the Truthlands and the Elysian Fields were the people who dwelled there. They were a people of humility, grace and hospitality. They were lovers of music, dance, and praise. These people would welcome anyone into their homes with abandon. They had one fatal flaw—innocence for lack of wisdom, for they had no teacher of the truth for hundreds of years. In their lack of wisdom, they were easily led astray by evil. Their numbers were growing thin, as birth could not keep up with the lost. Their need for a teacher of the truth was great indeed.

They had no teachers for ages because the prophets and priests had fled for their lives. When Eli asked why they fled so easily, Sol explained that it was not so easily. It was that they feared for the lives and souls of their families and themselves.

Sol went on to tell Eli about the lovely, strong and proud Aura, leader of the mountain nymphs, and her army who had been the great protectors of the true faith in this kingdom. They were imprisoned by the evil one inside the Banelands Caverns near the caves in which the priests and prophets fled. No one knew if the two groups ever reached one another within the passageways of those great underground tunnels and waterways, but there were rumors they had with the aid of the One whose name must not be spoken.

Sol explained to Eli that before the Great War there had been one like a man who often appeared to the people in times of fear or confusion. The people considered him both a prophet and priest-some were tempted to call him king. He was full of truth, wisdom and holiness. Apollyon put a curse over the entire kingdom concerning this holy man-anyone who might call on him or even say his name would turn to stone.

After many questions, Sol went on to tell Eli that the disappearance of the holy man after the Great War was all a part of the old prophesy.

Sol told Eli solemnly that it had also been prophesied that one by the name of Elijah would come from another place to free the water nymphs and restore them and the priests and prophets to their rightful place. The coming of the child was contained in the selfsame prophesy, and Eli, it was said, was this Elijah.

Eli and Sol talked of many other things during that time; their hopes and their fears concerning the prophecy. Their main decision was the pass best to use—the one closest to the Elysian Fields.

Life, Passion, and Mortality

As the news spread through the group of where they would depart the Passage near the Elysian Fields, all drew near together. Sol told the company, "Most of you have not made this departure from the Passage. It will not be an easy one. It is the most dangerous of all the Passage exits. There are those who have lost their lives here. For this reason, you go of your own free will. If you choose to go or not to, there is no difference. No one will think any more or less of you. That is what love is. It is unconditional. We love each other. Love never fails."

Sol continued, "Here the pass begins by traveling deep underground. There is no light for miles with many twists and turns, for we go beneath and through the hills, much as we did beneath the Styx only with less space to maneuver. The pass then turns upward to a rock wall climb. We will have partial light if we are timely. The passage is narrow and we of human size must go one by one. It will be a squeeze.

"There is more to tell. All along this pass are our enemy's minions, chameleons and others. We know what to expect from them. They are ready to prevent us from reaching the exit in any way they must. They have been in this pass for eons, they have burrowed out hiding places and live in them, awaiting travelers on the way to Elysian Fields. It is said that if they know of our coming in time, they have power to call upon the rain to flood the pass, making it impossible for us to enter it because of the rushing water. Or they could wait to drown us as we are half way through."

Sol said, "This is your time to think about and make your decision. As you see, it will not be an easy one to make. Remember, love is unconditional."

There was not a dissenter in the company. Sol asked each one to raise a hand who was willing to go. Everyone raised a hand, proudly and with shoulders back and chests out!

"I am very proud of each and every one of you," Sol said with tears in his eyes. "You will not be sorry for your decision, no matter what happens, I assure you, 'for to him whom much has been entrusted, more will be given.'"

Sol decided that the housecats would be the first to go. They offered to do this because they were able to change shape and size and could return with news of what lay ahead. After them would go the panther who would be a warring match for who or whatever might attack. The humans would go after her in the order of Sol and Eli with Anna between them for her protection. The Pyrenees would go before and after Jepetto, the green toads and the old owl. The falcons would stay back and go last in case of any attacks from behind for they are fierce warriors themselves. Their talons are able to claw and crush many pounds and carry the evil one's minions miles away and drop them elsewhere.

Soon, just as planned, the cats began their journey underground. It had been decided that within twenty minutes the next group would follow if all was well. All did go well, and in the appointed time, the panther left to go beneath. After twenty minutes it was time for Sol to depart, with Anna and Eli behind him.

Sol set out on all fours with the other two behind him. They crawled close to one another in the pitch darkness, feeling their way as they went. The further into the mountain they crept, the danker was the smell and the closer the walls. Now the gravel under their hands and knees was turning to wet stone. They could hear the dripping of water echoing far in the distance.

"Caverns," Sol said aloud. "This could mean a widening in the passage."

As they drew nearer to the dripping sounds, there was a sound of water and from above a tiny ray of light! Could it be true? As they looked up toward the light, they saw that they were at the edge of a cave opening filled with stalactites and stalagmites.

"I do believe I can stand up!" exclaimed Anna.

"Go ahead. Give it a try," Sol answered. They all three did and could.

Only Eli, who was well over six feet in height, had to stoop a good deal and finally sat down on the stones.

Glad for the openness and some light, they took this chance to rest. Within a few minutes, they heard the sounds of hopping toads and Jepetto and the Pyrenees, Mimi and Moses, coming up behind them.

"Hello," Sol called out to them. "Is that who I think it is?" he teased them.

"It is me, Jepetto, oh yes it is, and toads and our friends the great dogs. Yes it is! Is that you, Sol?" he answered.

"Come, Jepetto, Mimi, and my friends. Call to Moses at your back, for we have found a wonderful resting place!" Sol called out again.

Soon they could see the great white Mimi carefully entering the larger opening under the slim ray of light, four green toads hanging from her long white fur for dear life! Jepetto came next and then Moses with three toads more, the last one clinging to the end of his long, full tail.

Moses and Mimi looked at one another and at their small charges. Moses gladly reported to Sol, "All present and accounted for." Jepetto was extremely happy to see Sol, Anna and the ray of light. He hopped, jumped and danced around the stalactites and stalagmites like a swift little tornado. "Stop, stop!" cried Tobias, with Churchill in echo. "We have had enough. Enough! Sol, please do ask him to stop. It is too dense and close in here for dancing!"

At this Sol replied, "My good fellows, he dances for joy and thankfulness, and that is good. It is a form of praise. Oh, that we could all be so free with our praise and joy. I say let him dance!"

"Wait everyone," Tobias yelled out in his small toad voice. "Where is the professor?" Sure enough, no one had seen Huckabee the old owl emerge from the tunnel.

"He was with your group, was he not, Moses?" Sol asked.

"He was, yes. He was with us when we came into the light. I remember for he was muttering on about the excellence and age of the rock formations here in the cavern. He is probably examining more of the rock. He cannot have gone far."

Sol said, "Everyone, listen to me. Quiet and listen. Draw near and sit."

After Sol had everyone sitting and quiet, he said, "I am going to call out for Huckabee. Do not speak. Keep still until I give the word. We have no time to waste and must find our friend as quickly as possible. Stay where you are. If you hear his voice or any noise from the cavern, raise your hand or paw. Understood?" Everyone shook their heads yes.

Sol called out in a moderate tone, "Huckabee, are you here?" He walked a few feet to the right and called, "Huckabee, it is Sol. Can you hear me?" Sol went several feet to the left of the crowd and called, "Huckabee, this is not a parlor game. If you are here, say something!" This time Sol's voice was stern.

Then, from the cavern depths came an echoing sound impossible to pinpoint and a high-pitched shrieking laugh that faded into nothing. It sent chills down the spines of all the company. Churchill was by this time in Anna's lap asking in a whisper, "What was that, Anna? I'm frightened!"

Just at the time when Sol and Eli were fearing the worst and feeling totally at a loss for help, Borneo came doubling back, almost slithering, blacker than black, up the cavern wall. "Sol, none came down the pass on time," he breathed. "I was sure you were in some sort of trouble, stranded or attacked. Tell me that all is well."

"Not quite," Sol answered. "We have lost sight of Huckabee and have called for him. Our calls have made things worse! We have heard hideous screeching sounds from within the caverns but still no Huckabee." Sol bent down to the panther's ear and whispered, "I fear the evil one's minions are here, watching us now, ready to attack and have Huckabee as their prisoner or worse."

Borneo said to Sol, "It is surely evil minions, but I believe they are from the Banshee Faylinn."

Borneo reminded Sol of the legend of the Faylinn Imps and their Queen Le Annis the Banshee. Borneo was of the belief that the shrieks they heard came from the mutant fairies. He believed that Le Annis herself held her court somewhere in or near these caverns and it was she, by her wicked magic holding Huckabee in her evil Faylinn.

Anna had dealt much with fairies in her life, both graceful and evil ones, and she was wise to their differences. Anna's life had begun in the Faylinn of the evil fairy herself. Anna was a beautiful child of eighteen months when the kingdom fell completely to Apollyon. Both her parents' lives were lost in the battle, as many parents of children were. In those terrible days and weeks, children died or families took them in. Anna, however, being a gifted and seeing child was a powerless target for all the evil powers.

Le Annis saw and claimed her for herself at once. "Oh! What a beautiful child and so full of promise! We must have her, must we not?" She had asked her fairies as Anna was crawling outside the lopsided house where her parents had lived. There, using their magic, the baby was taken in by Le Annis the Banshee, treated like a princess, and taught fairy ways until she was nearly four years old.

Anna was named for Le Annis and knew no other mother. Anna sat at the knees of this banshee, and her gifts were perfected there. Little Anna was taught there was no difference between good and evil. Le Annis made no attempt to teach her the difference between right and wrong because she was pruning Anna as a pawn in her Faylinn. Le Annis would have had her hideous way with Anna had her plan not been thwarted. She would have had Anna grow up a tiny creature, marry a fairy or a dwarf, and have gifted and seeing children who were half-sprites to become her evil pawns.

With the life-saving help of a graceful fairy spy and Orla herself, Anna's freedom was attained just before her eighth birthday. The remainder of her childhood Anna spent in the home of another seeing woman, Goody Nightingale, and her family, not far from the Elysian Fields in the Arielian Hills. The graceful fairies found this loving and accepting family for Anna. The stories of Anna and her time with both Faylinns would be another book entirely, so we shall leave it here for now.

22

After hearing that Huckabee might be in the grasp of Le Annis, Anna spoke to Sol. "Husband, we have but two choices in the matter. You are aware that I know that of which I speak if the owl is indeed in the grasp of Le Annis." Sol gave Eli a quick background on Anna's childhood.

Anna continued. "Le Annis's purpose is not to kill, it is to intimidate, lie, and cajole. I believe by taking Huckabee she means to frighten us into turning back. Spies move between both Faylinns even hourly at a time of journeying. If Le Annis were to harm a feather on Huckabee's head, Orla's Faylinn would retaliate en masse, and a war between the fairies would ensue. Neither queen is willing to risk such as that over the life of one creature. This being as it is, I believe it to be fact and not conjecture that we can stay here and stage a plan to retrieve Huckabee, which would possibly start a war with Le Annis's minions. A war would cause chaos and tempt us with the evil deeds of another. We could also go on as planned. I hope and believe Le Annis will release Huckabee after she sees we have not fallen for her ploy."

Sol looked to Eli. "Her words ring true to me," said Eli. "Evil always takes us down a chaotic road and attempts to draw us in when we need to remain focused on our call. Do you agree, Sol? I believe that is what is happening here."

Both Sol and Anna shook their heads yes to Eli's question to them. Sol continued, "We leave Huckabee to his own and to the Most High and go ahead then?"

"Yes, I believe we do," Anna replied.

Eli paused. "What is on your mind, Eli?" Sol asked, looking at him queerly.

Eli asked, "Sol, may I address the company? I believe it to be important."

"Yes, of course," Sol answered with a slight frown because Eli looked so solemn.

Eli stood as close to what was the middle of the cavern clearing as he could and called for all to gather around into a tight circle. "My friends and comrades, Huckabee is lost to us. There is no time to waste. The Most High sent forth the Word and the world was made. His Word sustains it to this day. He has taught me that I was created in His image and that His Word has great power for good. If you have not believed this is true until now, I ask, do you believe it now? If you do, bend your knee and bow your head before I call on Him."

Unlike the creatures' usual responses to turn to see their neighbors' actions, each one did as Eli suggested at his own time in silence.

Eli continued, "Repeat in your minds what I say aloud, even if you do not understand the words or the language." All heads remained bowed.

Eli began to pray, "Oh Mighty One we come with one hope that You would reign in our hearts. We offer You our lives, as one living sacrifice that You would come now into our hearts and reign. We cry out to You! Loose our friend! Change the minds of his captors. We give You honor and praise with gladness."

Eli's words became unintelligible, musical, and beyond lovely. This singing began to infect the others until it rose above the sound of the dripping water and melded into the rushing of the stream flowing through the cavern. It was heavenly and unknown even to those who created it. It reached its peak in an intertwined mix of words, unknown sounds, tongues and music. The singing slowly returned to ordinary known words and meanings.

Each one was giving thanks to the Most High for the returning of their friend to them when they heard a familiar voice. All opened their eyes, and beside Eli stood Huckabee, dusting off his waistcoat and smoothing his head feathers!

"Well, what is all this chorus about in the middle of the day? Have you nothing better to do than have choir rehearsal?" the fussy old owl asked.

At this, everyone gathered around, hugging him and pawing at him, believing and yet unbelieving he was actually there and safe! Huckabee, being a formal and distinguished scholar of a bird, was quite put upon by all the personal attention. "Quite right, it is good to be back, I'll say. The queen of those fairies is no lady. I can vouch for that! I would not be surprised if she does not pursue us at her earliest convenience! I believe we should make speed from this place, ancient rock formations or no!"

Sol agreed as he patted the old bird on the back. "Listen, everyone!" Sol called out. "From here on out it will be an uphill climb and a one-by-one climb at that. I am not worried about you toads, for your feet will be of great help. I warn you only to stay together in front of Jepetto. Tobias, please be last in the toad line if you will. Churchill, you will be the lead toad."

Tobias and Jepetto were feeling supremely proud to be in some sort of charge with responsibility. Tobias began immediately to give them guidance on how to carry out their orders to perfection.

Sol continued, "We will continue in the same order as from the beginning. There will be no light. If one tires and needs to stop, wait until you find a place with a good foothold and lean there. Call out so that those in front and behind will know you are stopping. A rest can be no more than thirty seconds at a time for all the obvious reasons. You must remember, in the climb you not only hold your own life at stake but those of all the others."

Jepetto thought about this. He loved Sol and Anna, for they were the only parents he knew. The toads were his friends. So were the sweet Pyrenees, who would surely give their lives to save anyone in danger. He thought about what he would do. Jepetto knew. He would move if he had to and fall to save their lives, for his life would be nothing without theirs. He would rather not. No. He could not live knowing they perished because of him! He thought about this like the number games he and Sol played, and he thought, *The life of the one for the many versus the lives of the many for the one.*

"How did Jepetto figure that out?" he asked himself. He didn't think about it anymore because he knew in his heart it was right.

23

The panther and the housecats had been gone for a few minutes now, as well as Sol and Eli, with Anna between them. Jepetto was following along behind Tobias as planned and could hear the Pyrenees scratching up behind him. Climbing was hard—much harder—than he thought it would be. His broad, flat feet found little to no clinging spots, and he was mostly using his hands and knees. Jepetto remembered the words Eli had said and repeated them, "Oh, great and mighty one, help Jepetto. Jepetto's knees are bleeding. With one desire I come, that You would come. Oops!" He almost slipped. Jepetto kept climbing. Up. Pull. Up. Pull. Take a deep breath. Up. Pull.

Jepetto needed to rest, and he called out, "Jepetto needs to stop for thirty seconds!"

"Okay, Jepetto," he heard from both Tobias and Mimi. Jepetto leaned his back against one side of the wall, pressed his big, flat feet against the other side and began to count.

He was at eighteen when he heard Sol's voice a long way away calling, "Is everything all right down there?"

Jepetto started to answer him, but Tobias said, "All right, Sol. I am taking a small rest. Two or three more seconds now. Cheerio-o."

"That's fine," Sol echoed back. "Anytime, Tobias."

Jepetto nearly began to cry and said quietly, "I am ready to go now." The move was on once more. Up, pull, up, pull, bleeding knees, bleeding hands. Jepetto kept praying. He knew in spite of his pain that everything would somehow work out fine.

Out of nowhere, Jepetto heard the loud sound of many shrieking voices. The next thing he heard were Mimi and Moses barking and snarling. Then he felt tiny, dark, flying objects moving past him at light speed, stinging as they went. Something was falling and hitting him on the head, and then he heard Anna crying out, "You will not have me again! I am done with you!"

Jepetto heard Anna's voice again but now in a language he did not understand. She was speaking to another person—a woman as well—who spoke in the same strange tongue. They were yelling in anger and rage at one another. Jepetto was terrified. He wondered where Sol was and why he did not stop this thing from happening to Anna. The shrieking voices and the dark beings were still darting back and forth beside Jepetto's head. He did not care. Jepetto began to climb up toward Anna as fast as he could. He had thought the toads were between them, but they were gone. It was pitch black. Finally he gained on Anna's position and could see the being she was arguing with.

A shimmering glow encompassed the being. Its glow revealed Anna and parts of Sol and Eli. The two men held motionless to the cave wall like statues, mouths agape and wordless. Jepetto could now see the tiny shimmering being was a fairy queen. She obviously held some great power over both Sol and Eli, making them unable to move. As for Anna, she was holding her own with the banshee queen.

As the two women spoke, flashes of fire darted from the fairy's mouth toward Anna. Anna warded them off with a warm white light coming from the palm of her raised right hand. This infuriated the evil queen, who attempted to retaliate with fire from both her mouth and her hands.

Now Anna was calling her name loudly and with authority, for she had seen Jepetto there and that the fairy had turned her gaze upon him. "Le Annis, touch him and I will destroy you!"

The banshee turned, "Ha-ha! Now Anna, my love and my namesake, I see your Achilles Heel at last! I will have you for my own again and after all!"

Jepetto did not know what all this talk meant and neither did he care. All he knew was that this evil little being was threatening Anna. Without another thought, Jepetto jumped upon Le Annis as if she were a fly, catching her in his wide mouth. She burned his tongue like pure fire and red hot peppers, but it was no worse than his knees and hands. He took one good bite down before he could give another thought to it and jumped down the shaft. By the time Jepetto reached the cavern, they all heard the explosion and saw the light rising after it from deep below.

"Jepetto, no!" cried Anna in vain, horrified. At the sound of the explosion, both Sol and Eli grasped for the sides of the walls, for they were once again themselves, set free from the queen's spell.

"What has happened, Anna?" Sol asked in the half-light of the fire, looking at her shocked and agonized face. Eli gazed below and at what he could see of Anna and knew something had gone terribly wrong.

Anna did the best she could through her sobbing to tell them. It had all happened so fast. She could not be consoled over the fact that Jepetto had given his life for her. Sol, who could do nothing but try to comfort his wife, was in shock as well.

Eli saw that he must take leadership and gain control of the chaos for the good of the entire company. Jepetto could not have survived the explosion. It couldn't have been helped. "Sol. Sol," he said. "We give thanks for Jepetto, for his life, his tender and light spirit, for his loving ways and his great courage. We all know he rests now in the hands of the Most High, for he gave his life for all of us."

Sol answered, "You are right, Eli, my friend. There is no use doubling back. Now we must move on. Am I right?"

Eli answered to all, "Listen to me. We leave our friend behind, but he would want us to move on, and that is what we do now. Turning back or staying here is not an option. Pick up your hands and feet, for we climb! We climb for Jepetto!"

All those left, for who could count them in the dark, cried out, "For Jepetto!"

They once again began the tedious climb up the inside of the mountain toward the outward pass to the Elysian Fields and sunlight.

24

Queen Orla felt a deep sting and rumble in her spirit as her sister, Le Annis, fell dead on the cavern floor.

There is a fine line between love and hate in any kingdom. Orla hated her sister's actions and whom she had chosen to follow, but she did love her because she was her sister and cut from the same sprite at birth. Orla had never given a minute's thought that her sister's life might one day actually end or that hers would, for that matter. Well, it had happened and all of it over the child—this girl named Louisa who Dulci and Tania had brought to her court to meet her over a silly mistake. Orla knew now that none of this was a mistake. This Louisa was a very special child who had come into their kingdom for a very distinctive purpose. Orla's sister was dead for a reason that had to do with this child's safety, and as far as she knew, Le Annis had never had an audience with Louisa. Orla would know. Orla was no fool and was privy to her sister's evil ways, so she was sure Le Annis had some hand in her own demise. Orla called for her fairies.

Dulci, Tania, and Elva were outside the big tree as usual, flitting around the groups of toadstools, when they received word that they were summoned. Dulci said, "I guessed something was up! There have been rumors for an hour or two now."

"What sort of rumors?" Elva asked.

"Those of a death in the Truth Passage near the Elysian Fields pass."

Tania spoke up, "You both had better hold your tongues, for that is near the Faylinn of Le Annis herself, and you well know that our queen does not take it lightly when such as we talk of her between ourselves!"

By now they had gathered with all the other fairies inside the great throne room of Orla and were each perched in their places, wings shimmering brightly. Orla stood in their midst, her white hair pulled straight back from her head in many tiny braids and flowing down her back. Tonight she wore platinum and onyx crosses braided into her hair, and on her chest were two swords of platinum and onyx. Her ring was a simple platinum cross, and she wore no earrings. In her left hand she held the graces shield with a cross in the center and a background of the infinity. In her right, she held the sword of platinum inlaid with onyx.

Not a word was said and no wing made a sound. Orla said, "My children, Le Annis of Banshee Faylinn has fallen dead this day. We mourn her not. Like all planners of unrighteousness, she put a scheme in motion that brought about her own demise when she meant the harm of those seeking to do the right thing. I am convinced the safety of the child Louisa was and is involved. Le Annis's minion fairies are evil, as was she, and they will not stop until they revenge her death upon Louisa and those who protect her.

"Louisa's rescue company journeys at this moment through the pass up into the Elysian Fields from the Truth Passage, and they do not bode well. I send you all to fly like the wind, lift them up and out, say not a word, and return to me directly. There is no time for questions. Now, fly!"

And they flew! One by one, they zipped away on their shimmering wings. They went off through the great hall, out the tree, up through the sky, and to the pass, like the tail of a comet or a falling star!

~~~~~~~~~~~~~~~~~~~~~~~

Wormfly was hidden in Sol's cape, holding on for dear life as they climbed through the dark. He had been knocked off twice but managed to find his way back onto Sol's cloak using his antenna. The minute he sensed Jepetto falling, he followed. Wormfly was able to figure out what was going to happen, and he flew into the tightest place he could find in the cavern wall and waited. After the blinding explosion and all the dust had settled, he flew out and looked around for Jepetto, afraid of what he would find. Wormfly had seen death and gore all throughout his hundreds of years of life, but he did not want to see this. He had actually become fond of little Jepetto. Jepetto made him happy inside and even venture a laugh. Jepetto had been full of life! This was not fair.

He flew around in and out of the twists and turns, seeing nothing, and was about to give up. There! There, huddled in a corner like a baby, was Jepetto. His hair was burned, as was one of his eyes. His mouth looked— well it did not look like his mouth—and one of his ears was completely gone. From the way Jepetto was curled up, Wormfly could not see his legs or arms, but he saw dark red blood coming from somewhere.

Wormfly thought for a moment about what he could do. Then he used his chameleon powers and did it. Wormfly became a green toad. He spoke very carefully to Jepetto. "Hello, Jepetto. Are you awake?"

At this point Wormfly was not quite sure if Jepetto was still alive, for he got no response. He ran to the running stream and caught water in a bottomed-out tin he found on the ground. Then he put it to Jepetto's crushed lips. *No*, he thought, *first things first*. Wormfly as the green toad took the tip of his finger and placed it on Jepetto's lip. He looked closely and at first saw nothing. Then he dipped his finger into the water and tried again.

Wormfly the toad had his eyes very close to Jepetto, looking carefully to see what might happen. Jepetto's mouth began to change from a crushed and torn gash into its nearly normal, wide self. Jepetto still did not move. "Well, that proves that a healing might happen even to a strange creature like Jepetto," Wormfly the toad said aloud.

There was a little cough, and then a weak, thread-like voice said, "Who are you calling strange—you who look like a toad but have stupid wings? I wouldn't be calling someone else names," Jepetto said.

"Oh thank goodness! You are alive! I cannot believe it! Can you see? How is your eye? Can you walk?" Your knees look pretty bad!" Wormfly was so excited he could not contain himself!

"Jepetto does not know if he can walk, but yes, Jepetto can see. Yes he can! Who are you? Where did you come from? Jepetto is happy to meet you, yes, so happy! Anna, Anna! Where is she? Is Anna okay. Is she okay? Jepetto needs to know about Anna!"

Wormfly did his best to answer Jepetto's questions about Anna. He told him he was a long-lost toad-like cousin who had come to his aid but would have to return home as soon as he helped Jepetto get back to Sol and Anna. This satisfied Jepetto just fine, except Jepetto insisted on knowing Wormfly's name. Wormfly made up the name Truluck because he was feeling truly lucky for finding little Jepetto. He felt deep down like a being with a true heart at that moment. Jepetto said he would never forget Truluck as long as he lived and said he was sorry for saying his wings were stupid, even if they were!

"All right, are you ready to see Anna now?" Truluck asked.

"Oh yes, oh, yes! Jepetto is always ready to see his Anna!"

"Hold on tight. Up we go!" Truluck planted himself on top of Jepetto's head tightly with his suction feet, and with a little toad magic and charm, up the pass they went, bumping a few rocks along the way!

While Truluck was coming to Jepetto's aid at the bottom of the cavern, the Faylinn Graces swarmed into the entrance to the pass at the Elysian Fields toward Sol and company. They had flown so swiftly and quietly as to have gone undetected by spies of Apollyon.

Borneo was the first to meet them and understood why they had come. He moved for the fairies to pass. The mass of fairies lifted and flew Borneo and the cats out of the pass on into the light and onto green grass. They turned to see Anna, Sol, Eli, the toads, both Pyrenees, and Professor Owl Huckabee being lifted out of the pass on the wings of many tiny fairies!

Anna went to Borneo to tell him of what had happened and how brave Jepetto had been when another breeze and swarm came from the opening to the pass. Upon the wings was Jepetto! He was looking a little worse for the battle, but there he was, alive and well!

With the fairies hovering in the air, everyone ran to encircle Jepetto. There were toads hopping everywhere. Even Eli and Sol were hopping! Anna was dancing around in circles with Jepetto in her arms, smiling from ear to ear!

25

Orla was not the only queen to know and sense the death of Le Annis. Even though Aura, the revered leader of the mountain nymphs, dwelled within caverns too deep for sound to penetrate, she felt a rumble in her spirit as the evil banshee fell dead. Aura was the daughter of Gafir, a southern mountain giant, and Nora, a seer nymph from the Arielian caverns. Aura's grandfather had been one of the few seeing men from Arielia. He passed his gift to his daughter, Nora. Gafir and Nora still lived in a mountainside dwelling in the hills between the mountains and the Arielian caverns, where they offered as much leadership in the truth and aid to travelers as they could.

Aura's parents had seen the promise of leadership in her when she was a small child. Aura inherited her father's genes and grew to be a tall, strong, and capable young woman. Her long blonde hair fell to her shoulders, and she wore bangs across her forehead. Aura's clothing was a leather body suit with her sword at her side and boots on her feet. She also carried her bow with her at all times. Aura's women loved and respected her. She was not only their leader but she was their friend.

Most of the mountain nymph army had the same or a similar lineage. Not all of the nymphs were seers, but all were daughters of mountain nymphs and giants. These women were extremely strong, brilliant in mind and clarity of thought, beautiful to look upon, and fierce warriors.

Both the mountain giants and the seeing women were true believers and they taught their daughters about the one true God from baby-hood.

Their fathers taught them from childhood to wield a sword and shoot an arrow with exceptional accuracy. They must have had special gifts of marksmanship because there was no man in the kingdom who would dare try one of Aura's women in battle. As long as Aura's army was present, the good people and creatures of the Truthlands, Elysian Fields, and Arielia lived separated from Satan in relative peace.

Aura and her army lived at the very top of the southern mountains in a dwelling cut out from sandstone eons ago. Rising hundreds of feet into the air, these elusive, towering dwellings were covered with green trees, flowering succulents, and vegetation. Under them, and running down toward the sea, there were rivers that dug great craters through the mountains, leaving huge, gaping caverns with bottomless lakes and shimmering walls of dripping minerals.

It was here, deep within the caverns and in the lakes, where the women trained for battle. They bathed in the underground lakes, which held the deep magic of healing, power, strength, and courage. In these waters, the women became extremely accomplished swimmers able to breathe water. Some say that it was from these lakes that the women gained the power to fly. The nymphs could fly without wings. However, flying saps a nymph's strength greatly. The nymph must return to the underground lake and its powers to renew her strength. Aura taught her warriors to use their powers of flight carefully.

At the time of the Great War when Satan gained total control of minds and souls, Aura and most of her army were away within their own caverns. Walls of natural rock miles thick were placed around every exit by Satan and his minions. With no outlet even to their dwellings, Aura and her army tried to escape by following the rivers. They found every river diverted to flow in a different direction. By following each of them, they found themselves at the gaping mouth of Hades itself. Escape through the sea was impossible because Apollyon's sea serpents stood guard at the openings from their caverns to the sea. With no way out, the mountain nymphs remain imprisoned to this day.

Aura knew something was going on outside their prison. She had been having the dreams again—the ones about the girl and the mare. The girl was frightened. Now there was another with her—a man. Aura was sitting by the fire with her closest friend and advisor, Daphne, and she said, "There has been a change in the balance of powers on the outside, Daphne. I feel it in my spirit. I still dream of the girl, but now there is another. I sense he is a promised one."

Aura looked at her friend for confirmation, because Daphne was a seeing nymph as well. "Is this other presence strong? What is it that makes you sense a change in the balance in the powers?" Daphne asked Aura.

Aura answered, "I sense the death of one of our longtime enemies. I have seen in my spirit that it is Le Annis, queen of the Banshee Faylinn. There is a great disturbance there. There is something else. This girl, the one prophesied to come—she was to be of little or no faith. She is anything but. I sense a strong-willed child with her own convictions. This issue is already causing our enemy to change his plan. As we know, he is unhappy with surprises."

"And what sense do you have of the character of the other presence?" Daphne asked again.

"Oh, yes. He is a strong-willed one as well and is here, I am sure, for the child. I have a strong feeling that his presence in the kingdom will affect our imprisonment in some way. I do not want to put false hope into the hearts of the others, Daphne. Keep this between ourselves for now."

The two women smiled warmly at one another and continued their conversation.

All the while, in the darkest parts of the deepest lake in the caverns, a creature unseen even by Aura or Daphne was waiting for its opportunity to strike. It too had felt a shift in the balance of power. The creature was hungry, sad, alone, and seeking revenge for the death of its mate. It had waited for many years and could wait until the time was right.

26

Apollyon and his fearsome snake were still going on and on with their own beastly revelry, as if the chaos and eruption of mutated creatures produced by the boulder slide near our last camp was purposeful. As terrified as I was of what might happen next, somehow I had a feeling deep inside that all was not lost. Eli's face kept popping into my head in clear visions, and I was comforted.

After Apollyon had regained control and Little Horn, the creatures, and wolves had had enough, we set out again. As for me, I was very glad to leave that place! I asked Aprion quietly, "Aprion, have you been this way before?"

"No," she answered. "But I have heard that this is one of the roads to the place called Paradeisos."

"Oh, is that the same as Paradise, like heaven?" I asked.

Aprion said, "I cannot truly tell you, but it seems to me it must be more similar to the place of creation. I do not claim to understand these things, for as I said, I have never traveled this road or been to this place before." Her answer, as far as I could tell, was confusing me and bordering on purposefully vague.

I said, "Surely it is a good rather than another evil place then?"

"Oh yes!" she exclaimed. "Of that, I am sure."

We were entering a quite beautiful land on all sides. It was much like the landside near the lopsided house with rolling lush green hills, scatterings of wildflowers of all colors beyond the spectrum that we know and thundering, high, white waterfalls. I noticed at once many birds of all kinds and sizes, some in kinds and colors never before seen in the world. The music they made with their twittering and calling as they flew was unimaginable unless you had been there yourself.

The temperature of the air was close to perfection. If I had been alone and allowed, I believe I would have taken off every stitch of my clothes, just to feel that air on my whole body. Knowing that would be very unladylike and that Nimee and Cerena would certainly, oh, I don't know what … well, I only wish that I could!

The air was filled with wonderful-smelling flowers. That scent does not exist in the world we know. It had to come from the flowers that fairies or angels planted and were always popping up around the next turn. Everything grew more lush, green, and tropical as we traveled. Pines gave way to oaks and the oaks to scrub palmetto and finally palms, dates, fig, and pomegranate trees so large their tops grew into the clouds!

Succulents bloomed in the brook's raw dampness. Dark, sharp reds, yellows, and pinks were among lush roses of yellow, white, and deep vermillion. Around the ponds were lilies of orange, purple, white, and the bluest blue. Parrots, giant herons, white doves, and many unknown species of tropical multicolored birds inhabited the trees. I had seen these kinds of birds, plants, and trees in India and Africa, but they were only by accounts poor and pale country cousins to the ones I was now seeing.

We were traveling swiftly downhill now, into a deep and lush valley. From where I could see on Aprion's back, every waterfall seemed to pour into the valley, and I could see one river flowing out from it. We were traveling parallel to the river. The river ran as far as the eye could see until it disappeared into the thick jungle.

The sounds of the waterfalls and the birdsongs grew louder as we approached, and I was becoming mesmerized by it all when I noticed a sole ring tone, very beautiful, that was growing more pronounced in my ears. *Okay,* I thought. *Listen to this, Louisanna. Pay attention. It just might be a message. Or it might not.*

This tone did grow a bit but more in intensity than volume and was most certainly female. The sound had a silver tone to it, as if it might be coming from a flute or a viola with string made of the finest material and was surely in a minor key. I would have guessed either A or F# minor. As in the times before, I could make out no words, but a message was emerging in my soul as I listened. *Come to the water, come to the word, Come to the harmony. Remember the tree. Remember eternity. Let faith arise. Do not be afraid. Bring not a sword.* It was beautiful in timbre and depth. I thought about the meaning for a long time.

As this music went on and grew more intense, I looked at Apollyon to see in his face if he was listening. If he was, his face gave away nothing. His eyes were straight ahead, and he was, as always, talking and laughing with the snake.

Then I motioned Aprion to look at me and looked closely at her. She seemed oblivious to the sound, so I asked her, "Aprion, have you ever heard such beautiful sounds and singing? Where are they coming from?"

The mare replied, "The waterfalls and the rushing rivers make me feel as if I am at home in the fields. What do you think? Are you enjoying them? These sounds are lovely in comparison to some we have heard on this journey, wouldn't you say?" Aprion answered.

I continued, "You are right, of course, Aprion. The poor souls crying out for help, the beastly singing from Apollyon and the snake, and those terrible sounds while crossing the river was what I was comparing them to."

"You are right," she replied. "But what singing do you mean? The ancient chanting of Apollyon and Little Horn is the only sing ..." And then she stopped and started again. "Oh, yes, of course it was. Terrible, just terrible, was it not!" Aprion said, trying to cover her misunderstanding. She could have just told me she didn't hear it. I found it implausible that she could not have missed that!

Why did I have mixed feelings about Aprion? She had been my good friend. She comforted me and gave me good advice when I was under the influence of Apollyon's candies. Well, I thought she had. She told me she was a good horse and that she was my friend, and I had believed her. Just because she had been vague and forgetful gave me no reason to doubt her, I told myself, and I tried to put my mind to rest about it.

Just as these thoughts were swimming in my brain, Apollyon appeared beside me on his horse. "Well, how do you like these waterfalls, my dear? Did I not promise you the most glorious waterfalls ever? Why do you have that finger between your brows? That is too much frown for a lovely child like you and especially one who is as distinct and with such an exceptional a fate as awaits you!"

At this, I smiled as coyly as I could and said, "I did not realize I was frowning. Maybe the sun is in my eyes. It is a beautiful day."

"That it is. That it is. Is it not, Little Horn?" he replied as he turned his gaze at the snake on his shoulder. The snake made no reply. It only turned its horrible green eyes on me. Apollyon looked at me again as if he expected me to answer the rest of his question, so I said as courageously as I could, "I would like to know where you are taking me. This is a very lovely place, just as you promised, and the sounds coming from everywhere are beautiful and interesting, but we seem to be getting close, according to Aprion. She has not heard the beautiful sounds I have and I don't know why. She was kind enough to tell me we are going to a place known as Paradeisos. Is that true?"

At this Apollyon's face began to grow and change as it had once before when he became angry. His eyes turned red, and the horn stubs were showing out of his dreadlocks. The snake drew near his face and hissed something in his ear. Apollyon tuned his face away from me, and when he turned back, the horn stubs were gone and his eyes were normal—well, normal for him. He turned his eyes squarely on Aprion. She was shuffling back and forth on her haunches but did not move a muscle of her head. Not a word passed between them. Now I knew the truth.

Aprion had never been my friend, and Apollyon was no longer hers.

Arrangements were made in the hissing between Apollyon and Little Horn. Aprion was led swiftly back the way we came by one of the largest and most violent of the wolves, begging for mercy as her cries faded in the distance. My heart could not help but go out to Aprion even though she had betrayed me. I believed she had been brainwashed by Apollyon or at least his minions. I didn't realize what she was doing had put me in danger. She was a young mare and easily influenced.

As for me, I had already forgiven her and was so glad I had whispered it in her ear before the wolves led her away. She made no reply or gesture, but I did not expect her to with those eyes upon her. I suspected she was already in danger of losing her life—or worse.

As Aprion's cries died away, I could still hear the faint tone coming from the hills and tried very hard to keep track of the messages. Between lovely humming and Alleluias were the same repeating phrases: *Come to the water. Come to the word. Come to the harmony. Remember the tree. Let faith arise. Do not be afraid. Bring not a sword.*

As I sat by a brook with my bare feet in the warm water, Apollyon suddenly materialized beside me. I wanted to ask him what he would do to Aprion, but I decided it was too soon. He was all smiles, as if nothing at all had happened. He was very good at that. It was as if hurting someone terribly or breaking another's heart meant absolutely nothing to him. In fact, it brought him not joy, for he has no joy, but energy to hurt and destroy even more.

He said to me, "Well, now we must find you a pretty new mount, shall we?" I said nothing because I was still upset about what I did not know was going to happen to Aprion. "Oh, come now, come now. If you could have anything in the world, what would it be? And not Aprion, for she has proven herself untrustworthy to us both, has she not?"

I thought for a moment. It was true. She lied to me and was unfaithful to him as her master. She was untrustworthy! I was not ready to admit it to him, though. He was an untrustworthy master, but did that make it right for her to lie? I had asked her questions to try to trick her into finding out whose friend she was. Had that been fair to her? I was so confused! Apollyon, I hated to admit, was right. She was not my friend or trustworthy. How *could* he be right? Evil can never be right.

In the few minutes it took for this thought process to go through my head, Apollyon had been skipping stones in the brook like a little boy. He looked suddenly younger, like a sort of Peter Pan. His dreads even looked shorter and of a lighter color, and unless my eyes were deceiving me, he had become at least a foot shorter! As I watched him, it looked as if he was actually having fun!

He looked toward me and said, "Come on over! This is fun!"

I thought for a moment, took off my slippers, and off I went! We danced across the stones and laughed, sometimes holding hands. I lost my footing on a slippery stone and Apollyon gathered me up and took me to the bank in his arms. We sat breathless and giggled at what we had done. "Oh" I breathed, "that was fun! I didn't know you would ever play."

"I can play with more revelry than anyone in the universe, Louisa. I can dance upon the stars and swing from the moon, but today I danced on brook stones with you, and it was brilliant!"

"I had more fun than I've had in a long time myself," I said.

"Well," Apollyon replied, "and now for something to eat."

I have no idea where the food came from, but we had sandwiches just like the ones I have at home. There were cucumber, salmon, and caper with cream cheese and liver pâté with white crackers. I was so thirsty, and the drink, whatever it was, was wonderful! It tasted of every dainty tropical fruit in a perfect mix. For dessert, there was rich chocolate ice cream.

"I enjoyed my supper so much," I said. "These are some of my favorite foods. How did you know?"

Apollyon replied, "Aprion, you must remember, did not pretend to be only your friend. She did serve some purposes before she failed us, ay?"

"I suppose," I said, remembering how confusing it all seemed.

Still sitting by the brook with the sun going down and Apollyon younger and somehow more innocent, he said, "Well, and we do need to find a good mount or another beast to carry you. Think and tell me, in all your dreams and wishes, what animal have you wanted most to ride upon?"

The answer to this question did not take me one second to answer. I had dreamed and wished for it since I was a little girl.

"Oh! A white elephant is what I want!" I blurted out. "I have wished I could have one all my life! They are the most wonderful animals in the entire world! I don't want a full-grown one, though, or one with large tusks.

I am small, and it should fit me, please! I would also like a gentle one. The only elephant I have ridden was a large bull. That was with Eli behind me, and I was little frightened even then."

"Well, a white elephant and a small, gentle one, is it? I can see this is quite certainly the beast you desire. Yes indeed! Well, you shall have it!"

I began to hop up and down with excitement, clapping my hands and saying, "Thank you, thank you! When will it come? Will it really be a white one?" I asked in rapt excitement.

"Well." replied Apollyon, "come, directly around this turn in the trail." He was leading me as he spoke.

We walked up a small embankment around a group of lemon and palms trees, and there in the tall grass just ahead of us stood the most proud and enchanting snow white elephant I could have ever dreamed of! I stood motionless, hands over my mouth like a child seeing a decorated Christmas tree, gazing at him as he waved his graceful trunk back and forth and seemed to smile at us.

"Well, and what do you have to say?" Apollyon asked. "Is he everything you expected? And how do you like his embellishments, for he is a prince of an elephant, fit to carry a queen."

It was true that he looked like a prince! His headdress was of diamonds, rubies, and pearls, with one ruby hanging down his forehead from a string of snow-white pearls interspersed with ones of a raven hue. Around his neck and huge shoulders was a harness made of gold mesh with silver and gold stars, moons, and teardrop rubies woven through it. At the bottom of the mesh were golden bells that each carried a different ringtone when he moved. Covering his great, wide back was an ancient Turkish tapestry of reds, yellows, blues, and turquoise, with huge teardrop pearls, rubies, and golden bells at its fringes. Around his thunderous ankles were the widest golden and silver-hammered bracelets in the world. There were six on three ankles, and on his right ankle was a plain, wide metal bracelet.

He was so beautiful that I could not believe my eyes! "Oh please, what is his name? May I touch him? Can I ride him now? How do I get up there? He is so big!" I had so many questions all at once. As much as I wanted all these things, I was a little apprehensive of approaching the huge beast alone, so I asked, "Would you go with me to him and help me onto his back?"

Apollyon replied in good humor, "Well, and it seems you do like him after all. Yes, I will help you go to him and tell you his name and help you onto his back, and he will be yours. But first we must talk a little business, you and I." As he said these words, his likeness changed. He grew taller. His dreadlocks were long and dark again, and the youthfulness disappeared from his face. Along with the youthfulness, all play and fun were gone.

"What kind of business?" I asked, shying away. "You promised."

He answered flatly, "Promises mean nothing to me unless they are secured by another's promise. We must be sure of one another, am I right? Have you forgotten Aprion so quickly? She could not be trusted to keep a promise to either of us, could she? If her promise was no good, neither was she, to you or to me, yes?"

"I suppose you are right," I said. "But what promise?" I asked.

"The business we need to speak about is a person you know as Eli."

What does he know about Eli? I thought. *It may not be my Eli. Perhaps he is casting a net.* All this went through my mind in a second. Then I said, "Eli is the husband of my nanny and lives in my Grandmamma's house back at home, not even in this kingdom, so he shouldn't have much to do with anything at all, especially my elephant, as far as I can tell."

"Well, and surely you know that this Eli of yours is a prophet and has very great powers in whatever world or kingdom he happens to be?"

"Actually, no," I said. "All I know is that he is a kind and good man and I believe him to be very wise."

To this Apollyon responded, "And well then I can see that you have not the wits I thought you had if that is all you think of this Eli, for if you had one tiny brain in your head you would surely have known of his gifts if he lives in your own house!"

"I beg your pardon!" I answered in anger. "I am a very bright person. You may ask anybody you wish who knows me. You have known me only two days, and because you ask me one question and do not like the answer I give you, you call me witless!"

He replied as if I were a spoiled child, "I am quite aware you are not in the least witless, so be so kind as to answer my question truthfully and you may ride and have your elephant forever, young lady."

I hated the condescending way he had changed the subject back to the elephant from Eli. "Let me ask you, why and what do you need to know about Eli? It seems you already know more than I do. I am telling the truth when I say that I have never been told he was any sort of prophet. We do not talk about such things in our house. It would make my Grandmamma very uncomfortable. Has Eli done something I should be aware of, or is he in some sort of trouble?"

"If you do not know, you do not know and therefore cannot answer. It is all to be expected. I am quite sure your Eli would not wish for you to go without your prized elephant for a few unanswered questions, especially concerning him! Because I will find my answers in one way or another, what difference does it make to you? As you say, he is in another kingdom, and you will have your wish come true."

"What do you mean by saying you will find your answers in one way or another? Why and how would you know to inquire about Eli in any case?" I asked, not knowing why I kept this conversation going at all because we were seemingly going in circles!

"Louisa, Eli and his prophetic powers are known far and wide. These powers transcend the spiritual and the natural worlds. In your world and this kingdom, for example his powers can be put to use for good or ill."

I remembered Cerena telling me the same thing when talking about my gifts, as she called them. Surely if Eli possessed these gifts, he would use them only for good! I asked, "Is Eli here in this kingdom? How did he get here? You tell me what you know."

"Well, but first you must tell me a few things, yes? What of Eli's appearance? Is he a tall man? Is he white or dark skinned? Old or young? What does he believe, and from where do his people come—his birthplace? Does he have living children? You say a wife—does he have any other living relations? Who are those most precious to him? All these things I need to know, and from you now!"

I replied, "Why all these questions? And what if I don't know?"

Apollyon looked at me with his red eyes, and I noticed that there were just the two of us standing there. "You will tell me what you know, and I will know if you tell one lie. These answers are far more important than an elephant, and well you know it!"

He was growing angry, so he stopped, caught his breath, and went on. "Sol and Anna and their little friend—his name escapes me—Eli has been traveling with them to a place not far from here. Because of Eli, the family and all those in his path are in great danger. Do you not know my minions are persuasive and cunning? Do you not believe even a prophet can be persuaded by a silver tongue and promises of riches for eternity? His powers would be multiplied by joining with me! Don't you see? Eli is lost to you. You have no need of loyalty to him. A promise to me of truthful answers to a few questions and you shall have your heart's desire, my precious lady."

"I don't know," I answered. "It is a hard thing to believe that Eli would do anything hurtful to anyone. His heart is as pure as gold, and he is good."

Apollyon, with much patience and in a very gentle voice, said, "I know. He is a good man. My minions have told me as much. Now we are talking. Tell me more about this good man and what he believes and the things he has done."

Falling into his trap, I told him, "Well, Eli is kind and gentle. He is an honest and good husband to Cerena, who is a very beautiful African, not as dark-skinned as he is and not as old. I would say Cerena is about forty, so I guess Eli to be sixty. He grew up on a plantation in South Africa, where he was born, and was a spiritual leader in his church there. He could speak and hear in tongues, whatever that means. On the Sundays we do not go to church, Eli reads the morning prayers and gives what Nimee, that's my Grandmamma, calls a homily—a sort of short sermon about the Scriptures. I think Eli would make a good prea ..." I stopped short before going on because I realized I had said much too much already! I might as well have gone ahead and said he was a prophet as much as I had told! Gosh! What damage had I done?

"Well, and now then, was that so hard? Of course not and no harm came to anyone. Am I right?" He took my chin in his hand and drew it up so my eyes were on his. He was smiling broadly. Tears were streaming down my face, but I refused to let out one cry or sob.

"Oh, oh, come. Now you have your wish, your handsome white elephant forever. I will take you to him and help you get on his back when you are ready and not before." I turned my head away and lay down on the grass, curled up like a baby.

27

There was much celebrating and recounting of the battle inside the Elysian Pass. Everyone was excited about Jepetto's bravery in swallowing Le Annis the banshee, saving all their lives, and returning with his own. There was also great talk and speculation about who this Truluck was. Where had he come from? Was he a mortal or an angel? Was he a toad or something else? Jepetto had no answer. He only knew he had healed him and helped him, so what difference did it make? Jepetto told everyone how thankful he was for Truluck, that he would never forget him and would try to be like him.

The company began to climb the soft incline of the hill on the green expanse. The toads were sitting astride the two great white Pyrenees, Jepetto was holding Anna's hand, the old owl, Professor Huckabee, was atop Sol's head, the falcon was on Eli's shoulder, and the cats, large and small, were dancing among the wild birds as they moved toward the Elysian Fields. Someone was watching, listening, and thinking. He had to make the final decision.

As Wormfly watched the company disappearing over the hills, he flew off in the opposite direction toward the River Styx. In no time he was there. Unlike anyone else, there was no need for him to wait for the Ferryman or anyone else in order to cross. Wormfly blended perfectly into the mist and deathlike gloom of the horrible river's surroundings. After continuing for several miles, Wormfly saw Apollyon and his snake and looked around until he spotted the child, curled up on the ground, alone. Wormfly wondered, *Can he tell I am here? How would he know? He has the power to do things to put me in more misery than I have ever been in before. But here is this child. Her plight has brought life back into me. She is afraid and should be. She needs help, and if I have one ounce of courage in this pin body, I must, I must come to her aid! How? How? Who would ever help anything like a wormfly?*

As he finished these thoughts, a pattern of words seemed to come streaming out of nowhere. It was hard to tell if they were words, music, or both. Wormfly thought they were the most beautiful sounds he had ever heard. He had no idea how long the sounds went on. As they began to fade away, Wormfly opened his tiny eyes and looked around. The entire world had a difference about it. In fact, it dazzled! He knew that from now on he would have all the help he needed and who to call upon for it. He also knew it was impossible for him to resume his body as a monarch forever to carry out his mission. Wormfly knew exactly what to do, for he had seen God!

He gathered all his courage, took a deep breath, closed his eyes, and spread his wings. Up, up, up off the ground he went, fluttering in the wind exactly like the small, unobtrusive moth he had morphed into to find Aprion. He retraced his steps and saw Aprion led away by the wolves. The wolves did not see him as he lit upon Aprion's ear. He whispered to her, "Aprion, I am a friend here at the child's service. Will you trust me and not be afraid?"

Without moving a muscle, the mare answered, "Who are you? You must tell me from where you come."

Wormfly should have expected these questions, but answered with some authority, "My lady, there isn't time to spare, and well you know it. I fly for the Elysian Fields to join the child's champion. He is Elijah and is with Sol, Anna, and their company. He will not only champion the child and free her, but it is said he will also free the prophets as well as your family, brothers and sisters and friends! My speed is excellent. Where were you to be at day's end?"

"We knew very little, for the evil one spoke in riddles to us," answered the mare. "Perhaps you could hover about him and find out?" Aprion suggested, looking sad.

"Do you know where these wolves are taking you?" Wormfly asked the mare.

"You know as much as I do. I only do as they say," Aprion replied.

Wormfly knew her fate would be worse than death if she had angered Apollyon enough to be sent off with wolves, so he said, "I hope to see you again and do not lose hope. There is always hope." Off he flew, still a moth, toward the evil one and the snake.

Wormfly morphed into a housefly, which he could do easily, and lit upon the snake's hard, spiny back. After listening to the conversations between the snake and Apollyon, he deduced the evil plan and the evil one's timeline. As far as he knew, he had escaped unnoticed.

After finding out all he needed to know, he went back the way he came as Wormfly again, so as not to be noticed. From deep inside of him, he began to sing a tune he once knew in his younger days, *I'm free, free-fallin'. I'm free, free-fallin'.* As Wormfly hummed, he heard another voice also singing an old familiar song, *"Hummingbird don't fly away, fly away. Hummingbird don't fly away, fly away."* Wormfly loved this old tune, but the voice was that of his old master and sounded as if it was directly behind him! Wormfly was seized with the old, familiar, contemptuous fear of being in the presence of pure evil.

"Hello, you pinprick, you needle-bodied varmint with the wings of a half-grown nat. That pin head of yours has not the room for a brain, and well I know it, so tell me and I will know if you lie. Where do you think you are going, and from where did you learn to produce a tone thinking it to be music? That was the most piteous pretense of humming ever produced, you wretched and useless insect."

This was Apollyon's greeting to Wormfly as he came up behind him in the form of a crow. "All I need to do is make one move with my beak and you are my breakfast, but the taste of you would turn my stomach! We shall have to think of a greater punishment for I have a suspicion of where it is you are headed and what for. Tell me now and I might be merciful, you little twit," the crow said as they were perched on a nearby tree branch.

Wormfly had grown accustomed to this disdain and verbal abuse from Apollyon and his minions. His heart that had been earlier awakened now sunk and nearly withered under this humiliation and thunderous hatred bellowed out upon him in one fatal swoop.

Wormfly spoke out, "But how did you know? When I came among you back there, I was a fly. You could not as much as have seen me."

Now Apollyon's form began to grow and change into his half-full demon form, the one I have always been allowed to see. He towered over the tree itself and began, "Does your tiny pin brain think I have only you as a spy and that you are best? Ha! Ha!" He laughed. He bore down on Wormfly so close that the breath coming from his mouth, hot and venomous, was enough to kill. "The mare Aprion, the one the child had come to believe in as her friend and best caretaker, consider Aprion. Did you ask the mare who brought her to the child? Ah ha, you simpleton, you did not!"

At these words, Wormfly was for one second confused and then immediately understood the terrible ramifications of what he was being told. The child had been in even graver danger than he ever thought and was without any protection.

Apollyon went on, "You have listened to whispers on the wind as many have, thinking them to be messages from something merciful and with greater power than I possess, promising life eternal, joy, and freedom from bondage. Say I speak the truth, you worm?"

Wormfly thought before he spoke, but alas, his master was right. He had. "Yes," he answered.

"Yes who!" Apollyon bellowed.

"Yes, Master."

Wormfly spoke with great sobs and a completely broken heart. He had allowed himself to be led astray by some voice in the wind, something he could not even see! Did it really happen? Why had he not asked Aprion more questions? Why had he not asked the child herself? He could have trusted her to tell him the truth! Was it too late for him now—again? Was it too late for the child?

Apollyon was standing with his half-winged hands on his hips, waiting for Wormfly to explain himself and staring straight at the tiny creature. For an outsider to come upon this scene, it would have looked preposterous;

a seven-foot man holding a half-inch fly hostage! How absurd. The man could certainly have done away with the insect with a thump of his finger, and yet this standoff was in the making. It would make one wonder what was really going on behind what we have eyes to see.

Up until now Wormfly had said nothing more than his, "Yes, Master," to the last question or rather series of questions. Apollyon did not want to give him any time to think more about it. Rather he had designed a test for Wormfly to pass in order for him to live or die.

28

Through many dangers toils and snares I have already come. 'Tis grace that's kept me safe thus far And grace will lead me home.

When Apollyon had once again taken on the body of the crow and left Wormfly alone, he had time to think over the conditions of this test that were put before him. It never occurred to Apollyon that Wormfly would choose anything but his conditions! First of all, he was sure Wormfly would do exactly as directed or he would surely die. If he did carry out his evil covert mission, he would be given the body of a monarch butterfly once more and would live forever under the kingdom and conditions of the master.

Second, Apollyon had put a stinger in Wormfly filled with a deadly poison. Wormfly was told he could sting only once, and then he would die. Depending on whether he did as he was commanded, he would be reborn as a monarch and live forever to serve Apollyon or become forever a sandworm, and all hope would be lost. Sandworms were the lowliest of minions. Their fate was to be devoured and reborn, only to be devoured again.

Third, Wormfly was to travel to the Elysian Fields, find Sol, Anna, and this champion who was to rescue the child, and travel silently with them. His name was Eli, and he was the one Wormfly was to sting and kill. Apollyon would tell him of the exact time and place, for they would all be in that one place together, including the child.

Last, in the case that Eli did not live to arrive at the place of meeting and another attempted to step in as her champion, Wormfly was to sting and kill that one in Eli's stead. Under no circumstances was he to waste his stinger, and above all, he was forbidden to sting the child.

Wormfly had begun to ask where he was to report once he was reborn as a monarch, but the bird had already flown away, leaving him, as usual, feeling incomplete and extremely agitated.

~~~~~~~~~~~~~~~~~~~~~~~~~~

The banquet table was set to overflowing with the best of every harvest when Sol, Anna, Eli, and their company arrived at the great Downing Valley in the Elysian Fields. The bees had brought their best honey and the trees their thickest and sweetest syrup. There was, provided by the fairies, magic time dust to sprinkle upon whoever liked the fare and enchantment of a tea under the tiniest toadstools in the world.

The wine was flowing, the children danced with streaming colored ribbons in their hair, and the boys played what boys will play in the grass. Sol exclaimed on the pot roast, Eli ascertained that the coconut cake was the best he had ever tasted, and Anna declared that it was impossible for anyone to have had such a wonderful tea as she and the toads had with the fairies. They had been brushed with fairy dust and become small enough to join in the enchantment of tea under the tiny toadstools.

As for Jepetto, there was nothing he did not enjoy to the fullest extent possible, and he hopped and pirouetted about so all would know. He did exclaim the muffins were tops and decided to sing and dance for that. As he sang and hopped and danced around the table and down and up the hill, he sang, "Do you know the muffin man?" Well, soon enough every child was following him and singing along. It was as if Jepetto were the Pied Piper of Hamlin. The children did all he did, and it was a joyous afternoon! Sol came to Jepetto, who was actually sitting still on the grass, as the afternoon was coming on strong.

Jepetto said, "I changed one word in the song to match the name of where we are. Is that all right for Jepetto to do?"

"Oh my, yes," Sol answered. "It proves you are on your toes—pardon the pun."

Jepetto looked at him with his head tilted to one side and said, "Pun? Not pun. Not bun, buffins! Buffin Man!"

Sol chuckled and sat down beside Jepetto, put his strong arm around him, and said, "Jepetto, I am so glad you belong to us. You fill us with joy every day, and you make my heart glad just because you are who you are. There is nothing you could ever do to stop my love for you."

Jepetto laid his strangely clad head against Sol's firm shoulder. His five-pointed hat, which never left his head, gave Sol a few good sticks and jabs around the neck and arms, but the little creature went on. "Jepetto is the luckiest boy in the whole kingdom! Jepetto had no home, was lonely, hungry, yes, so hungry and so, so, yes, so afraid of the dark when Sol and Anna found him and loved him. Did Jepetto tell it right? Did he, Sol?"

"Yes, you surely did," said Sol, giving him a confirming hug and smile.

Jepetto was not finished, for he went on talking, "Well, Jepetto is funny, funny, and he loves oh yes, love, loves too, but Jepetto is worried. Alarm! Alarm! Jepetto needs to tell Sol!"

Sol looked Jepetto in the eyes and asked, "Has something happened, my boy? Tell me what has upset you."

Jepetto answered Sol in a whisper, which he had never done in his entire life, "Jepetto had a dream that was true. Sol's friend Eli is in a very bad danger."

Sol asked him if he could tell him more about this dream. Jepetto said, "Sol and Anna must, yes must, keep a close, close watch on Jepetto's new friend, yes, on Eli. Jepetto's dream was about poison, about bad poison. All that is, all and all Jepetto knows."

The little creature was clutching Sol's arm with both his large, long hands and was obviously waiting for Sol to reassure him in some way. Sol, knowing what to ask him, said, "What did you *see* in your dream, Jepetto, and have you dreamed it before?"

As Jepetto answered, he was perfectly still, looking up into Sol's face with eyes as wide as saucers. "Jepetto saw the dream in two nights' sleep. Jepetto saw only big, beautiful butterflies."

"Thank you, Jepetto," Sol said and hugged him tight. "You are not to worry about this. I will take care of Eli, and angels are watching over him, just as they look over you. You only let me know if you have any more dreams that worry you. You were a very good boy to tell me, and I am very proud of you." Jepetto looked up at Sol and smiled his funny, crooked smile.

"Up you go!" Sol said cheerily to Jepetto. "There is time left in this glorious day for you to run and play in the fields with both your old and new friends! Run, sing, and dance; eat and be merry until we call you for the night, but stay close, my sweet boy!"

"All right!" answered Jepetto, happily straightening his crown and pirouetting on his toes. Off he danced, calling the toads as he went.

As the long day in the Elysian Fields ended, all the dwellers of that place went their way toward home. One very special family had invited Sol and company to be their guests for the night and were glad to do it. Their house was on the hillside, ancient, and made of stone. It was covered with moss and roses, and the rooms went on forever. Jepetto was put in charge of the speaking creatures for the night, and they were all sent up to the top of the stairs to the roof. There they found grass growing, thick and green, and plenty of straw. Jepetto was proud indeed to be the one in charge but had had a strict and simple talking to from Sol and Anna about humility, love, and remembering to lead everyone in prayers before sleeping.

Sol, Eli, and Anna visited for a while after supper with their hosts, shared in a bit of field wine, and said their good nights. Afterward the three held back in the sitting room to talk of what Jepetto had shared with Sol of his dreams.

Anna and Sol both had had similar insights within the last two days about Eli being in some sort of danger. Anna's insight had been through something one of the women serving at the banquet had said to her and another she had seen as she was in prayer. The woman at the banquet had asked her if this dark-skinned man was a prophet from of old, and whether he was or not, she had seen something like a glow about his head as they approached. She went on to tell Anna that later in the afternoon she had seen him talking with one of the townsmen and on the side of his head just above his right ear, she saw blood flowing down his face onto his neck. This had startled her so that she looked away quickly to see if anyone else saw it, and when she looked back at him, it was not there. Anna told Sol and Eli that she discerned in her spirit that this woman had the seeing gift because she saw that Eli was a prophet at first sight.

"Well," proffered Sol, "I cannot speak for you, Eli, or for you, my dear, but as I hear this, she is right that Eli is a prophet. Now, what do you make of this blood? What say you, Eli?"

Eli spoke up about these things being said about himself for the first time, "You and all say I am a prophet. I do not know this about myself. I do know that I once had a gift of healing and of tongues and of interpretation of prophecy in tongues. I do have what you call here seeing dreams and encounters with the Spirit as well. However, the blood this woman saw on my face and Jepetto's dream and caution of poison, is all a mystery to me."

Sol had to speak up, for he had not yet gathered up his thoughts into his words. "Well—and how I pray I did not have this to tell—but there have been things in my visions in the last day or two of a similar nature about your safety, Eli. That is why I pressed little Jepetto as I did and knew he said the truth."

Anna looked at her husband quizzically and said, "You nearly always share your insights with me, Sol. Did you not wish me to worry about Eli and take it all upon yourself, knowing my heart and prayers have been with and for the child? We cannot and must not lose our focus."

Sol went on, "We must not forget that not far from here the Truthlands end. The land between here and the Banelands are populated with naysayers and those who worship the evil one without shame. It has always been this way." Eli listened sharply and with growing understanding as Sol continued, "Eli, you must understand that in this kingdom there are many more of those under Satan's lordship than not, for he truly rules in this place. There are so few who stand for the truth and seek the Most High and that in worship, their hearts are not in it. Therefore the evil one does not pursue them. He has nothing to fear from them. If they had any faith at all, enough to move him to worry, then he would be at their heels. It is a sad state of affairs."

Eli did not speak for a moment or two, for he was thinking. Then he said, "Perhaps Satan means what he has planned for Louisa for evil, but the Most High has a greater plan yet. Maybe He plans to count it for good!"

At this thought, Sol and Anna quieted and drew each other close once more.

Sol began to tell Eli about his visionary encounters of the last days. "When Jepetto was telling me about his dreams, he said two words, 'Alarm! Alarm!' This gave me a sudden, clear flashback of being in a classroom at the university where I taught years and years ago. When we gave out examinations, a bell would ring when the students' time was up. My belief is that the evil one is testing one of his spies for credibility, which includes poisoning Eli, and one that can kill with its sting."

Anna said, "Hence the butterflies and a butterfly that stings."

Eli responded, "But butterflies don't sting."

"I agree," answered Sol. "We also know that our enemy is a copycat. He knows how to do nothing new. We have chameleons that are of nothing but goodness, so it would follow that he would use chameleon spies as well, and in his depravity, make them mutants of the original."

Eli and Anna agreed all these theories to be possibilities to pray about and put to use in their planning, starting immediately.

The first order of business was the appointment of night watchmen, preferably ones who dined on insects. As luck would have it, there were several close at hand. Up the stairs Sol went. He borrowed two of the oldest toads who were the most advanced at bug-snapping and set them up for night shifts. The toads could not believe their ears! They were so excited to be of service that as Sol went down the steep stairs with Archibald the toad on his shoulder, Archibald had his chest broadly displayed and cheeks puffed for his shift. The rest of the toads were quite unruly, hopping up, down, and all over and giving Jepetto a hard time at being in charge!

Early the next morning, Churchill was doing his best to awaken Archibald, to no avail. The toads had proven worthy of their duties all night and had bravely taken turns standing watch for murderous flying demons. Not long after the house was quiet and Archibald began to get lonely, Churchill came hopping gently down the steps and joined him. They made an executive toad decision that it must require them both to properly contain the premises from this probable attacker of Mr. Eli. All night they hopped around and about the outer perimeter of the house, looking up and down and often up to the roof to make a stand of defense there as well.

"Arch," Churchill called out in a quite loud whisper, "you must get up, my man! The day has begun. Our duties have ended, and now we may have breakfast!"

The elder toad arose, stretching and yawning. "Bring my spectacles, if you please, or I'll trip over my own feet. Yes, and breakfast it shall be. Point the way!" Archibald answered.

"By the way, a rather chipper job last night, Church."

"Yes, thank you. Rather," replied Churchill. And off they went toward the smell of good food and morning conversation.

Watching them through a window as they hopped toward the voice of Jepetto was a tiny, pin-like insect with unusually long, thin legs and wings so pitiful they were barely visible in the dawning light. Wormfly had been spying on these two toads hopping about hither and thither since the house went to bed. He had listened to their thick British conversations in which they continually went in and out of kingdom to toad language, both of which he understood and could speak fluently. Wormfly thought it quite a conundrum that they had gone on believing that they, or anyone else, for that matter, would be able to thwart his attempt to sting and kill Eli if he chose to do it. After all, he was worm, a fly, and chameleon. Therefore, they knew not what they were protecting Eli from or if he needed protection at all. Wormfly was watching and waiting.

29

The entire family was standing at the door of the stone house waving their good-bye to Sol and their company. Jepetto and the toads were leading off, along with the pair of Pyrenees, down the hill when a group of women came running toward them shouting, "Eli! Eli! We must see Eli the prophet! Is he still among you?"

These women and their loud voices frightened Jepetto so much that he turned and ran to find Sol and Anna, not far behind and gaining fast as they heard him calling. "It is all right, Jepetto. I will talk with these women. You go and stay with Anna," Sol told him.

Sol and Eli met the women and calmed them, telling them no one would talk without a peaceful head and a quiet spirit. The two men walked three of the most sensible of the women off to the side.

Eli said, "I am the man known as Eli. Why do you seek *me*? Can I be of service to you? Are your families ill, or is someone in need or trouble?"

The women all began speaking at once. Sol stopped them and said, "Please, ladies, we do want to hear you, but it is difficult when all of you speak at once." He touched the arm of the woman who had not spoken with the others and asked if she would speak for the group. "My dear, what is your name?"

"I am Martha Titherspoon, sir."

Sol continued, "Please be so kind, Mrs. Titherspoon, as to explain to us the urgency of your need of Eli, and please be thorough."

Martha Titherspoon was a round woman, certainly a wife and mother of many children. She wore an apron over her simple ankle-length dress and her hair was neatly wrapped in a white scarf. She began breathlessly, "We have been told since we were children at our mothers' knees that at the time appointed, a prophet whose name is Eli would come into the kingdom from another time or place to release the priests and prophets long held captive in the caves in the region of our homeland. That he would also free the mountain nymphs from their cavern graves so we may once again have protection from Satan and his evil minions. We saw this Eli with our own eyes yesterday. We have met in prayer and meditation all night and have been sent by the other women who are seers to speak with him concerning this prophecy." She stopped to take a breath and looked around at the other women for their opinion of what she had spoken. The other women nodded their heads in agreement, looking at both Sol and Eli.

"Is there anything else?" asked Sol.

"Yes." Martha went on, "We are in hopes that Eli will come with us to the caves and call the captive prophets out today, for we are in great need of teachers. This is our sincere prayer and request."

"I see," Eli replied after a few moments' contemplation. Eli knew the story in 1 Kings in the Old Testament when a man called Ahab commands Elijah to call forth and set free the captive prophets of Israel. In that Scripture, the prophets Elijah called from their captivity and set free were false prophets of Baal, a pagan god. Surely these women did not put their hope in prophets of a false god?

Eli looked quizzically at Sol, who already knew Eli's mind, and said to him, "Sol, you have called this an upside-down kingdom. Do you wish to change your mind now?"

Sol said, "We have these women here waiting. Do you think there is worth in their request?"

Eli thought another moment and then said to the women, "Please, dear ladies, if you would give us a few minutes to ourselves." Then he gently bowed to them.

Since Eli had arrived at the lopsided house, he had been wearing Sol's clothes. He was dressed in a robe of raw and knotty linen, and a hooded cloak of heather grey, made from linen and wool held together in the front with large wooden buttons and loops. Everyone wore sandals in the kingdom, and those worn by both men were of an old Hebrew style. "Sol, are the caves these women speak of far from our route and of any delay and danger to our mission?"

Sol answered, "They are not far—a quarter-day's journey to the east, I would guess. The people in that region are inbred, Eli. That is my concern."

"What concerns you about that? They are mixed in race?" asked Eli.

Sol went on to tell Eli about how in the Banelands, where the caves are, men took Nephilim as wives in the very early days. The center of Apollyon's wickedness and stronghold, which remains over the entire kingdom, lies close to this region. Danger would certainly not be a strong enough word. "So," Eli said, trying to understand. "The prophets held captive in this realm are then true prophets?"

"Yes," replied Sol, "and would be at the mercy of the enemy the moment they stepped forth into the light of day."

Eli looked at Sol and at the terrified group of women. He saw the fear and lack of faith in their eyes. Eli said, "Sol, I believe we should go to the women."

Eli and Sol returned to the group of women, and Eli said to them, "Ladies, we will travel to the caves today and do what is good in the sight of the Most High. Go, gather up your group of women and wait here. We have business before we leave." The women began to shed tears of joy and thanks, and all came to shake his hands before going for their friends.

Eli led the women back to their group, and on the way he said, "Sol, you will not mind if we pray?"

"Please and we must," answered Sol and the women agreed as well.

Eli asked the group to stand in a circle and hold hands. They all did this with no problem. It was only when Eli began to pray that he saw their misperception of prayer itself. There was confusion on Eli's part as to what god the group was praying to, for it seemed Eli, Anna, and Jepetto prayed to one and the women were praying to a different god. The animals were certainly addressing their petitions to yet another deity.

Eli thought to himself, *Why should this surprise me in this kingdom where evil rules above all? Was it not true even in Scripture that where evil reigned the Spirit was absent or squelched, false prophets would teach and false gods worshipped? How do I reach these lost people quickly and is it my calling to do so?* From deep in his spirit Eli heard his answer: "Set My people free!"

And Eli did.

The women and Sol, Anna, and their company listened as Eli prayed to the one true God. They wept as he sang in tongues as beautifully as an evening songbird. They listened to him recite Psalm after Psalm of praise as they walked together toward the caves, for he reminded them that evil flees at the sound of praise to the Most High.

Eli could feel the Spirit of truth growing stronger as they traveled and as the others joined him in singing. One of the women came to the front of the group with a wooden cross, lifted high in both hands. Their praise and prayers grew louder and stronger as they drew closer to the Banelands.

It was high morning now. Groups of townspeople gathered on a hilltop with their hands over their eyes, shading them from the sun as they heard Eli and the women approaching. When they heard the praise and saw the cross, some fled, some stared as if in shock, and others ran to meet them. There were men in this group as well. Eli and Sol were to find out when they reached the village that only women were seers in this region of the Banelands.

Anna's home and family had been here but were long dead or moved to other parts by now. Anna had been a seer as a child of eighteen months and of a seeing mother before Le Annis took her away. It was said that among the women were the Nephilim and all were seers. Therefore all seers were evil and all seers were women.

It had been decided long ago that all seeing women were not evil and each should be given her own account by the other women. So it was. As for the men, none had ever claimed to be seers here by anyone.

Eli could tell this region had been a matriarchal society since ancient times. Why were they putting their trust in him, a man, as a prophet and a seer? Maybe there was a difference in their eyes? Eli had been discussing these things with Sol and Anna as they finally reached the edges of the Banelands caves.

30

Hidden inside Eli's hood, Wormfly was nestled as close to his temple as he could get, resting, watching, listening, and waiting. Wormfly wanted to whisper in Eli's ear and tell him exactly what was going to happen when he called forth the prophets from those caves. Or he wanted to go ahead and sting Eli, get it over with, and not have to agonize over this decision one second more. No, he wanted to sting himself and set Eli free and himself as well. If he did that, how would he be of assistance to the child? He was not sure what was in his heart. Sometimes he had kind thoughts and sometimes the most evil of all thoughts. Had he just thought about being kind to someone? Is that what he had in his heart? Wormfly had forgotten the meaning of that word, just as he had forgotten the meaning or feeling of life! Living also meant to hurt and not know what to do. Wormfly needed to know how to pray. If this one true God was real, Wormfly needed Him now!

As Wormfly was pondering this, he was suddenly surrounded, and completely encompassed by a brilliant white light. In this light he could see nothing else and yet his eyes were not strained. In the light was music so beautiful that it made him want to cry and laugh at the same time. Out of the light, there came something like a voice, but it was not a voice but more like a knowing. All of Wormfly's questions, doubts, and hurts were taken away in a second. Something else took their place—something he had never known before. There was joy, peace, rest, gladness, forgiveness, and a love and a hunger for this new Love, which was the light. The light faded into glorious colors until it was gone. Wormfly could not move or even think for a good while. He might have even fallen fast asleep.

The Banelands Caves

The Banelands Caves many sons of men and prophets held;
Call upon Eli to draw them out as Ahab and Jezebel.
Ancient seers cast lots on the close of the play.
All believe to know. In the end, all obey.

Eli and the woman seer, Martha, had established a bond of the spirit on their way to the caves village, and Eli felt that Martha would be a strong force in helping him not only gain the trust of the villagers but also in the deliverance of the captive prophets.

The one thing Eli did not understand was the strong compulsion he had to set these prophets free. After all, he had every reason to believe they were false prophets and teachers and that their allegiance was to the evil one. Eli did believe that Martha would in some way play a large and powerful role in what transpired afterward. Therefore, Eli put Martha to the forefront.

Standing before the caves with all the villagers and those from surrounding areas looking on, he said, "Martha, call upon the one true and Most High to release these men from their bondage."

Martha, in a loud voice full of authority and faith, called out, "Sons of men and prophets of old, come forth!"

You could hear a pin drop, for every man, woman, child, and creature were silent and waiting. There were many caves within the walls of the tombs, and they looked from one to the other, wide eyed. Eli said, "Martha, call them yet again."

Martha called, "Sons of men and prophets of old who have been held captive, your freedom is now. Come forth in the name of the Most High!"

At this, a deep rumbling started way down low within the tombs. Small stones fell from the tops of the walls. The ground beneath them shook. Out of the openings of the caves came rock, sandstone, and gravel until the dust was too thick to see the openings. As the dust settled, out of the caves walked man after man, hunched over and hiding their eyes from the sun. Many were very old and feeble while others looked as if they were but adolescents and in their prime. All were pale as sheets and covered with the clay and sandstone dust from head to toe. They were dressed in loincloths or long, tattered robes.

The women ran toward them, bringing water as they sat upon the ground, still shying away from the blinding sun in their faces. Martha and Eli looked at one another with serious questions. Every other soul was exclaiming, "Miracle!"

"She is a saint, a prophetess."

"What need have we of Eli?"

"Martha, Martha!"

Eli and Martha made no reply to these remarks but saw that provisions were made for the men. There were twenty-one all counted, and they were taken into a large meeting hall where the women tended to their needs for food, water, bathing, and clean clothes. The seeing women, including Martha, talked with these men as well to try to get a feel for where their allegiance stood.

Eli was waiting outside the meeting hall for news from the women before they continued on when Martha came outside and told him that she and the women believed all the men to be trustworthy.

"Martha," Eli asked, "have you and the women prayed with these men?"

Martha lowered her eyes and said, "It was my sincere intention to do so, and I knew it right to do, but some of the seeing women could not agree to pray to the same gods. Because they now think so highly of me and called my name saying, 'Martha!' and 'She has worked a miracle,' I stepped back and did not pray."

"Martha," continued Eli seriously, "we do not contend with flesh and blood. We fight against powers and princes in the places where even God and evil dwell. We must stand and call on the name of the Most High. It is His name that freed those men, not any person. Do you understand?"

"Will you pray with us before you go, Eli?"

"I will pray with you all, including the men we have released," Eli replied insistently.

Inside the hall Martha, Eli, the thirteen women, and the twenty-one prophets had room to gather in a circle. Eli asked everyone to hold the hand of the person next to him or her, and they did with some opposition.

Eli began, "We give thanks and praise to You, the Most High, for Your goodness and loving kindness, for Your almighty works. The winnowing fork is in Your hand ..." At these words, the shadowy glass in the windows began to rattle. Stones fell from the giant hearth that covered one wall, and low growling came from the throats of at least half of the men in the circle. The hands of everyone grew intensely hot. Clasped hands dropped at once, and every eye looked at his or her neighbor in fear and judgment. The faces of those from whom the growls were coming grew red, and their eyes blazed fire. From six of the women came high-pitched screams of horror as intense pain was upon them and the hair on their heads looked electrified and glowed. Eli, Martha, and the other seven women stood firm without fear and continued praying and singing high praise.

This took place within three or four minutes time of those men who were growling falling to the floor dead. The dead prophets, who were obviously evil, each had a prick, dripping red, at his right temple. Once the power of all of these men was squelched, the screaming of the six women stopped. They appeared to be normal, and all was quiet except for the songs of praise.

Eli, Martha, and the others who were singing had never opened their eyes because their praise and prayer was so intense. When they did and saw these men lying dead on the floor and the screaming women quiet and themselves again, Eli asked of anyone, God maybe, "How? Who? Did anyone see how these men died and who drew these women back to us?"

"No," was the response from everyone.

"Look. See their temples," said Martha, who was bending down at the body of the man beside her.

"What could have done this, and to them all, and so quickly?" asked Eli.

One of the other women offered, "Some flying thing, a stinging insect of some kind."

"It would surely have to be very venomous and known exactly what it was doing!" said Eli in amazement. Eli asked of the women, "Are any of your women chameleons, able to change form at will? An undetected insect is the only answer."

The woman looked to one another and to Eli, shaking their heads no. Martha said, "If there is such a one, we have no knowledge of her."

Eli looked around at the faces of those in the room. At the door, he saw Sol, Anna, and Jepetto. Eli greeted them, saying, "Come! See what has happened here! See what our God has done and what else has happened as well."

Sol and his company left this mystery to the women and villagers, as they were already making preparations in the hall for all to come and hear the prophets after centuries of silence. Martha Titherspoon and her women friends' hearts were changed from the inside out by their experience. They wanted to share it with everyone they knew!

As Sol and his company were moving on towards finding Louisa, Wormfly was rejoicing in his service to his new master. He was already flying towards Paradeisos and giving thanks to the Most High for keeping His promises.

31

I turned and twisted with dreams that left me burning with sweat. In my dream, I heard thundering and rumblings of the earth underneath me, terrible shrieking, and growls that tore the life out of my lungs. I was afraid Eli was dying and that I could not catch my breath.

I woke up to the sound of air in my ear and something nudging me in the back. I suppose I had slept right there on the ground after exposing nearly everything Apollyon needed to know about Eli, trapped by his tangled words. As I turned to see where the air in my ear was coming from, sitting on the ground beside me was my gigantic white elephant. I looked directly into one of his great, sweet brown eyes and gently rubbed my hands across his body, speaking to him in soft, quiet words. I said, "Hi there. What is your name? Mine is Louisanna, and I am so very glad to meet you and that you are here with me. Can you talk? I have wanted to ride an ele—"

A voice like the pitch of a masterfully played French horn interrupted me, saying, "If you will give me time to get a word in, little lady, I will gladly tell you all these things and more." I jumped to my feet, dusted and straightened my dress, and patted down my frazzled hair so I would look quite like the lady he called me. I felt I was in the presence of Grandmamma when she was not to be addressed as Nimee.

"Oh my goodness!" I exclaimed, sounding like Dulci, "I hope I haven't offended you."

"Not in the least. Rest yourself against this smooth stone, and we will get acquainted."

"Okay. That sounds good to me!" I replied, as he moved his great white body into a comfortable position. "Permit me to sit, if you will, so that we will be in closer eye contact."

"Certainly. Now go on and please tell me your name," I said.

With his lovely golden brass voice, he told me all about himself. "My name is Airavarta. It is an old and proud name meant only for white elephants of the court of kings and queens of ancient lands who believed in the one true God, and as you have seen, I speak very well, though you may detect a hint of my Hindi accent."

"It is Hindi, isn't it? I knew it! I lived in New Delhi up until a few months ago, and so you see, I do know some Hindi myself!"

"All things work together for those who put their trust in their God," Airavarta replied to this.

"What was the business of the white elephants in the courts of the Hindi?"

"The Airavarta were the bearers of the kings and queens," he replied.

I was quiet and thinking to myself, *Does Apollyon know this Hindi history, and is this the reason he was so quick to please me? Should I and can I trust this animal not to be one of his? I am growing exhausted of never knowing who to trust.*

Airavarta drew me out of my thoughts by asking, "Little lady, would you care to try my back? I will not rise until you say so nor walk until you give the word."

"Airavarta, would you mind if I asked you to answer a few more questions for me? I am a young girl and alone and have been put to the test many times in the last two days, and this is the third. I do not mean to be—"

He stopped me and said gently, "My lady, it is no burden to me and certainly no offense. I expect and welcome your questions as if you were one of my calves, my babes. I would watch over you with my very life."

"All right," I said. "I will ask one at a time, and you answer as much or little as you will. If it is enough, we will go on. If not, I may want more."

"Whatever you wish, litt—"

I stopped him and said, "Please, when you call, call me Louisa. That is my nanny, Cerena's name for me."

"It will be so," he replied. "Louisa," he said. "That is a beautiful name."

"My first question is, how did you come to be here to be my bearer?"

He replied, "My herd comes from south of the Banelands where it borders the Arielian Plains in the Heleos Desert. There are many whose will is to stand for the one true God, and others who have no stand at all. We abide there in peace, both sons of men and beasts. In this kingdom where the evil one rules, when one is called he comes and keeps his faith in his heart until an opportune time when he can possibly make a stand for truth. There are those who have made their stands, countless numbers of them, but as a whole they have been ineffective in changing anything. Apollyon himself flew to my home in the form of a crow and told me to come to Paradeisos to carry a princess through its gates. He spoke certain strange words over me, and I became a crow as well. We flew together just yesterday when I saw you through the clearing."

"Did you want to come?" was my second question to him.

"We who know and put our faith in the one true God always wish for an opportunity to make a stand for Him. Yes, I did. I wanted to come for myself as well, to see Paradeisos. Who would not? The center of creation itself closed and barred from all beings by angels of God since the fall of man! An opportunity to see this place, enter its gates with a princess on my back! No Airavarta, no matter how distinguished, in all of history has ever had such an honor bestowed on him as this!"

"What else has Apollyon told you about his plans for me once we enter the gates? If you lie to me, I will know!" I said this to him with as much authority and belief in my gifts and my God as I had.

"Louisa, Apollyon as you call him, commanded me that I must be gentle with you, for you were not a rider. I must be obedient to him at all times, and that once through the gates, I was not to stop. He said he would tell me exactly what to do, where to stop and what to do then. After entering the gates, I was to take orders only from him. He also told me he has taken away my special gifts."

I asked further, "He did not tell you where inside the gates we were going?"

His answer was no to this each time I asked.

"Airavarta, did Apollyon say when you should carry me through the gates?"

"He said we would enter the gates today. May I ask you a question, Louisa? It is really more a courtesy. Would you like to call me by my shortened name as they do at home?"

"Well, your name is hard to pronounce," I said in a hurry. "I think your name is beautiful and exotic, but a mouthful! What is your shortened name?"

"Varta is what I am called by my family and my friends."

"Hum, Varta," I said. "I like it very much! Varta, you had some special gifts that Apollyon took away from you? Were those gifts others had given you?"

He said, "They were gifts every true and faithful Airavarta has from ages down the line. These gifts are born into us. The growth and caring for them is up to the individual. We must stay attached to the root of the tree that gives us sustenance, which is the Great Line of our fathers and our fathers' fathers. The use of them is at the will of the Most High."

I thought to myself, *It seems that every creature or person I meet in this kingdom has a spiritual gift and takes it for granted as if it was just eggs and toast for breakfast!* This taking away of his gifts was the last thing Varta mentioned about what Apollyon had done to him. As I thought, I wondered, *Does Apollyon have the power to take away gifts given by the Most High? Does he actually have the power to cut people off from their very faith?* I was about to ask Varta what his gifts were when Apollyon and three of his wolves came walking toward us.

It was not a good morning for questions at all. Apollyon had had dreams as well, but his were waking dreams. He had not worried too much about an insignificant fallen fairy queen, but he felt the earthquake and heard the thunder as the prophets were released and cursed Eli and his God. He knew also that his own prophets had fallen dead, but to his utter amazement and bewilderment, he did not know how or why.

No! This could not be! He was the master and ruler of this world! He knew all things! He always had and he always would! He would wipe off the face of the world anyone who stood in his way, but first he would torture him to death, little, by little and take extreme delight in doing so!

No, it was not a good morning at all when he approached Varta and me. "Well, and it seems the two of you have now become friends. And I knew it would be so," Apollyon announced, hands on his hips. "And how do you find him in personality and beauty, Louisanna? Is he a good companion and bred well enough for you? Gentle and kind as you wished? He is, as I am sure you have found out, from a line of elephants of royal blood, both valiant and courageous. Do you find him to be all these things as well as pleasing to carry you?" All this Apollyon asked in his typical condescending way, smiling broadly with a twinkle in his eye.

I got to my feet and looked at him without saying anything. Varta stood up slowly while Apollyon was talking, and I saw that he was not as large an elephant and with shorter tusks than I had expected and with much smaller ears, but still quite amazing. Varta looked at Apollyon as well, keeping his silence.

"Cannot either of you speak this morning? Has some ogre come overnight and taken away your tongues? Has an evil witch cast a spell upon you, leaving you idiots? Can you not hear me speaking to you? Answer me!" he demanded, growing red-faced.

Not wanting him to dissociate to his violent other self, I said with my arms crossed against my chest like a child in a demanding tantrum. I thought, *Two can play at this game.*

"I want to know what you are planning to do with me inside the gates of Paradeisos. You want to know things. Well, I want to know, too!" Apollyon said nothing but stood laughing under his breath at me.

At this I lost my temper completely and nearly shouted at him, my voice rising as I spoke. "I told you everything you wanted to know about my friend Eli. I exposed Aprion's lies to you and have no idea what will become of her now. I have been your prisoner since I came into this kingdom two days—no three days ago. My whereabouts have been kept a secret from my friends and family. I have been made to see and experience all sorts of horrible things no one in the world should have to go through. Now my fate is in your hands, as I am in your grasp, and you refuse to give me the courtesy of telling me anything, thinking me too stupid, I suppose, to figure it out otherwise. But you are wrong! I have! I have figured it out all by myself! I know exactly what you are about to do with me, and I am not afraid of that or of you!"

Of course this last bit was completely false, but I could play games as well as he could, and besides, I wanted to see his reaction. I was so undone that I was shaking. I was in high hopes he could not hear the tremble in my voice.

Apollyon, with one hand rubbing his chin replied, "Well and if you do know, please tell me what you are so sure of. I would hate for there to be a misunderstanding between us."

I expected this question from him and had my answer ready. "I will tell you nothing that I know. Why should I? You share nothing with me and presume I should tell you everything. What gain is in that for me?" I answered.

"Ah ha, it is a compromise. A mutual exchange of ideas is what you want. And as you said, you are in my grasp. Why should I compromise with you when you are in no position to do so?" As Apollyon answered this, he actually stepped back just a little. It was barely noticeable, but he did step back. I knew I had hit some nerve with him or struck some weak spot in him. What did I say to prompt that? Before I had any time to think on it more, he said, "Enough of this! Rise upon your beautiful elephant. We go!"

Varta sat down on his haunches. With no help and without fear, I held onto his bridle as he had instructed me to do and sat astride him upon the Turkish tapestry. "Hold tight. Are you ready for me to rise?" Varta asked. "Do you feel secure there?"

"Yes, I do. You may get up, Varta."

He rose on his huge front legs as gently as could be. I felt his back slowly rising and me with it! "Are you still comfortable, Louisa?" Varta asked again.

"Yes, go ahead," I said.

Now I felt his back legs begin to lift me up. I felt a bit dizzy, and being so far up off the ground was going to take some getting used to, so I said, "Wow, it's a different world from way up here!"

"Yes it is. It is best to remain relaxed. Look around you on all sides and behind you. You may try turning your body this way and that as I stand still. Speak to me as you do all this and breathe normally. If you do this, it will help you acclimate yourself to the height and to being on my back. When your head feels still and your ears no longer ring, let me know and we will try the next step."

"Varta," I asked, "how did you know my ears were ringing?"

Varta laughed. "It is a normal reaction for most all first time riders. It will soon pass."

I did as Varta told me, and soon my dizziness subsided. The turning of my head was like ballet lessons. You move your head as quickly as you turn on your toes to keep the room from spinning. The height on Varta's back was a little frightening, but the ringing in my ears subsided slowly, and I was happy to be getting used to riding an elephant!

32

I was opening my mouth to give Varta the word to walk on ahead when Apollyon appeared beside us, hovering in mid-air. This was the only time he had actually used his wings in this way since I had been in his company. His feet now appeared more as the talons of a large bird, and as for hands, he had none that I could see. He was gloriously handsome, so graceful and beautiful, in fact, that I did not want to take my eyes off him. The braids in his hair were so shiny that they looked wet, and among the golden and silver stars, diamonds and lengths of ivy were woven in. He wore no clothes, but his body seemed covered in a glittering substance not known to me before. It blended in between and through the multicolored blues, purples, forest greens, and shades of black and silver of his feathers. His face had a soft look again. It was not as youthful as before when we played in the brook, yet still younger and in a way, vulnerable.

"Well," he asked in a lighthearted voice, as if we had not had harsh words just a while ago, as if he was quite a different person! "The two of you make a lovely pair, the lovely lady and her elephant both, the princess soon to be queen and her royal Airavarta. If I were an artist, I should set up my easel and paint your portraits!" he said with glee.

He asked right off, "Do we move along to the gates? Is all well? Are either of you in need of anything before we go?" As he asked this, he flew around and about with the grace and unpredictability of a dainty fairy. The sight of him like this was totally out of character. It made me think he might go tumbling to the ground at any moment! It was all I could do not to laugh, so I put my hands over my mouth and pretended to sneeze.

Varta said, "The lady may need a few minutes to gain her balance as I begin to walk. She has just gotten used to the height of my back."

Composing myself, I said, "I give the word, Varta."

As he put one foot in front of the other, it was as if the entire earth was moving beneath me and swaying at the same time. I gripped his wide sides and balanced myself as best I could, and before long, we were walking along, up, down, back and forth, and on and on.

"And how are you up there?" Varta asked.

"Oh, I'm just fine," I fibbed. I was feeling sick to my stomach.

"Don't forget to turn your head now and then," he said.

"Oh!" I choked out. Doing this helped quite a bit, and we were off to a good start.

Apollyon was still hovering along beside us without the wolves or the snake in sight. He was now making small conversational chat about anything that he could think of. Suddenly I asked him, "Where are Little Horn and your wolves? I have not seen Little Horn since yesterday morning, I believe, and I am sure I have not seen a wolf today at all. I thought Little Horn was your best friend and that the wolves were your guards."

"Oh, what made you think those things?" he asked as if it they both were not obvious to anyone in the world. "Little Horn thinks he is very special, so I let him believe it," he continued. "He is as useless to me as a piece of clay that has dried up. Serpents are very stupid creatures and only know to do what they are told. They have not the ability to think of anything on their own. Little Horn is an expert imitator, however. Everything he does he has seen someone smarter than himself do before."

I interrupted, "So, what is he doing now?"

"I have sent him on through the gates with exact instructions for a few small things to do. Nothing of difficulty, I assure you."

"And what about the wolves?" I asked him.

"Well now, wolves are a different matter. A wolf cannot be trusted. It has a mind of its own and is not easily trained or tamed. Even a few of the ones I have had the most success with have turned on my comrades, and

I have had to destroy them. Wolves serve no one except themselves. They are rebellious and in their wildness place themselves at the top of the food chain. In other words, my lady, they believe themselves rulers over all other animals and in doing so, make fools of themselves. Their rebellion and self-serving knows no bounds." As I heard Apollyon's opinion of his wolves, I was thinking it was a good thing they were gone, as far as I could tell.

"Apollyon," I said, "I am glad to know all about wolves' personalities, but you have not answered my question! What have you done with them or where have you sent them as part of this plan of yours?"

Still hovering along beside us like a giant fairy, he said, "Now do not worry about those beasts. It is no trouble to you. I have sent them to a place where they can do no harm to themselves or others outside my command, for I am the only one they answer to."

We were now approaching the gates of Paradeisos. I could see them in the distance through the dazzling sunlight and the trees. Apollyon was no longer hovering. He was flying like a hawk. Up he soared until he was nearly out of sight, his black and silver wings shining in the light. Like a hawk, he would come sweeping down, out of nowhere to hover beside us again. He seemed to be playing again and having a grand time at what he was doing!

I thought to myself, *If only he were not so evil, I could fall in love with him, when I am a little older, of course. I believe he is the most beautiful creature in the entire world. It seems that I bring out the best in him. After all, he plays with me and becomes young and happy when he is with me.* These thoughts came to the forefront in my mind. I kept looking at him more and more. He noticed it and was returning my looks in a way that sometimes made me laugh and giggle. Other times those looks gave me a feeling of total confusion.

As I thought and we walked slowly up and down and back and forth, I had a flashback to the "its" who had helped me on my first journey up the green hill. They had been fairy-like and told me not to be afraid. Those were words of truth and grace. Somehow this hovering thing beside me now telling me not to worry myself about wolves or the snake seemed to be the greatest of all imitators!

"Well and now it is time for a rest. What do you say, Louisa?" Apollyon asked.

"Okay with me. I am getting tired and thirsty, and I am sure Varta is as well!" I answered.

"Here it is that we will rest then," he said.

Varta said, "Louisa, I will lower my front legs first and then the back ones until you are on the ground. It is the same when I let you down as when we rise."

"Oh, all right. I see," I remarked. I had never quite thought about it, but it did make sense!

"Are you ready?" he asked as we drew close to a large pool with soft grass on its bank in the shade of a huge willow tree.

"Go ahead, I give the word."

With this the world began to fall forward very slowly, and I found myself leaning back hard and digging my feet into Varta's sides. Once his front was down, I felt the back dropping, and I leaned forward until all was level and we were on the ground. "That was not bad at all! Very well done Varta," I said, and I patted him on the sides.

"Now sit there for at least a minute before you hurry off, my lady, for your legs may be a little weak," he instructed me.

My know-it-all-self took over, and I did not listen to what he said. I slid right off his big back. The minute my legs hit the ground, they felt as if they were made of water. My tummy tickled all funny, and I keeled right over! The next thing I knew, Varta was sprinkling water in my face with his trunk and I was waking up from a dead faint!

"How are you feeling?" Varta asked. I sat up slowly, feeling fine but very hungry, and said, "I feel very foolish. If I had listened to you, this would not have happened. I am sorry."

He said, "I believe you were overheated and need to eat and drink. It takes a lot out of a young rider on her first Airavarta ride!" He seemed pleased, proud, and to chuckle at this somewhat. It is true that an elephant can chuckle.

"There is lunch and water in the bags on my carrying pouches. There are also towels, soap, and a hairbrush. Are they yours?" Varta asked me.

I looked over at Apollyon quizzically and said, "No. They are not mine. Apollyon only provided one other picnic for me and it was on a day that he played. Let's see what is in these bags!"

Inside the bags of food were all my favorite things to eat! It was just the same food I had eaten at Sol and Anna's that first night—cream cheese and cucumber sandwiches, salmon with capers, shrimp with egg, and of course water crackers. For dessert there were Anna's lemon and dandelion tarts. Apollyon had even put in a small napkin with two of those marvelous candies he had given me from the gold and marble box.

"What is the liquid you are drinking?" Varta wanted to know.

"It is nectar that is really delicious. It has the taste of every fruit you could think of that is or ever could be all mixed up together in just the right amounts. It will quench a thirst quicker that anything in the whole world as far as I am concerned," I said.

"What do elephants eat for the most part?" I asked.

Varta said, "We are vegetarians by nature and live on plants, beans, and root vegetables like potatoes and turnip roots, but I would not turn down the offer of a rare mutton chop, boiled crayfish, or a fine Turkish sausage!" We both laughed. Varta was munching away at some wonderful cabbage, rutabaga, and pole beans that were in our lunch bag for him.

I saw Apollyon looking at the two of us eating together and laughing. An elephant can indeed laugh. Apollyon looked at me, straight in the eyes. I had not seen an expression like this from him before. I had never had anyone—no, not any boy—look at me like this before. His eyes were beautiful. I could have drowned in them. I wanted to pull my eyes away. I felt uncomfortable. I felt warm. I felt confused. I was totally lost to him.

Airavarta saw all that was going on between the two of us. He knew exactly what Apollyon was up to. He also knew that his window of opportunity to make me believe the truth had passed, at least for now. And so, in his wisdom, Airavarta kept his silence.

33

An awareness arises from within the mind
where God hides, waiting to be called,
Whispering hauntingly, "Come deeper, find me!"
The world is a butterfly's wing.
Be gentle and come deeper.
—Allen Cohen

Wormfly was on his way to Paradeisos morphed into the form of a common moth. Being a chameleon is only fun and satisfactory if you have the choice of what to be, he was thinking. Bats were everywhere in the air tonight, so the little moth was having a bit of trouble maneuvering so that he would not be someone's dinner. He had done what he believed to be the will of the Most High in the Banelands meeting house. The six false prophets were dead from his sting. As he dodged bats, there was one and only one thing he did not understand about what took place in him actually killing the prophets. Apollyon told Wormfly he had the ability to sting only once to kill. After once stinging, he would die.

He thought to himself, *The evil one drilled that into me, and I believed it. Why did I believe anything he said? Oh, I must stop thinking about him in any way at all! He is no longer my master! You, the Most High, are my master and God, now and forever! I am still alive, so therefore he lied to me. I will leave it at that.*

Wormfly had wanted to whisper into the ear of Eli or Sol. He had wanted to let one of them know he was there to lead them straight to the child, but in his spirit he had the knowledge to go on ahead and to say nothing to them before he left. Wormfly had again been obedient. He had proved to be a good and faithful servant with the things the Most High had entrusted him. Wormfly heard the words, "To those whom much has been given, more will be required." Wormfly knew where the child was at this very moment. She was approaching the gates of Paradeisos, so that was his destination as well.

Morning had come, and Wormfly arrived to see the child, an elephant, and a bird-like creature moving at a moderate pace toward the gates. The child was astride the great white elephant. The bird-like creature was flying alongside them in a slow and gentle hover. Now and again it would take a sweep up into the air and down again, as if in play. Even in this boyish guise, Wormfly could not help but recognize the beast himself. *I should have known he would take this way with her*, Wormfly thought. *He knows the weakness in every person and plays it well to his advantage.* He had certainly done so for centuries with Wormfly and every other minion Wormfly had seen him use. Wormfly thought, *Perhaps the thing for me and this elephant to do if he is good and has a bright spirit is to outsmart Apollyon's evil mind. He believes himself clever, but his tricks are ancient and he knows of nothing new.*

Believing all things possible when meant for good in his newfound faith, Wormfly flew to a nearby tree. There he lit on a limb, quickly laid the egg that was promised to him, quickly wove a cocoon around his moth body and the egg, attached it to the limb, hung, and waited. Inside his cocoon, Wormfly prayed, "Your will be done." His cocoon was stretching, growing longer and wider. Even with the cocoon's larger size, Wormfly's body was outgrowing the cocoon rapidly. *Have I been inside it long enough? This is too soon to be opening! This process should take at least a few hours*, Wormfly thought desperately. His cocoon was already opening! He began to wriggle out, all sticky from his lost pupa. As he emerged, his wings wet and his body straightened itself out, Wormfly felt much different. He felt heavier, and his legs were not as long, making him have to balance carefully.

Wormfly could not see what he had become, but his wings were dry and three times as big as before, multicolored, and three-fold. He had wings of peacock hues and long, lovely feelers at his brows. If Wormfly had a mirror on that limb, he would have seen in its reflection a huge swallowtail monarch butterfly. His wingspan was now nearly seven inches across. His colors were black, red, and yellow. At the tips of his tails were round red dots, just at the beginning of his descending swallowtails, which were three inches long. These tails were black and yellow with a slight orange tinge. He was a beautiful specimen indeed!

Without wasting any time and as soon as his new wings were dry, Wormfly put them to use and up into the sky he went. In his dreams he could never have imagined this experience! He felt light as a feather. The breeze took him up and his wings took him down. His long tail helped him maneuver ever more easily, and he was soon directly behind the child and her elephant again. This had taken a total of fifteen minutes! *A true miracle; a transition from a wormfly or a moth or whatever I was into a butterfly*, he thought.

Apollyon, Louisa, and Varta were a quarter mile from the gates now. Wormfly flew to meet them, and as he had planned and thought best, he lit on Apollyon's head fearlessly. He was as light as a feather and for the moment went unnoticed, at least by his host. Wormfly heard them talking.

"Look! The gates are so, so big and tall and beautiful," said the child.

The gates into Paradise were made of solid gold and the entirety of them that surrounded the garden itself was inlayed with vines of roses, ivy, and symbols of fish and eternity intertwined. There were symbols of God and musical instruments of all peoples and cultures intertwined with ancient depictions of every animal, bird, and swimming thing in the worlds. Wormfly was so amazed at this handiwork and its beauty that he could scarcely take it all in.

As they arrived at the gates, Apollyon asked me as he hovered beside the elephant on my eye level, "Louisa, would you like to stand here for a while and see the beauty of the gates or enter now, for more joy and beauty than could fill your imagination awaits you inside?"

I said, looking at this beast with the eyes of puppy love, "Tell me all about every symbol on the gate and what it means." These are the words the beast spoke to me:

> As is the heart that dwells deep and unknown
> The Morning Star like the giver of all gifts
> Of old, will open for thee the Rose of Sharon bound
> For thy hand in mine is like unto the ivy and the round.

I gazed at him with huge cow eyes for what seemed minutes. The elephant stood, obviously disturbed, rocking back and forth on his haunches. Wormfly was horrified that this beast had just spoken love poetry of blasphemy to this innocent child! *Did she understand what he said? Was she that taken by him? Did she think it a love poem?* Wormfly thought, and then he had his confirmation. He heard me pleading with Apollyon, "Please, will you recite that to me once more?" And he did.

I beamed back at him, and as I did, he picked a rose growing nearby and put it in my hand. Wormfly looked at the elephant to get some idea of his thoughts, hoping to find by that whose camp he might belong to.

At this point, the gift of the rose, Varta put his ears over his eyes and blatantly shook his head as if to say no. Thinking this an opportune time, Wormfly moved daintily and lit on his opposite shoulder from the beast. In his quiet butterfly voice that he had practiced only once before now, Wormfly whispered in Varta's ear, "Do not move. I am here beside your ear, a friend. I have come in hopes that I may be of help. I am a butterfly."

The animal made no response. Wormfly continued, "I am aware that you cannot speak at this juncture, but I am sure that you do speak. If I am right, wiggle your right ear a bit. If not, wag your tail. Those will be our signs for yes and no. Understood?" The elephant slightly wiggled his right ear.

"Good, very good," Wormfly said. "Has the child been this enchanted with him long, over a day?" His tail moved. "Well, that is to be thankful for, we can suppose. Have you been any influence to her at all in any way?" At this, his ear wiggled a good bit. Having a clue, Wormfly asked, "Has he been with you and the child since this seduction began?" Another hard wiggle from Varta. "And you have not had any chance to make sense of it to her?" Another ear wiggle was the elephant's answer.

Wormfly gave all this some thought as the beast and I continued in our talk of the gate and all I loved about it and all that awaited me inside. Wormfly wondered why he was waiting to take me in and what his plan was exactly. His heart was losing hope, which he knew he should not allow. This liar of liars had convinced me that he cared for me. I was too young to completely understand. Wormfly thought, *He is the father of lies and does it well. He has kept our entire kingdom in his grasp and without hope for ages upon ages, even keeping the true prophets imprisoned in the Banelands Caves. Hopefully the people there are once again hearing the truth, coming to believe, and passing it on to others. We still have hopes of the mountain nymphs being set free.*

If Apollyon's plan for me came to fruition, the good that had been accomplished and the many souls who were now hearing the truth would be once again bound by the beast. This time he had a human child with her own will—or did he? Was he bending the rules by seducing me so soon? Of course he was! From what Wormfly had seen and his years of being mastered by Apollyon, he could tell that I would follow Apollyon anywhere and eat right out of his hand, just like a lap puppy.

Here I am. Wormfly. Where is everyone else? We are entering the gates of the garden. Am I really to be on my own? Wormfly thought.

As Apollyon said words of the ancients in unknown tongues, the gates opened. Bright light streamed out at us like a flood. In the light there were three beings like angels from high places speaking back to him also in tongues, with authority.

At these words he drew back his left wing and stretched it out, and as he did this, it became a long feathered and muscled arm with fire flowing out from it and flashes like lightning bolts toward the angels. The angels now spoke so we could all understand. "I will not kill him or defend against him any longer since there are the lives of the others to be spared." After they said this, the brightness drew back and with it, the golden angels. Apollyon had the way open to him. It was exactly what he had hoped for.

34

Little Horn had gone through the gates before us and was deep within the midst of the garden. He saw the reflection of the light coming from Apollyon and the angels at the gates. He overheard what the angels said and knew Apollyon and I would be joining him soon. He had been lying in wait for quite a while and was anxious and bored. He knew what he had to do. It sounded simple enough to him, and he was ready to perform his duty and obtain the rewards he had been promised.

There he lay under the shadow of the gigantic shade tree in the balmy breeze listening to the rippling water of the nearby stream, the birds in the trees and the many insects chirping around him. He looked up toward the sky and saw that the tree was laden with purple figs so ripe they were about to fall to the ground. It was then he realized that the insects he heard were bees and wasps buzzing around the over-ripe figs both on the tree and on the ground near him. Little Horn was just about to fall asleep when he heard sounds coming from the gate.

His orders were to stay at that tree no matter what until they arrived. At least, thanks to the all the supernatural commotion, he was now wide awake! It was a good thing, too. In the clearing and down the path, he saw approaching a large elephant carrying me and Apollyon riding his horse.

The elephant was adorned as if he were carrying Persian royalty. Apollyon looked as if he needed a bath. His hair was dirty and needed to be re-braided. His body feathers were molted, and his wings singed as if by fire.

I had obviously been crying, apparently from fear, Apollyon's apparent anger at me, and everything else that was happening. My eyes and nose were red and swollen, and I was sniffing and breathing hard, fast breaths. We were a motley looking crew indeed as Varta, Apollyon, and I drew near Little Horn.

I saw the ghastly snake as we approached him. Apollyon called to him, "Come, serpent. Tell us where to bathe! Prepare food and drink from the elephant's bags. Can you not see we have need of you? Get up on your legs and hurry!"

At this, the snake's back stretched out to form legs and small feet so that he stood upright. His front parts formed short arms and claw-like hands so he was now more monster-like than ever! I felt sick to my stomach and was about to retch. How could I think about food or eating? Little Horn did as he was told. He led us toward the brook and began to prepare the food in Varta's bags.

I looked at Varta and said, "Something has happened to change him since we entered the gates. When his form altered to fight the three angels, he came back victorious but physically scarred. His splendor is gone. His loveliness has disappeared as well. He is angry and resentful now. I am worried about him. He has refused to talk to me about the fight at the gates or anything else. 'We often take our frustrations out on the ones we love' is what Cerena used to say, so I suppose he is taking it all out on me, for I know he loves me. I am sure because he has shown it in everything he said to me and did today. The love poem he recited to me is proof enough! That and the playful mood he was in, plus the way he looked at me! Now he is injured and discouraged and needs my help and support. I have to be there for him."

All these things I thought were true at that time. There was not a person or creature on earth who could have convinced me differently. How terribly wrong and hopelessly lost I was! I was the one who needed help and was blind to it!

"Apollyon, come and let me help you. Your wings are singed and burned. Let me put medicine on your injuries. After all, I do love you," I said to him as tenderly as I could. I could not recognize my own voice as I spoke. It sounded like the voice of an older girl, even a woman. The feelings I had for him were feelings I had read about but had never experienced myself. Maybe I had changed since we entered the gates to this garden as well!

At my offer of help and comfort, he turned and looked at me with fiery red eyes in his evil anger and said haltingly, "Go! Leave me in peace. Can you not see with those beautiful, important eyes of yours that I need not be bothered by the likes of even the perfect woman?"

I was cut to the heart. Little did I know that coming from the beast himself, these were the kindest words anyone may ever hear from his mouth, for he had not planned to be injured. It shamed him, and his vanity could not take shame.

He disappeared off into the brush in an instant with his head down, but not without warning us, "Do not attempt to leave this place, for I am watching your every move. Do you and your albino elephant understand me?"

"Yes," we both answered as I choked back my sobs.

"Varta," I cried after Apollyon had left us, "what has happened? What can I do now? One moment he loved me, I know he did. Then after his confrontation inside the gates, he is not the same."

Varta led me to talk on. "Yes Louisa, I see very plainly he has a totally different air and appearance about him as well. His entire mood is different. Is it not?"

"Yes," I sobbed. "Those angels who met him at the gates must have said awful things to him, and his wings are burned because of them."

Varta continued, "Louisa, can you try to contain your sobbing? I cannot have a conversation with you nor can you think coherently until you are able to compose yourself."

I took a lovely hand-embroidered handkerchief from Varta, blew my nose, took a deep breath, and said, "All right. I think I am all right, Varta. I apologize. Please, go ahead."

"No need for apologies or thanks. I ask you to think about this. When we entered the gates, what was the first thing you saw?"

"It was the blinding light and the three angels, of course," I answered.

"You are correct," Varta answered. He went on with his next question. "What do you remember happening next?"

"Hum," I said, beginning to get a grip on reality. "Apollyon's form changed, and he began to speak words I could not understand."

"And then?" Varta asked.

"The three angels appeared and spoke strange words to him, and after the words there were flames and lightning bolts going toward …"

"Yes, Louisa. And then?"

I stopped before I answered and thought, *It was Apollyon who sent out the flames. It was then that the angels said something about not attacking him because of the rest of us.*

"Yes. Do you remember, Louisa?" Varta pushed me to answer.

"I do now. The angels could have destroyed him and us with him, but they spared his life because of the two of us. That is what really happened, isn't it, Varta?"

"Yes, it is," Varta answered, "but there is more. The angels gave Apollyon free entry into Eden itself. The angels gave him permission to bring *you* in as well. That is the root of your heartbreak and the ultimate crux of what may become his victory."

I looked at Varta questioningly and asked, "What do you mean, Varta? My only fear and concern is that I thought Apollyon and I were in love and his encounter with the angels has caused him to turn against me. I only wish they had left us to enter in peace! What sort of heartbreak and dilemma do you mean? "

At this, Varta turned his great head away from me, and turning back, he said, "Louisa, it is time for us to rest. I am hungry and I thirst. I am sure you do as well. Am I right?"

As for me, I was not, but I agreed to eat what had been prepared, slowly dismounted, and ate by myself, thinking of Apollyon and all that had happened.

A Good Decision

"Ah," Varta sighed as he and Wormfly sat together on the ground out of earshot of anyone. "She is not to be reckoned with in her state. When we met she was a girl of precociousness as well as good sense."

"What is her age, eleven or twelve?" asked Wormfly.

"Yes, I believe so, and since she has been with this beast it appears that she has begun to mature at a rather rapid pace. When she and I first met, her innocence was clearly visible. By this I mean that nothing or no one of the male gender affected her any differently than a female. All things to her were fairytales and tea parties. She did talk of the things of the Spirit being important in her life and that of her family. Truth, justice, wisdom, and honor were ideals she admired in me. She did as well in her grandmother and a manservant named Eli.

Wormfly knew Eli, of course. Wormfly and this Eli had even fought together in a spiritual battle, although Eli knew nothing of it. Wormfly remembered somberly the days when he had contemplating killing Eli as Apollyon's minion and gave thanks and praise that day had never come!

Wormfly came out of his reverie and asked Varta, "Did you have a chance to speak with her, I mean in a way to share the things of the spirit that are important to you with Louisa?"

Varta answered him, "Please tell me your name, for I do not know it as we were not properly introduced, and these are deep matters of the heart that we speak of."

Wormfly was at a loss all of a sudden as to his name. Then he remembered the quick name he had thought of for himself when Jepetto asked him. "It is Truluck. My name is Truluck," he told Varta proudly. After that moment with Varta, he never thought of himself as Wormfly again.

35

Truluck moved through the air until he found a spot quite near Apollyon. The beast had moved as far away from the gates as he could and still be inside the garden. He was licking his wounds and talking to himself. Little Horn found him but was crouching in the brush nearby, too afraid even to speak a word to his master. Apollyon was drawing with a stick on the ground and chanting ancient, wicked, and abhorrent canticles known only those of the underworld.

All around him were fiesterhogules, mutated evil fairies, known simply as hogules. These fairies were filled with such rage that they had left their Faylinns hundreds of years ago and joined forces with Apollyon himself.

The head of this kind of hogules is much too large for the body and is hairless and football shaped. The body itself is that of a shriveled-up old man with backbone and ribs showing over stretched skin. The tail is that of a serpent, as are the claws on hands and feet. The wings are shaped as fairy wings in being two-fold but thick and serpentine as well. These hogules are furious flyers, and their shrieks are so high-pitched and offensive that they have been known to make those who hear them completely deaf. Hogules are loyal to Apollyon and will perform any evil he asks, even torture a person to the death.

Apollyon's canticles had summoned them, and they swarmed around his head, waiting for his destructive direction. As close as they swarmed to his head, he did not seem to notice them.

Truluck knew the bestial canticles, but the ones Apollyon spoke were too deep for the likes of a minion. Truluck could tell one thing about Apollyon and the present circumstances. The beast was fearful he had lost power or authority and was despairingly attempting to regain it. He even feared the loss of his prophets and the rise of Eli and the rise of the prophets of the Most High.

Truluck thought that now would be the perfect time to attempt an escape with me from the garden and flee. Then he re-thought. I did not want to leave him. If I saw Apollyon now, I would only take pity and want to comfort him. My mind and will was his. Unless a miracle happened, I was lost to my friends, and with me, the entire world.

The Second Red Door

Eli, Sol, Anna, and their company were nearing the north gates of the garden as Truluck was hoping for a miracle. Apollyon and Louisa had entered the garden from the south. Because of their mighty impact in the Truthlands and the news spreading of the miracles into the Banelands, they had decided to enter the Passage as soon as they could to continue their journey. They had made excellent time with more help from the Faylinn Graces with whom they were now fast friends. Orla had come with them on this last leg of the journey, knowing the hogules would probably attack with full force.

It is not always easy to find a pass way into the Passage from the outside because there is not an entry sometimes for hundreds of miles. Between the Elysian Fields and the garden, the only pass was the Banelands caves pass, at least a half day's walk away. At this or any other point, that was not an option. The caves held many dangers, and they had not the time to spare.

After a discussion and much perplexity, Orla asked, "Gentlemen, would you allow me to grant you a grace? All you need to do is wish for an opening in the Passage, and with my grace, I believe we shall have it!" Eli and Sol talked this through and to allow fairy magic in this instance, to the thankfulness of Anna, Orla, and everyone else!

"All right, I wish for an opening in the Passage," said Sol. With that, all the fairies beat their wings, and the light grew so intense as to believe it was mid-summer.

Orla said to the company, "Your pass, my friends." Then she motioned to the right. Everyone looked in that direction to see a parting in the woods like a pathway, tight and close.

"Can we?" Sol asked.

"Of course," Orla answered. "Follow the path."

The company followed the opening in the woods through the tight trees and brambles. Sol, Anna, and Eli had to stoop, because the branches of the trees were hanging low and thick. Jepetto was in front hopping as best he could. Sol had given Jepetto and the toads permission to scout things out. Jepetto's voice was pretty soon heard, "Red door, Anna. Jepetto sees a red door!"

Sure enough, there it was a red door with yellow trim, much like the one into the main Passage from the lopsided house. As they approached, the door swung open for them, and beyond the door was a most astonishing sight!

Inside the door was a huge, fragrant, well-lit, warm, and welcoming home. There were family members bustling around preparing the meal and greeting their relations, whom they had not seen in ages, it seemed. Each person, from Sol to Churchill, imagined his own family there, and saw and experienced only what he wished. It was fairy magic and grace combined.

Eli saw Cerena in a mirror where she came to life in her beautiful madras dress. He sat and ate with her and told her all that he had experienced in the last few days. Cerena sat and listened quietly and reminded him how much she loved him. She offered him his favorite foods from the huge table piled high with every savory meat, bread, cheese, good vegetable, and fruit from the earth and all the pies, cakes, and strudels one could wish for.

Tobias saw his son, Franklin, in a living picture there on the table by the fire, Franklin, who was in the King's Academy of Merchant Seamen Toads. Tobias and Franklin had been separated by hard feelings for too many years. Tobias told Franklin how proud of him he was as they shared a tall glass of dark ale.

Everyone who wished for a loved one saw and shared time with them that night. It was a time of feasting, fierce joy, sweet tears, and finally, as the loved ones disappeared, fairy grace-induced sleep—restful and deep indeed.

~~~~~~~~~~~~~~~~~~~~~~~~

Truluck flew as fast as his wings would carry him in search of help to rescue me while Apollyon remained weakened and feeling defeated. Truluck naturally headed toward the Elysian Fields and just northeast of there in the direction he thought he could find Sol and Eli. He reached the area, and from high above the earth, he saw no one. *How can this be?* He thought. *Unless . . .* He was thinking there might be a hidden opening when a tiny voice startled him.

"Hello!" Truluck turned to see a tiny, red-haired fairy hovering in the air near him with two of her comrades.

"Hello yourself," Truluck responded. "What's your name, and where did the three of you come from? Are you following me?"

"Well, we were sort of following you, I guess, but we mean you no harm! Why are you all by yourself? Don't you know it is dangerous in a place like this? If you are a good butterfly, are you? Good, that is."

Truluck answered indignantly, "Of course I'm a good butterfly! I am trying to find a group of my friends who are traveling this way, that's all. You still have not told me who you are or your names and where you come from!"

"Oh my goodness gracious," exclaimed Dulci, for of course it was Dulci, Tania, and Elva that Truluck had met. Orla appointed them to keep watch around and about and report back if necessary. "Please forgive us! My name is Dulci, this is Tania and Elva," she said, introducing her friends to Truluck as they all hovered. "We are from the Faylinn Graces. Orla is our queen, and we are traveling ourselves."

"Oh, I know of Queen Orla and her Faylinn. I have heard many wonderful things about the Graces all my many years of life. I am very pleased to meet all three of you! My name is Truluck, and as you can see, I am a giant monarch butterfly. Do you mind telling me with whom you are traveling? I need to find my friends as quickly as possible because it is a matter of life or death for a child that I do."

The three fairies looked at one another and formed a tight circle, hovering in the air. After a few moments, Dulci said, "If you can tell us the color of the trimming of the main door of the Truth Passage, we will take you to the travelers."

Truluck answered, "Fair enough. I respect your sense of security for the travelers as well as the mission. The color of the door trim is yellow. I have seen it myself."

At this answer, the three fairies flew to him, threw their arms around him, and nearly kissed all the butterfly dust off his wings, quickly replacing it with shimmering fairy dust!

"Oh goodness gracious," said Dulci. "We are so, so happy to have a new friend, especially one as beautiful as you! All you need to do is tell us your wish and we will grant it. We are full of graces!"

"Are you sure it is that easily done?" asked Truluck.

"Oh my, yes!" the three answered at once.

Elva added, "Be sure to ask exactly what you want. Do you want to *be* where they are or to *know* where they are? There is a difference. Think about it."

Truluck did think about it because it made a lot of sense. In a moment, he looked the three fairies and said, "Thank you so much for being here when I needed you. I believe you are not just fairies but angels. I will not forget you. Now, I want to *be* where Eli, Sol and Anna are, please."

Before Truluck could finish saying please, he found himself in a different place.

36

Orla's fairy-induced sleep was over. Truluck happened upon the scene inside the Passage as the travelers were setting out for the northern entrance to the garden. He knew he had to stir them up to enlighten them to the present situation.

Their time was drawing short. Truluck felt that I was sandwiched in between the beast himself and my own wrong thinking brought on by his evil ploys with my mind and heart, even near to my very soul. At this point, there was a strong possibility that I could have walked out of the garden on my own, but Apollyon's grasp on my will was strong and my faith blinded by his lies. Others were coming to my aid but by the opposite direction, and they might well arrive too late.

Truluck had thought about this for quite a while, and he knew Eli was the one with whom he should speak. He also knew he would have to confess to Eli what he had nearly done, but there would be time for that later. He knew my fate was more important now.

The Passage here was a tropical, dense jungle. There were waterfalls, lush lakes from flowing and gushing river basins, and huge, brilliantly colored birds that flew through the air, and it was thick with moisture and the scent of flowering trees and dampness. Banana trees blew in the breeze, and as they walked on, the company saw the northern gate of the garden and the flame blocking the entrance. They had nearly reached their destination with no sight or sound from me.

Eli could feel me. He knew I was close by now. Yes, he could feel me, but something was not right. For a while now he had sensed it and let it pass, but now it was too strong and too wrong to deny. Eli was afraid for me. Yes. He had been afraid for me all along because I was in the presence and company of the evil one. He was afraid for me now for a much deeper and darker reason. Eli feared my will and soul were being lost and that meant hope for me might already be lost.

Just as Eli was having these thoughts and praying for me, a beautiful butterfly lit on his shoulder and spoke to him of all he knew. As Eli and Truluck talked, they had a deep spiritual meeting of the mind and heart at once, for death and life, hate and love, lies and truth, and finally hopelessness and faith known by two have all things in common. The Most High takes great joy in sending his servants out two by two joined in a singular mind and heart for truth and His glory. Eli and Truluck found this bond as they sought my rescue.

Truluck flew ahead to the garden, passing through the northern gate in another form, hoping to go unnoticed, to plant a reminiscence of faith into my ears. Eli and Truluck had made this decision together, for they knew everything hinged on my own acts of will.

Within the hour, Truluck returned with the news. "I have safely given Louisa the words we decided on and escaped before I could be detected for her sake more than for mine."

He went on to report what he had seen and heard of the anger, bitterness, cruelty, and pure hatred in Apollyon, the serpent, and the dangerous hogules he had seen in the time he was with them.

"Do you believe she understood you were there to help her, or did she indicate in any way that she understood your words, Truluck?" asked Eli.

"I know that she was listening closely to me. As to her understanding, she understands that her fate will be left in the hands of the Most High and that we leave her very soul in His hands."

"Could you tell which tree it is where this event will take place?" Eli went on.

"From what I know of the layout of the garden and the direction they were headed, I believe she is being taken to the tree of life by the beast himself."

"In that case," said Sol, "we must prepare for a long spiritual as well as physical battle!" All eyes in the company were upon their leaders, Sol, Eli, Anna, and Queen Orla. As for Truluck, he took his new and rightful place upon Eli's right shoulder!

Orla called upon her brother, Gaspar, and the Faylinn Knights who could defend along with her fast flying Graces against the hogules. Gaspar and the knights were known and feared in the kingdom for their bravery in battle and their agility and speed. They did pick their battles and were not seen much in common or local mischief, as some male Faylinns were. They were considered royalty among fairies and would only come forth and fight for an honorable and mighty cause.

Gaspar and his fighting knights all had white blonde hair, dressed in platinum fairy mail, and wore shimmering platinum helmets and boots. Their fairy dusting was royal purple and gold and shone as the northern lights! In their last battle with the evil one's hogules, they had defeated at least four thousand in one day! Yes, they would be of great help, if needed.

Eli, at the suggestion of Orla and her brother, Gaspar, had their company divide into three sections as they continued toward the gate for protection as well as keeping watch for what was ahead. Gaspar and his fighting knights knew it would not be long before they would encounter the enemy. They meant to be and were prepared in many ways unknown even to Eli and Sol, for fairies have special friends with unbelievable powers and weapons.

37

Well, there I was sitting in the garden waiting for him. I had bathed in the pretty pool in the garden, redressed myself in a bare ivory silk slip, and braided my hair with flowers and ivy. I had crushed roses and rosemary, along with mint, and made a sweet, earthy perfume. My feet and arms were bare in the sun, and my cheeks and nose had begun to blush from its heat. If I sat there too much longer, I would get too hot, get sunburned, and ruin it all. Where was he? Why hadn't Apollyon come to me? Varta told me not to worry about him right now because he was angry. Why? I could have helped him not be angry anymore. I could have made him smile and be happy again. These were the thoughts going through my mind as the beast was planning with Little Horn how to serve me up as an offering to himself.

Little Horn had lain in the grass cowering as long as he was willing. He took up his courage, knowing his master's sulking would last only so long, and slithered to his side in the tall, lush grasses. The canticles Apollyon was murmuring were too deep for him to understand, but he began to recite those he knew. As he did, he felt power rise in himself, slower, then more, building.

The hogules grew frantic, shrieking louder and louder. Apollyon lifted his head and looked toward Little Horn, and a broad smile crept over his horrible face. The two chanted in unison now. More power came into them, building and growing stronger and stronger. Apollyon was gasping, and his breath was coming fast and hard. The serpent looked quickly enough to see him in his full ghastly appearance—horrific and terrible in every way, and fully evil.

"Enough of this! Where is she?" Apollyon demanded of the serpent, the hogules, or anyone who would listen. "Come here, girl!"

I heard him calling to me finally! I ran to him with my arms open, thinking myself the most beautiful girl waiting for the open arms of her lover. Where was he? I could hear his voice. I had my head turned as I was looking, and then I ran into something as hard as a rock and bounced off, falling back onto the grass.

"Well and there you are. Are you going somewhere all dressed up with those flowers in your hair? Do you think you have dressed so beautifully so someone will notice? I do not see anyone in this garden who cares what you have on, do you, Little Horn?" Apollyon addressed us as I got up and brushed my silk slip off.

He continued, saying to me, "We have no time to lose. Louisanna, get in front of me and follow Little Horn. There is no need for talking, for no one will answer you. I do not want to hear your voice. Do you understand? Shake your head yes."

I shook my head indicating yes, but I did not understand what had happened to him to change his mind about me or his feelings toward me. My heart was totally broken, and yet I was afraid to cry or to show emotion of any kind. I fell in behind the snake and in front of Apollyon, and we walked directly into the center of the garden.

Ahead I saw two gigantic trees. From where we were, one of them appeared to be laden with some sort of purple fruit, some of which was turning orange from over-ripeness and falling to the ground. The other was without fruit as far as I could tell. Both of the trees were set apart from anything else in the garden by their sheer size. They were larger than even the tallest palms. The area of their shade was at least four or five times that of the oak where I found the Faylinn Graces.

I was wondering which one of these trees was the tree Apollyon was taking me to when I heard a small buzz by my left ear. It was an ordinary housefly, and I shooed it away. As we travelled a few feet closer to the trees, the fly was back at my ear! What a nuisance! What else would I have to deal with today? I shooed it again, but it came right back. This time there were words in the buzz! It flew away. What had it said? There it was again. I listened closely as it buzzed,

"Remember the music. Remember the word. Let faith arise. Remember the harmony. Remember the tree. Remember eternity. Be not afraid. Bring not a sword."

I looked back to see where the fly was because it was gone. "Well, and what are you looking for?" demanded Apollyon. "Have you seen something that enthralls you more than the trees? You had better hope you have not! The tree up ahead is your death or your life, Louisanna. You best do as I say and keep your face upon it and not some buzzing fly!"

"What tree?" I asked him frantically.

But I got no answer. For suddenly he grabbed me with both of his huge arms, jerked me around to see his hideous face and said, "Fly? What was it? Was it a fly? What kind of fly? What did it say to you, Louisa? I will know if you lie to me, for I know all things! Tell me! You tell me now, I command you!"

I was so terrified and he was hurting me with his hands. My arms felt as if they would break. I cried out, "Oh, you are hurting me! Please stop!" With that, he let go his grip so that I was no longer cringing and could speak. "Louisa; you, you, tell me what the fly said to you!" He was holding his temper now, very cautiously.

I was equally as cautious and said, "The fly was a plain housefly. I have seen many like it before. It buzzed in my ear, and some of it sounded like words. I did not understand it. I did not understand what it meant."

"Just tell *me* what the words were and let me understand what they meant, *Miss Priss!*" This was his tempered answer. His horns were starting to come out now. Even the snake was looking warily at me, hopeful this exchange would soon be put to rest.

"I believe it was something about remembering things, but I couldn't understand what it was I was supposed to remember," I said.

"Well, can you venture a guess?"

"No," I answered. "And I'm not really sure now that I think hard about it that the fly said anything at all. After all, why would a fly want to speak to me? I hate flies and always have. They are filthy and carry diseas—"

"Oh and enough! You are exasperating and wasting good time. Let it rest!" Apollyon shouted. "Little Horn, if you see another fly, snap it up with your tongue! Do you understand?"

"Yes, Master. I will see that no fly lives to pass," the snake replied.

As for me, I remembered everything the fly had buzzed in my ear. I had heard it before. Was it in a dream? I hadn't remembered before, but I did now. I repeated the words and their possible meanings over and over in my head and my heart as I walked toward the trees between the serpent and the beast.

38

Then I saw another beast come up out of the earth. He had two
horns like those of a lamb. And he spoke with the voice of a dragon.
He did astounding miracles such as making fire flash down to
earth from heaven while everyone was watching. He required all
the earth and those who belonged to the world to worship the first
beast, whose death-wound had been healed. He deceived all the
people who belong to this world and required all to be given a mark,
which was his mark, the mark of the beast, for it is the number of a
man. The number is 666. Wisdom is needed to understand this.

—Revelation 13

The trees had not looked so far away! It seemed we had been walking
all day. The garden was so beautiful and the paths lush. On each
path was a waterfall or a giant pool filled with plumed birds singing their
hearts out. The paths twisted and turned, so I could hear the chirps and
the cuckoos until we got near, and then all was quiet. As the snake drew
near, each pathway darkened. Every sound stopped. Even the waterfalls
grew quieter. I hated that the sounds of nature stopped by the approaching
of these two evil beings, so I began to imagine my own sounds. It was
very hard at first because Apollyon took all imagination from me long
ago—ages and ages, it seemed. I even seemed older to myself.

Who was I? I thought. *How in the world did I get to this place, and why
me?* I was getting angry—very angry! *I will not let these creatures have any*

more to do with me, no matter what they say or do to me! I would rather …
Oh I do not know what!

I wanted to go home and see Nimee and Cerena, and Eli! Eli! *Eli.*
Eli. Eli. I thought his name and felt peace wash over me. Why was that?
I closed my eyes and thought as I used to. Not closed all the way … *Eli,*
Eli, Eli, are you near? Eli, are you near? Eli yes? I could see him. I could
tell he was nearby. How? Never mind how. *Eli,* I thought. *Are you here?*
I waited, and slowly a beautiful harmony began in my mind. I heard the
song-harmony I had heard before the rock-fall incident and Aprion leaving.
Oh, yes, *remember the music, remember the words, the tree.* Oh and what
else was there? Was it the song? What were the words? All I could think
was let faith arise. Why that? Where was my faith? Where was my God?
They were the words the fly buzzed in my ear! I tried to put it all together.
There must be a connection. I was so confused right now about Apollyon
and about God

I was very angry with Him. I didn't want to talk to Him or about Him
now. Any god who would allow all of these horrible things to happen to
me was not a good god, and must not even exist! Yes, I was angry! What
would Eli do or say if he knew these thoughts? Well, I needed him here to
ask him that right now, and he was not, so that was that.

I was totally confused and lost, and the serpent and Apollyon knew
it very well. Well they knew as long as they were on either side of me, the
evil in them would keep me from calling out to the Most High in truth.
Confusion reigned in my soul and spirit. That is where they wanted me,
for if I had been hopeless I might have cried out to God for help indeed.
Yet, confusion and chaos are always best, according to the beast.

I kept my eyes ahead and tried not to cry. No, I would not cry, no
matter what happened. I didn't care what they did to me. I refused to
cry. These were my thoughts as we rounded the last loop on the pathway
before the trees.

The shade was already upon us. I could tell now that the trees were
actually so far apart they cast separate shadows. I would have had to walk
for a good three or four minutes to get to the other tree from where we
now stood.

The tree we were approaching did bear fruit. I had been unable to see it from a distance. This tree was laden with tarnished crimson, nearly black pomegranates. The leaves of the tree were broad and so green that they were nearly black. The trunk of the tree was gnarled and obviously ancient, as were its branches. The knotted and contorted roots burst out of the ground for at least ten feet around the tree, making it impossible to stand close to the tree at all without losing your balance and falling either backward or forward because there was nothing on which to hold to steady yourself.

The closer we came to this tree, the more intrigued I became with it. This tree and everything about it drew me in. It had an aura about it that was captivating and almost sensual. The fragrance it gave off was fleeting and lilting. The way the breeze moved through the branches made its leaves dance like prima ballerinas. The grand shape of it and its sheer size cried out wisdom and authority, and yet I could not touch it. The thought of tasting the seeds of the pomegranates made my mouth water.

I had not realized what was happening to me, but the snake and Apollyon did. The two of them spoke quietly between themselves as I stared at the tree, mesmerized.

"Well, and she is up to her ears in the tree now, is she not?" Apollyon asked the snake.

"I do not believe she sees anything else. Look at her eyes."

The beast replied, "Yes, and I am sorry they are no longer on me, but this is the way it must be, my brother. We must call for the others. The time is soon. We have nearly accomplished our plan! She stands in front of us, the perfect lamb for my purpose."

Apollyon, the beast, turned aside, raised his wings, and in all his hideous fury yelled out, "It shall all be mine now, at last! All mine!" Then he laughed. Even the serpent drew back in utter terror as that shrieking laugh echoed across the ancient garden.

Two Trees, One Choice

The Lord planted a garden in Eden, In the East, and there he placed the man he had created. And the Lord planted all sorts of trees in the garden-beautiful trees that produced delicious fruit. At the center of the garden he placed the Tree of Life and the Tree of the Knowledge of good and evil. The Lord placed man in the garden to tend and care for it. But the Lord gave him this warning, "You may eat freely from any tree in the garden except fruit from the Tree of the Knowledge of good and evil. If you eat of this fruit you shall surely die."

—Genesis 2:8, 15–17

And the angel showed me a pure river with the water of life, clear as crystal, flowing from the thrown of God and of the Lamb, coursing down the center of the main street. On each side of the river grew a tree of life, bearing twelve crops of fruit, a fresh crop for each month. The leaves were for the healing of the nations. No longer will anything be cursed. For the throne of God and of the Lamb will be there, and his servants will worship him. And they will see his face, and his name will be written on their foreheads."

—Revelation 22: 1-4

Oh yes, the tree had me under its spell. Knowing that I could not reach the fruit was driving me crazy! As hard as I tried to balance myself on the roots long enough to get close enough to jump up to clasp onto a branch, I could not do it. The smaller knots on the gnarled humps turned my ankles. It was almost as if the roots had grown like that on purpose—just so that no one could ever get close enough to reach the fruit. I also thought it was strange that there was no overripe fruit fallen onto the ground around the tree. All the other trees in the garden were laden with overripe fruit falling to the ground.

It had not occurred to me that this could be a magic tree—the tree of good and evil or the tree of life. It was one of the two largest trees, and it was near the middle of the garden. Regardless, I did not intend to ask Apollyon, the snake, or God which of the trees this was. I did not care!

Apollyon and his snake were watching me and laughing at my pitiful antics as I tried to reach the fruit from the tree. Apollyon's plan was eventually to help me to reach the fruit so I could eat to my heart's content. He saw himself as the new savior of the world and me as the first born to new life by eating of the fruit at his bidding. At his command, I would have eternal life, and by this act he would again place himself on the same level as the Most High. His gift of eternal life would be wrought by theft and lying, by deceiving me and mocking the Word and the free gift of God. In truth, not even he knew what would happen if I or anyone else ate from the Tree of Life, but he was willing to give it his old copycat try. He did not care what happened to me—his puppet, his pawn, his sacrifice. All he could think of was greater power and standing in the ranks of heavenly powers and principalities. The life of the child meant nothing whatsoever to him.

His plan was working perfectly so far as he could tell. The small setback at the garden gate was nothing now compared to how far he had come! Try as he might, he could not see this Eli who would be my champion. Some powerful spirit blocked Eli from Apollyon's visions. This was the one issue that gave Apollyon pause. Like any great and successful warrior, he did not like surprises, but he had a plan for that as well.

39

"Vanity of vanities, all the world is vanity."
—King Solomon

Apollyon's self-absorption, false pride, and certainty of victory over all were so great that he wished for every one of his minions and all of his warriors to be present to see the final enactment of his clever plan. He was so confident that his plan would be successful that he decided to wait for my champion to arrive. Yes, for exactly that and all of my foolishly dedicated friends. And so he set the time, sending out a call for all his followers to join at a certain place inside the garden. He was proud for them to know that the angels had given him full access to pass into the garden.

Then Apollyon's thoughts turned to Wormfly. He knew Wormfly had failed in his test to kill Eli and now would come his recompense. Wormfly would come under a guise to take this message to Eli and suffer his violent and torturous end. Apollyon would send another minion to Eli to root-out Wormfly and to tempt Eli to come to the garden for his precious Louisa.

Apollyon's choice for the messenger was Hogholke, king of the hogules. Hogholke was a man and not a fairy. He was a direct descendent of the Nephilim, whose bloodlines are ancient. Some say they have lived in the Banelands since before the great flood on the earth. All Nephilim were angels of evil origin, and a few of them intermarried with fairies. Hogules are the offspring of their union.

Hogholke was a horrible creature who looked just like his name. He stood only four feet and nine inches in height and was of a stocky build. He weighed over two hundred pounds, and all of this weight was pure muscle. He appeared to have no neck whatsoever, and his head was square on his shoulders. Hogholke had a broad and flat nose and two small, deep-set eyes. His ears were those of a fairy. They were quite large and pointed at the tip and turned outward. His legs were short and stocky, and his feet were flat and wide. Hogholke was always dressed for battle in mail, helmet, breastplate, boots, and kneepads, also made of mail. His long red hair streamed down his back from his helmet and was worn gathered together in a wild ponytail.

Only Apollyon and Hogholke's wife were able to understand him because he mumbled so harshly when he spoke. It was also said that his temper was so volatile that even his wife was afraid to ask him any questions. Of all of Apollyon's warriors, Hogholke was one of the most feared for his own brute strength and because he had full dominion over the hogules. Apollyon had summoned Hogholke and he had come at once. He was taking his orders to locate Wormfly with his flying masses—to bring him directly to the master and then remain with his hogules until further commands.

Hogholke was too massive to fly, but he rode upon an ancient beast called the fawshyvon. The Fawshyvon had the dark pink head of a flamingo. The body of this beast was that of a flying serpent similar to the triceratops. Its flamingo beak was wide and pointed and contained three sets of razor-sharp teeth with which it could tear flesh from bone, and if enraged, it could blow fire from its mouth. The fawshyvon's tail was very long and grew thinner at its end, with row upon row of reptilian scales. At the tip of the tail was a stinger much like that of a scorpion. Its poison could maim and kill. Hogholke rode this beast like a horse and commanded it well.

Apollyon called the fawshyvon to the garden. I watched the fearful creature approaching from the north. As I saw it coming, I ran to the opposite side of the tree and bent down under the grass and leaves. No one noticed me because all eyes were on this giant flying reptile with a pink face. Hogholke had his orders. Apollyon gave the fawshyvon his orders as well, and Hogholke ran and leapt onto the wide back of the beast. Away they flew, turning westward toward the Elysian Fields.

Each of the thousands of hogules wished to serve and obey Apollyon, but they feared retribution from Hogholke if they did so without his express permission. This kept these tiny misfits in a state of confusion and temptation at all times, especially at a time like this.

One of the fiesterhogules who had been in the garden flying around with the rest of the swarm was watching me trying to get to a piece of the fruit from the tree. This young hogule, whose name was Hartsap, was ready, willing, and able to help me. He wished to impress Hogholke and certainly Apollyon with his ingenuity and strength. He knew he could lift me up on his wings to reach the fruit of the tree. Hartsap was smart enough to know that it was Apollyon's wish for me to eat the fruit. He was too prideful and compulsive to think it might not be the right time. Thinking all Apollyon needed was someone to help get me to reach it, he decided to approach me with the idea. Several other hogules were flying around me with Hartsap, shrieking and crying as they always did.

At my surprise and horror, Hartsap spoke to me in his shrieking voice. He sounded like the wheels of a long train trying to come to a sudden stop—metal against metal. "I," he shrieked, "could lift you up there."

I looked around to be sure it was this repulsive creature that had spoken to me. "What did you say? Was that you? What are you doing here?" I asked, continuously turning my head because he would not keep still.

"It was me, Hartsap. I was summoned here by the master to help you reach the fruit," he lied. Then he continued, "Of all the fiesters I am the master's favorite and come from a long line of the house of Hartsap. We are of royal blood. It would be a great honor if you would allow me to lift you up to the fruit. I can see that you are trying very hard to reach it on your own. You would only have to say yes, and the fruit would be in your hands!" he shrieked.

"Hartsap," I said. "What do you know about this fruit? Is it some kind of magic fruit, or is there a legend about it?"

The renegade fiesterhogules finally hovered in front of my face and spoke to me. "The fruit of this tree is said to give eternal life to anyone who eats it, only if he or she has the master's command so to eat. No one knows what the fate may be to eat of the fruit without command of the master, but we all know the master." Hartsap answered with a look of fear in the beady little eyes inside his baldhead.

"Hartsap, if this tree really will give eternal life, then why wouldn't the master want all of us—I mean those who are his minions, as he calls them—to live forever? If so, he could be sure to have a kingdom of minions to serve him for eternity. And what about his own future? I suppose he already lives forever—isn't that right? Sometimes I feel so confused!"

Hartsap looked me straight in the eye as I asked him these questions, and I could tell he was thinking hard. In his metal-on-metal voice in a quiet sort of whisper, he said, "It is a sad thing for me to tell you, but all of the master's minions will already live forever—just as we are. This is the way we are. It is our nature and by no choice of our own. His kingdom in this world is secured forever. I am sorry, but I am afraid to say anything at all about the master's life. If he knew I was talking to you at all …"

Apollyon heard the shrieks and saw Hartsap talking to me. Without warning came a stream of fire—hot, red, and flaming. It hit Hartsap dead on. He fell to the ground not twelve inches from my left foot. As I saw what was left of him between the roots of the tree, I could still feel the heat on the side of my face. I looked up to see where the flame had come from and saw Apollyon stopping several feet away from the tree to the right of me with the snake catching up behind him. At the same instant, I saw more than two or three dozen hogules swarming away in fits and dives from around me, in fear for their lives!

I could hold back no longer! I wasn't crazy about those horribly ugly things shrieking around my head, but one of them was trying to help me reach the fruit. I had been making friends with him, and now Apollyon, that nasty thing, had just zapped him to ashes! I yelled out at Apollyon, "Hey, that was totally uncalled for! Why did you burn that poor ugly thing up? He or it or whatever was trying to help me get a piece of this fruit. What was wrong with that? You are so mean. You really are!"

Apollyon stood now with his hands on his hips and seemed totally composed and able to take on my ranting and raging. "Come out here, Louisanna. I will not yell back and forth at you. That is no way for a lady such as yourself to carry on a conversation."

I lowered my voice and called back to him, "Tell your snake to go far away, because I don't like him at all. Then I'll come out a little further."

"Oh, and so you will be my master and boss now, will you? Little Horn, go." Then he shooed the snake away. The snake moved about two feet. "Go, you imbecile! Go when I tell you!" Belligerently the snake slithered off into the brushes, looking back at me with his slanted green eyes.

I nearly fell again walking over the huge roots. I made my recovery and only went as close to Apollyon's evil presence as where the root line ended. "All right, here I am, and I'm not yelling. Why don't you want me to eat that fruit? Is it poison? Will it give me powers over *you?* I know there is a very good reason or you wouldn't have zapped that poor, ugly creature who was trying to help me reach it."

"Louisanna," he said, very calmly and condescendingly, "you always think the worst of me. I did not fear you eating the fruit. You may have all of it you want. Those small, bothersome hogules are, as you said, poor and very nasty creatures. I was afraid Hartsap would hurt you—maybe pluck your eyes out or gather his friends and pick the very meat from your very pretty bones! That is all. What is all the fuss about the hogule, ay?"

"It was mean and cruel for you to kill that poor, ugly creature. I wish I had never known its name!" I said.

"Louisanna let us forget all this foolishness. It only muddles my purpose. What do you say? I want to tell you the reason we are now here—the reason we have come this long way. I want to tell you why I have brought you here, to this garden, to this very tree, and for the exact reason. It is a story that will live forever, and you and I will be the players that all in eternity will remember. We, you and I and that tree, are going to change the fate of the entire world for all time! Do you wish to hear more?"

I stood there looking at Apollyon and listening to him. He had grown more boyish again—younger looking in many ways. His smile was more genuine and his body less offensive. Actually, he was becoming more attractive to me by the minute. We were alone, and I felt uncomfortable again. I always felt uncomfortable around him. That is an understatement. This was a different discomfort. It was a kind of shyness and desiring to play coy with him at the same time. I remembered this feeling. How I let it take me over and made me think he loved me. I remembered too how badly my feelings had been hurt—how my heart hurt when he changed and became the beast again!

I was feeling confused and helpless, but I did want to know what in the world all this Lopsided Kingdom was about, as well as the garden and the tree. Most of all, I wanted to know, why me?

Apollyon went on telling me what was going to happen and how I would, at the appointed time, eat a piece of the fruit of the tree. I took a step closer to him with every word he said. He cast a spell over me with his every word!

"Louisanna, my heart," he sighed. "You are the loveliest of all human women I have ever had the pleasure to meet in my eons of being alive and king of this world. I have chosen you for a high place of honor in all eternity. If you choose this, you will be to the whole world a woman set apart from all others in power and beauty, who is mine alone. Many will bow down and worship you! You will have the entire world at your command. All nations and peoples will do with as you please. You will be a new queen, set high above all queens, known and unknown."

He continued, "The one thing you must choose to do to gain all this is to eat from the tree. That is so simple, now isn't it?" He looked at me dead on with an expression that was so appealing and piercing that I could not turn my eyes away from his.

I stared into his deep, sea-blue eyes for several moments, dumbly ingesting all he said, and then I answered him with this question: "How will I reach the fruit?" still staring into his eyes.

He smiled and said, "I am able to give you the power to reach the fruit if you so desire it for my purposes, Louisanna. All you must say is yes to me."

"Well that sounds easy then." I responded. "Tell me more."

Apollyon said, "Louisanna, look around and welcome all those who have made the journey to see you become the new queen."

As Apollyon was beaming proudly at the arrival of his first group of guests, as he called them, Hogholke was arriving at his destination to meet Sol and his company in the Elysian Fields.

40

Jepetto was the first of the company to spot the fawshyvon flying in high from the east with Hogholke on its back. He began to hop and twirl and pull at the hems of Sol's cloak. "Jepetto sees something, Sol. Yes! Look! Look up!" At this announcement, everyone looked to the direction Jepetto was pointing. There they were in plain sight and starting to land.

"What in heaven's name is that?" asked Eli.

"It looks like one of the leaders of the hogules riding a creature called the fawshyvon. I hope they come in peace, or we could all be dead in several minutes. Hold up your right hands, everyone. That will show we intend no war strike!" Sol demanded of the company.

Everyone did as Sol commanded, and Hogholke and his dragon landed as peacefully as they could and not far away. There was a terrible crushing of brushes and trees, and part of the dragon's wing was washed in one of the waterfalls, but other than that, it was a smooth landing.

Sol and Eli, along with Gaspar and Queen Orla, moved out in front away from the others to meet up with this leader of the hogules and to find out why he had come. They stood in a line, in a stance of protection of their friends, as they watched the sturdy warrior approaching them on foot. The ground shook at his every step. As he lifted his sword, and laughed, the flying serpent gave a loud, deafening cry.

Once Hogholke was several feet away, Sol cried out to him, "We have no quarrel with you. Call down your fawshyvon, put your sword away, and let us talk in peace, man."

Hogholke answered in his mumbling voice, "Show me your pockets, open your cloaks, and let me see that there are no fairy weapons about you, and I will down my sword."

Everyone did as he asked. As for Orla and Gaspar, they removed certain signets from their heads and waists, dropping them on the ground beside them. Sol and Orla spoke to him again. "We have done as you asked. Down your sword now," they commanded.

At this, the hogule dropped his sword and continued to move toward them until he was only a few feet away. "I do not know if my reason for coming to you will be considered peaceful to you or no, my fellows," Hogholke told them candidly.

They all listened intently, and Sol said to him. "Go on, tell us why you are here."

"I come in search of a minion of Satan and will not leave without him, for I must return him to the master this day. Do each of you understand? This must be done. If you are harboring this minion, good or bad, he must be turned over to me now or it is death to you all. I am familiar with the kill and have savored it from my cradle. I am Hogholke, leader of the hogules, also ruler and king of the Nephilim and mutant fairy colonies. I warn you as well that the fawshyvon who brought me here breathes fire and stings poison from his tail. He stands at my command."

Eli whispered something into Sol's ear and stepped forward. "Hogholke, we appreciate your loyalty to your master and understand that you must return this minion to him today. I assure you that we have no minion of Satan among us. We would know because we are people of the Most High, and any consort of your master would feel uneasy at best and be very unwelcome here. I am sure there has been some mistake."

Hogholke's voice boomed back at them, "There is no mistake! The one by the name of Wormfly is here! He pretends to be your friend and is not, as he pretends to be loyal to my master and is not. He is a traitor to both camps and deserves punishment! His form is that of a thin fly with small wings and too-long legs. My master believes his last disguise was that of a butterfly. He has the right to be chameleon, which the master sees he also misused, as he did many other of his privileges. He is a traitor and must pay!" Hogholke's voice boomed louder and louder.

The four leaders kept solemn faces and looked straight ahead when they heard these words, but they refused to give in on Truluck. Hogholke asked each one of them individually concerning Satan's missing minion.

Sol stepped forward first and Hogholke questioned him. He told the hogule that they had suspected that this minion had been in their midst in the form of a dried-up looking fly before they left the lopsided house, but he had seen nothing of him since.

As the hogule was questioning Sol, Gaspar received a sign from Orla to stand ready to call his knights if Hogholke found Truluck among them. Orla herself sent out a silent call of a fairy wing shimmer to her Faylinn, who hid in the trees nearby.

As Dulci, Tania, Elva, and the hundreds of other fairies of the Faylinn Graces heard Orla's silent command, they quietly moved out of the trees and began to scout about. Hovering to the left of the company and far above them, they could see all that was taking place. The fairies all knew of the hogules and Hogholke and their reputation for warring and mercilessly killing anything in their way for the sake of Satan.

The Faylinn Graces remembered that it was Truluck who saved Jepetto after he had done away with Le Annis. They also remembered that Orla knew this minion of Satan was now a righteous believer and hero in their midst. The Faylinn Graces would do anything they could to prevent Hogholke from returning Truluck to Satan's grasp.

"Look, Elva! Oh my gracious goodness, over there behind the waterfall. What is that huge creature?" Dulci asked her friend. The two fairies hovered together near a fig tree leaf, looking in the direction Dulci pointed.

"I can't see it all together, Dulci. Let's just get a little closer and take a look. Be sure to keep your wings on silent shimmer," Elva responded. The two silly fairies flew around the bend toward the waterfall. The booming and rushing of the falling water would surely cover any sound they might make!

"Oh goodness, have we lost our senses!" cried Elva. "That is one of those flying dragons! Do you think it can breathe fire?"

"I'm sure from seeing it that it could eat us in one gulp! I don't believe it has seen us. At least it isn't looking at us!" announced Dulci.

"I believe we should go and alert Tania of the dragon's location, just in case it has seen us!" breathed Elva. Away they flew with this news at light speed toward Tania and the rest of the Faylinn.

If Tania had been with these two, she would have reminded them that the fawshyvon had perfect peripheral vision and that they were in fact in grave danger, for he had seen them both even as far away as they were.

The fawshyvon had no fear of fairy folk. He had been known to eat an entire Faylinn in one battle. Besides, these were women. What had he to fear from them? Yes, he had seen the two hovering in the trees spying on him, but they were not worth wasting a long breath on.

Fawshyvon was resting in a cave's entrance at the foot of one of the many waterfalls near the north entrance to the garden. He was thinking about all these things and that he would be able to destroy the entire company many times over with one word from Satan, his immortal master. Fawshyvon awaited the word. Yes, these two small nothings—he had let them pass without hesitation. He was dozing off when he heard Hogholke's call.

41

Warriors are made in a young man's dream
Where honor and right are on trial.
Tables turn when in the hearts they yearn
Truth and Justice to spar
When the prize grows a 'haze in tally of good and
Masters chameleons be.
The warrior wakes to see his face and the glass shows
A blazon scar.

Eli stepped forward, ready to speak with the leader of the hogules. He did not fear for Truluck's appearing or him being found on his person if he was searched. Truluck was safely out of sight. "How may I help you, Hogholke?" Eli asked.

The hogule squinted his beady little eyes and stared at Eli for a long time. He looked him up and down and asked him to turn around. Eli did so. Hogholke asked gruffly, with hands on his hips and feet apart in a stance of pure authority, "Who are you? From where have you come? You are not of this kingdom. I say in truth, I believe you know where the traitor is!"

Eli said coolly, "That is more than one question. May I answer one at a time, sir?" The hogule shook his head in the affirmative. "My name is Eli. You are right in saying I am not of this kingdom. I have come here to find a good friend, here also and not of this kingdom. We have both stumbled into this kingdom. We mean no harm to anyone. I journey to find my friend who is a child so she and I can return to our home."

"Ugh!" was Hogholke's reply. "Go on. Tell me more of this," he mumbled.

Eli continued, "The people I have met here say I am what is known as a seer. The child has this gift as well. I believe she is in danger. I have helped care for her all my life, and now I want to protect her from any danger. Can you understand that, Hogholke?"

"Do you believe I who would hurt a child?" Hogholke boomed. "Do you think me a savage, man?" he boomed again and stamped one of his huge feet.

Eli answered, "I do not know. There are many different kinds of people here, Hogholke, and many are cruel and heartless as far as I can tell. I do not judge. I ask, and I hope."

Hogholke answered nothing to this. He simply thought. This not judging, but hoping—well, those were powerful words. Hope. What was that really, he wondered? Hogholke had instantly forgotten the tens of thousands of women and children he and his hogules had murdered and slain at Satan's command over the ages. Well, he did give it a thought, but he was only doing his master's bidding. He knew nothing else. What was there to do? Hope. Hope was a concept Hogholke had forgotten about long ago. To not be judged, to have hope. This man believed these things and had spoken them out loud. Hogholke looked at Eli and Eli was smiling.

Eli thought the hogule had forgotten his question about Truluck being here. He hoped so. No, that would be too good to be true. Hogholke turned back around, facing Eli once again, and said, "I think about this hope, yes. But for my master I must find this traitor, Wormfly! Hogholke is no fool, Eli. I can smell this traitor on you. I am not this seer as you say you are, but I know what I know. The traitor is here with you. Why do you harbor him? Do you not know that he will turn on you as well? Disloyal to one is disloyal to all. Is it not true in your world?"

Eli had been hard in prayer and listening for an answer and believed he had received guidance that would be of great help. "Hogholke, how long have you been in the service of your master?"

"Many more hundreds of years than I care to count," he answered.

"Your master entrusts you with important business and missions he can trust no other with. Am I right?"

The hogule cocked his head to one side, motioned for Eli to sit, and they sat on the ground, he with a humph! He answered, "The master chooses those of us he sees fit for his missions. We do not and are not allowed to discuss them between ourselves, so I do not know how important mine is in accordance to another."

Eli went on, baiting him more, "Surely when you accomplish your mission in good stead, your master shows you great favor and rewards you, maybe with special privileges?"

Hogholke cocked his head again and asked, "Privilege, rewards? I am not sure I know what this might be."

"In this case, if you were to complete a mission concerning only one person or army and do it with speed and accuracy, on the next mission he would put you in charge of many persons and many armies because you showed him your loyalty, bravery, and faithfulness. That would be an example of a reward. An example of a privilege would be to be to rule over one of those armies yourself, no more needing him to be master of them, because he would then have put his trust over what was his in you."

Hogholke and Eli sat on the ground in the same spot and debated this issue for quite a while. They also talked about hope, forgiveness, and the absence of judgment. Hogholke asked Eli many questions, and Eli answered them to the best of his ability. In the meantime, Truluck escaped with his life. The fawshyvon awoke and let out a cry that made the ground rumble!

"Come!" was all Hogholke had to say to the fawshyvon. The sky became dark and overshadowed with the outline of the great dragon. Everyone covered their heads from flying debris. After a minute of relative silence, the company looked to see the fawshyvon standing on all fours with wings spread and neck craned. Its scorpion tail twisted back as if it were ready to sting. As it shrieked, the hogule called out to it, "Enough! Quiet yourself. They mean you no harm. We are not at war with these people!"

With that, the dragon laid down like a lap dog, curling its wings and tail underneath itself. He only kept his strange pink head erect, as if listening.

Hogholke had called the fawshyvon for that very reason. He wanted the dragon to listen—to listen to himself, Eli, Sol, and the others talking now as friends. A great shift had happened in the gruff hogule's heart and his thinking. After serving Satan for eons with no thanks, encouragement, advancement, or reward and often having to bear the brunt by being sent into drudgery and pitiful battles with his ugly mutants, he had decided to trust Eli, his friends, and his God—just for a while. He just wanted to give them a chance. The only thing he had to lose was his life, and what good was it—to go on forever as it was now?

Hogholke had to convince the fawshyvon. He had no idea if he had been listening or if the dragon would kill them all. Hogholke remembered the fawshyvon had a sister dragon who was taken from their nest by marauding hellhounds. These hellhounds were half men-half dog creatures of giant size, answerable to no one, that roamed the forests and highlands of the Banelands, taking for themselves whatever they wanted and going unpunished. Satan was very aware of these creatures and their destruction, but he only laughed and responded, "Men and dogs must have their fun!" His reaction to their destruction was to turn his head.

Hogholke told Eli and Sol of this and how the fawshyvon lost his sister to the hellhounds, thinking if the dragon overheard their conversations concerning my plight; it might strike a chord of pity in him for him.

The head hogule told Eli and Sol all he knew of Satan's exact plans for me as far as he knew them. He told them that Satan had summoned every one of his minions, every warrior and warrior angel under his command to come to the garden to witness the event, which he announced would change all time and raise him even higher than he who sits at the right hand of the Most High.

"It is blasphemy," said Gaspar, who had kept quiet up until now. "I am sorry to interrupt, but I can hear no more of this! He knows there is nothing that can raise him higher that the Son of the Most High. He is the Savior of the world!"

"If I understand Hogholke, what Satan plans to do is to use the child to steal eternal life by his means and therefore bring her and many more to eternal life without faith in him as the Most High commands us, which is the one and only way," Eli answered Gaspar.

Gaspar was incensed. "This is impossible! How can he force this child to do this for him? And if he does, is she not condemned forever as he is, not called into eternal life at all?"

Eli answered Gaspar as best he could. "Gaspar, we fight against powers and princes in the high places in the heavens. We do not know what is and is not possible in that realm."

"The Most High has given each of us free will," continued Eli, while Gaspar tried to interrupt. "The child cannot be forced. Eve was not forced, and neither was Adam. The rules have not changed. She has her right to choose. From what Hogholke has told me, Satan has wooed her until she believes herself to be in love with him and that he cares for her. When Hogholke was sent away to find Truluck, he tells us that the child was also trying on her own to accomplish the thing Satan has in mind for her to do—on her own."

Gaspar answered, "Is the hogule with us or against us, for we must move now to help rescue the child."

Eli, fearing this was severely premature, reached his hand out to calm Hogholke, only to find a large and rough hogule handshake, and a strong one. "We will go together to aid the child," Hogholke said, shaking Eli's hand quite sturdily and looking Gaspar in the eye.

With his other hand he motioned over his shoulder for the fawshyvon and said, "These people need our help. I have agreed and given my word and handshake that we together will help them deliver the child from Satan, your master. Will you go together with me as her champion against him and his hellhounds, for the child's life is in danger?"

Hogholke must have known the words to use, for the great dragon rose up on his wings, stretched them outward, stood upright on his great birdlike legs, tossed its head, and cried aloud in a new voice, shrieking a sound like yes!

The entire company shouted for joy and began hugging one another all around. Jepetto and the toads did their normal jigs, of course. These made things seem even more cheery in some way.

Hearing and seeing all this, Gaspar said, "Very well!" Excellent! Welcome to our company, Hogholke and Fawshyvon."

Gaspar also added, "Eli, if you believe it right, a few of my scouts and I will fly to the garden, find the location of the child and the beast, and return to decide on a plan of decent upon them."

Eli looked to Sol, Orla, and now to Hogholke. All agreed, and Gaspar and his scouts vanished like the speed of light, leaving streaks of blue fairy dust shimmering behind them like the tail of a magic jet plane.

42

Apollyon had positioned me beside him at the foot of the huge tree, watching the first of the groups arrive. They were those he saw as the important guests he had invited to the special event that would make me queen of the known kingdom and world. As for me, I could not tell if they were human or animal. When I asked, Apollyon's answer was not to worry; they were only some of his acquaintances from years past. They were not guests at all. He had commanded them to come.

These beings were both male and female. They had very little hair on their heads at all. The hair that they had looked singed, as if it had been burned. From what I could see of them, as they were at least fifty feet away and approaching slowly, they had to help each other stand and walk. There was also something very strange about their faces, as if their features were scabbed or missing entirely. As they drew close enough for me to see their faces in full, I was horrified!

These beings had no mouths. Some of them had healing scars where a mouth should be, and others had nothing in the place of the mouth; there was only tightly drawn skin there. They were obviously in some constant pain or discomfort. Others were gesticulating wildly with their hands, trying desperately to get the attention of Apollyon. He looked at them and simply waved and smiled.

I turned to him and said, "How can you just look at these poor people and not take pity on them? Can't you see they are in pain and need help? Why do they not have mouths? What happened to them? Are you the one responsible for it? You should be ashamed of yourself! No one deserves to be treated this way no matter what they have done!"

"Well, Louisanna, if you will have some patience after everyone has arrived, I will tell you about each group, who they are, and what has become of them. Until then I command that you keep your peace for that is best for you. Do you understand?"

He spoke these words to me, looking deep into my face. The blue Netherlands of his eyes mesmerized and placated me into silence. I would have done anything he asked. All anger, indignation, and questions were gone.

The next group was already coming along the path to the tree because those with no mouths had been set off to the side in their assigned place by the snake. They stayed there, continually writing in pain and agony. No one, including me, took any notice of them.

A second group was arriving by wagon pulled by huge boars with tusks like elephants. There were eight boars to each wagon, and the wagons were loaded to overflowing with men who were both tremendously fat and as thin as zippers. There were both groans and screams coming from those in the wagons as the fat men crushed the thin ones with their great weight. As the wagons drew closer, I believed I could actually hear bones being broken as a fat man rolled onto a stick man's leg or arm. This was accidental; these men were either so obese or so very sticklike that they had no control over their limbs or bodies at all. As far as I could tell, these were nearly as pitiful as the creatures without mouths, because either fat or thin, they were unable to walk or even stand because of their condition. They were therefore completely dependent on others for whatever they were given to live on or left to die.

I looked at Apollyon and was about to ask when he said, "Remember. You must wait." I did not want to wait, but I did not want to displease him at the same time, so I kept silent.

Before I could absorb the condition of those still arriving in the boar wagons, the next group flew in from every direction. A small, dark patch in the sky grew into a horde of flying rodents. These creatures were similar to the ones I had seen in the clearing after the rock and boulder slide.

Hundreds of them descended around the tree, but none of them dared to land in the tree or even fly very near it.

These creatures would have descended upon and attacked the men in the boar wagons if Apollyon not abruptly stopped them. With horrific shrieks and pitiful cries, they reluctantly obeyed. A good look at these creatures proved them to be mutants. The fronts of their bodies were like rodents, but they had small, pointed ears and protruding, sharp teeth. The hind halves of the creatures were that of giant wasp with wings and long protruding stingers. Their stripes were colors that looked like blood and pumpkin seeds. The insides of their mouths were always open, showing their sharp teeth, and were bright pink in contrast to the color of their bodies.

After one look at these guests, I would have to call them the ugliest and most repulsive creatures I had seen. I made no comment about their ugliness but asked Apollyon if these creatures had a name.

"Wagnarts," Apollyon told me. "They live to feast on those being carried in the boar wagons. That is why I had to call them down," he continued.

"Why does all this go on? I want to know more," I said.

"You will have to wait until all arrive!" he said again sternly.

"How many more of these horrible creatures do I have to suffer through?" I said out loud "Why do they even have to come at all? This is too much for me or anyone!"

"It is all a part of the grand plan, my dear. If you will only be patient as I tell you, you will under …" But before Apollyon could finish his sentence, he stopped and said, "Look! Up there!"

Coming from behind the tree from the right side were flying creatures, both male and female. I couldn't understand how they stayed in the air, for they had no wings. They simply moved through the air the way we move through water, only with less effort. Unlike the visitors before them, these creatures were very beautiful and graceful.

The women were young, with delicate features and lovely bodies. Their clothing was gossamer, thin, and very revealing. The men were young and strong. They were clothed only in loincloths. The men and women flew around and around one another in graceful circles, but never near and never touching, even though they reached out to each other in a beseeching way.

Apollyon called them to the ground, and when he did, I could see tears falling steadily from their eyes. He told them where to wait, and I noticed that they immediately formed two segregated groups. Even with the groups of all men and all women, no one dared touch another, yet everyone reached out all the time, obviously wishing that only they could.

"Well and do you think these creatures easier to look upon, Louisanna?" Apollyon asked me.

Not wanting make him angry, I teased with him about these that I did not understand at all. I crossed my arms over my chest and turned on my heels, and with my back to him, I said, "They are beautiful, but why are they crying? There is always something wrong with all your so-called friends! Don't you know anyone who is normal?"

"Oh yes. You are quite normal, Lousianna, but not for much longer!" he said as the last of the small groups the guests began to arrive. As for me, I could not bring myself to turn around and look at anymore. I already felt as though I was in a torture chamber at some sort of circus of misfits or else in the middle of a terrible nightmare from which I would never wake up!

I could hear them arriving anyway. It went on for at least an hour more or longer. I heard voices as well as animal sounds, but I did not know what it was I was hearing and did not care! It meant nothing when Apollyon told me over and over how rude I was and commanded me to turn and greet my guests. Keeping my back turned and my hands crossed over my chest, I utterly refused to move. It made no difference to these creatures. They were there only because he had summoned them and they knew they must come or a fate worse than death would await them. How much more they could suffer than they already did, I had no idea!

The one thought that sustained me during the waiting was this: if the plan was accomplished as Apollyon hoped and somehow I became queen over these creatures, maybe I could have influence enough to set them free from their pain and suffering. If I had to be in bondage to Apollyon and these poor creatures could be set free, it would be worth it to me.

I suddenly heard a loud swishing of wings and the sounds of singing. Apollyon began to echo their songs in the same strange harmony and tongue that was both grotesque and beautiful.

I looked up and saw what appeared to be angelic beings flying in from the sky from every direction. They looked much like Apollyon himself. These were all male. The closer they came, I could see their bodies were half bird and half man. They did not have human feet as he did but talons. Their heads, torsos and arms were human as were their hands. They had different coloring in their wings, from brown to dark grey. Some had brown hair, some red, and some blonde, but none black. None wore braids, as did Apollyon, but their hair was held in short ponytails at the base of their necks. None of the wings was black and silver as Apollyon's and none were as tall as he was. They needed no clothes because their feathers covered them.

These beings flew very fast and gracefully, which made you believe they spent the most of their lives in the air. Their singing was so perfect in pitch that you would also believe they were a classically trained choir, but their harmonies were melancholy, dark, deep, and in a minor or diminished key. Their music was lovely but grim and devoid of any joy.

These male singers did smile and appeared to be quite contented, which was very refreshing to me! Apollyon looked happy to see them arrive and smiled his broad, relishing smile as he motioned them toward us.

"Come, my comrades. How good it is to see you here! It has been much too long!"

The beings touched down, one by one, and greeted their master with a bow and a handshake and then moved aside. They each shared a few words with Apollyon and then stood in an open circle around him. He drew me hard and close to his side and said, "This, my friends, is the lady."

At this, they all bowed to me as if I was royalty. I felt very awkward and shy. He went on, "When the deed is done, she will be your queen. You are to obey her in all things as you would me. Do you understand?"

Each of the creatures replied in turn, "Yes, my lord."

"Good. It is well that we understand one another from the start. Introductions will begin right away. Please see Little Horn because he has refreshments for you." After this, he drew me hard and close to him again and said, "These are my knights in arms, very beings of my being. They are fine musicians as well, yes? However, they are warriors to the end. They will lay down their lives for me and now, for you. It is a great honor, Louisanna." Then he pulled me even harder toward him. "I do hope you understand me." Then he squeezed my arm until I whimpered in pain.

Then he changed and looked at me with a warm, calm and sweet expression in his eyes, and with my hands in his, he said, "You will know all their names in a very short time, and I will answer all the questions you have, for I am exceedingly anxious to tell you all these things." And then he kissed my hands. "There is but one thing left to do—just a small loose end to clear up just before we begin the final enactment. It is nothing for you to be concerned about. Fairy women are here, ready to bathe and dress you. They adore you, so there is no need to fear, my lady." Again, afloat in the sea of his eyes, I totally yielded.

43

Gaspar and his flying knights had flown ahead into the garden to aid in planning my rescue. They had been watching and had seen enough. The groups who were arriving gave Gaspar great pause. These souls were among those who were damned to Hades forever and were at the mercy of Apollyon. They stubbornly refused to ask forgiveness for hurting their fellow man, and therefore, had no advocate for them before God. Their fate was now sealed forever.

Satan would never tell me the truth about these poor souls. I had a heart that would make me naturally want to reach out to them. He knew that until I was completely his, I would feel this way.

It was not supposed to have happened this way. The child who was to come was to have had no faith, no commitments, and to be devoid of such sentiments. Apollyon hated every second he had to spend feigning love for me. His patience was growing short with it.

The fate of the damned made him glad, for he was surely their ruler now and forever. He could do with them as he pleased, and the display of this was keeping his spirits up. The Most High had delivered them into his dominion. Why should he not continue to torment them if he was so pleased?

He was tired of waiting and waiting for centuries. For hundreds upon hundreds of years he had been waiting for a human being to stumble into his world so he could seduce her to follow him into his new rule as savior as well as king of this kingdom. All would then look to him as even higher than the other one who had to die, for he would still be alive! There would be no cross for him—no suffering and shame. No pain for Apollyon. That was not his way! Not in the least! He would take it by force! But this young girl, this Louisanna, had been the one to come in. I was perfect—innocent and pliable, trusting, and easily frightened. There was also something sturdy about me that he both liked and feared. I knew of spiritual things and could argue quite well about them. Then there was Eli. Apollyon was certain now that Eli was a deeply spiritual man and his source of strength came from the Most High. This man loved me and I loved him. This was a problem. Apollyon did not like problems.

All the guests were assembled, and everything was in its place. He could wait no longer to hear from the hogule! He was beginning to look like a fool, putting things off as he was!

He had made up his mind. From the top of his lungs, he cried in a voice that sounded like a thundering waterfall, "Come, one and all. The time is soon. Gather around the tree, and soon you will see the salvation I bring to you all!"

44

Eli, Sol, Hogholke, and company listened as Gaspar reported to them all he and his knights had seen and heard in the garden. Sol commented that he had read of such beings in the Netherworld in old and long-destroyed poems. Hogholke testified that he knew Gaspar spoke the entire truth, for he had seen these people with his eyes. They were actual people indeed or once were. Hogholke and Gaspar were sure that I was about to be offered up as the sacrifice of Satan and that they should waste no time.

"What of a plan?" asked Gaspar.

"Well," boomed Hogholke, "it seems to me the best plan is to have Fawshyvon simply fly in and swoop her up and out of his grasp. It is simple as that, and he can be quick about it as well!"

"That does sound like a good enough plan, but I am afraid it will not work as simply as that. There are other factors involved," retorted Gaspar.

"And why will it not work? Of what particular factors do you speak, you pint-sized shimmer soldier? Are you the smart one, ah," barked Hogholke in reply.

"Who are you calling pint-si—"

Before the two could go at it again, Eli cut it off. He said to these two warriors, one gigantic and one smaller than small, both with hearts of champions, "Stop and listen to yourselves. I will say this again and again until you think in this manner. We are at war against powers and princes in high places—the netherworlds themselves. They want to prevent us from getting to Louisa, keep us from stopping Satan, and they want to create chaos and grumbling between us. We must have eyes to see this every day, especially today!"

Eli drew a deep breath and looked at the giant and the tiny warrior. "Do either of you have any more ideas? I really think we need a plan, and I trust you both." At this, Gaspar put his hand out to Hogholke. The hogule touched it in a gesture of camaraderie, and all was well again.

Gaspar offered, "Hogholke, your idea of using the dragon is good. Listen to what I have in mind to distract the others without the loss of life." The two warriors drew up a battle plan and had it approved by Sol, Eli, and Orla.

Orla said of them, "I never thought I would see the day when my brother would go into battle beside a Nephilim warrior. The Most High moves in ways that are not ours to reconcile and reclaim, does He not?" Her entire Faylinn hovered nearby listening and did not forget her words, for they were wise words and full of truth.

Gaspar called to Orla and her Faylinn Graces and his Royal Knights that the time had come to adorn battle armament and fly to the garden. They waited only for Sol's word. Even the Graces were dressed in fairy mail. It was, of course, beautiful and made of platinum and ivy. Their helmets were engraved with intertwined ivy and roses, and were topped with the infinity symbol. Gaspar's royal knights' helmets were identical except that they were topped by the cross itself.

"How will we travel the distance in time?" Anna asked.

"No problem my lady," the hogule answered. "Fawshyvon has a long wide back, and it is not as uncomfortable as it looks!"

"Gaspar, the time is now. Borneo," called Sol, "you cats and the dogs run like the wind to the middle of the garden and meet us there. Falcons! You do the same and take the toads on your wings."

"Oh no," cried Tobias.

"Oh, let's go, another adventure," said Churchill, pulling him up and hopping onto the back of the largest falcon.

They all set off at once, running and flying and waving, "For Louisa, to the garden!"

Suddenly, up from his perch came the dragon, and Hogholke cried out, "Hold tight onto your brother's hand!"

He jumped astride the dragon, and all the others followed in turn, Jepetto dangling from Anna's arm. They disappeared into the clouds.

45

There was a bumbling rumble of voices and sounds in the garden as Apollyon's many guests waited. There were casual conversations, there was coarse disagreement, and there were outbursts of rage, including biting, stinging, and clawing to the death.

This scene reminded me of the old Roman games with the gladiators, having two or more men in a ring, fighting to the death for the entertainment of others. Those who were not fighting were indeed enjoying watching it, especially Apollyon and his snake. They seemed to be the cheerleaders, as far as I could tell.

This chaos went on unabated while I was being dressed for my enactment of Apollyon's plan. As I made my entrance onto the scene, a man who had long ago lost the ability to see was groping around pitifully in an attempt to find another man, horribly thin and starving, holding a large piece of roasted meat and running from him. The man with the meat had no mouth and yet refused to give it to the other. The entire crowd, even those who ran with the meat, applauded, and cried, "More, more!"

Something stopped Apollyon. He saw me approaching. He bellowed out, "Quiet! All of you! She is here! Look to your new queen!" He waved in my direction.

All eyes—every single one of them—was on me. Apollyon came, nearly waltzing, toward me, and as he did, his demeanor changed before my eyes. Every bit of black in his wings turned to the deepest red in the world. The silver seemed to become more pronounced, and the stars and moons in his hair sparkled brighter. He grew at least a foot taller, and I saw his braids grow an inch or maybe two. His feet, which had always been human before, became large talons with pure white feathers. I looked to see his hands and they were human but covered with white feathers as well. His wings were clearly visible and ready to carry him at a moment's need. I saw that his wings had tripled. He was the most beautiful creature in the world, as far as I could tell. There was something different about his eyes, though. I couldn't tell what it was, but it frightened me.

As Apollyon came near, the ground on which I was standing began to rise up, little by little. I put my arms out to steady myself, and as I looked quickly at him, he shook his head yes to me. The ground finally stopped, and he was there at my side.

"Well, and how lovely you look, my lady," he said to me, looking me over. I felt very self-conscious and said, "Thank you." In these clothes I felt undressed. I had come to realize the purpose of the sheerness of the clothes was to make me look as if I had none on!

The dress was a flesh-colored silk with thin lace straps that crisscrossed in the back, making an X there. It was knee length and had lace around the hem. I had no shoes to wear and was told I was to become a queen in my bare feet. I had several thin chains of gold and silver to wear on my left ankle. The women had pulled my hair up as best they could and wrapped it in a ball on the top of my head. They set my crown there. Wisps of curls had fallen and were hanging loose around my neck and ears and on my forehead.

The crown was a living one, or once was. The women wove it from lavender, eucalyptus, rosemary, chamomile, and other herbs they use in their spell-making. The scent of it was nice but unpleasantly strong. Into the crown were woven tiny daisies the exact color of my hair with white centers.

Three of these women brought me a looking glass so I could see myself. When I did, I hardly recognized that it was me, Louisa. I looked older, more mature. Had my neck gotten longer, and was my chest beginning to grow buds? It made a shiver go up my spine, and I gasped with my hands over my mouth at the young woman I was becoming. Would Apollyon think I was beautiful? Did he really love me? As for me, now that he had seen me and told me I looked lovely, I was more certain than ever that he loved me!

"Here," he continued from where we stood on the rising ground, "take my hand. Do not hesitate to be proud of your beauty."

As we stood there on the raised ground, I thought Apollyon and his evil women, those fairies from Lee Annis's Faylinn who helped me dress, had cast a spell on me so that I would rapidly become a woman. They played at a game with me while I was being dressed. As I bathed in their herbal concoctions, they sang verses and had me repeat them. There were magical moves like dances I was told to do as I put on my dress. The women repeated the verses again as they put my hair up.

I could hear many other voices joining with them from places unseen. These sounds were grotesque and still very alluring to me. Now that the spell-casting was over, it was very unreal. It was as if it had never happened, and I imagined I had dreamed it.

I had been and was maturing into a young woman very rapidly. They had woven their spell so that my growth and age would stop at sixteen years old, the age of universal consent. Even Satan would not have the kingdom and world talking of him playing with and preying on the affections of a child. He would not have them *talking of it*. He had for a fact been doing this all along.

Apollyon knew I was no fool and knew he had been playing with my heart. So that I would never tell, he and his banshees had also wiped all remembrance of these things from my mind. All I could remember was that I loved and adored him above all others.

"The more beautiful you are, the more they all will love you!" He took my hand, and in a flash of a second we were on the other side of the crowd in front of the tree.

46

"I am the way the truth and the life.
No one comes to the Father but through me."

John: 14:6

Before the tree where we now stood were massive roots, spreading out for many feet beyond and around the tree. Grass and moss covered these roots and I discovered a Faylinn of fairies within and under these roots that only I knew were there. These fairies were terrified of Apollyon and were deep inside the hollow of the tree when we arrived on the scene.

Apollyon snapped his fingers, and the roots rose up, making two chairs that had the appearance of thrones. "Sit down, my lady, and listen to the stories of your soon-to-be subjects. It is important to know who you will rule."

Varta was beside me on my left, and our chairs were on a level with his back as he was sitting. He wore regal raiment. His jeweled head cover and Turkish tapestries with brass bells covered his huge back. On his ankles were his hammered brass and silver bracelets. Varta was magnificent and made me feel safe!

I took a seat in the chair-throne on the left. Apollyon stood and called out, "Quiet! And again I say, quiet! The time has come for each to tell the reason he must live as he does forever in his pitiful state. Remember when you tell your story to lay the blame where blame is due and not on me!"

All throughout the crowd was a murmuring and growling sound, and then all was still. "Quiet!" Apollyon demanded once more. He pointed to the group who had come in the wagons drawn by the sniveling boars and said, "Send up your spokesman! And do it at once!"

This group had apparently chosen a spokesman ahead of time, for one of the stick-like men who could actually sit and barely stand on his own came forth, leaning on a cane. He was so terribly thin that his body reminded me of a zipper, and under his slight overalls and shirt, every bone was visible. He leaned heavily on his cane as he spoke to me.

"My name was once John Carney. I was a strong and healthy man who raised many crops and stored them in my barns. My crops grew so well that I built barns and more barns to store them. My neighbor's crops failed. He needed food for many years. His wife and children eventually died of starvation. I kept all I had for fear that I might one day need it for myself. When I grew ill and died, the grain had rotted in my barns. I committed the sin of hoarding and wasting. I refused to repent by helping my fellow man who was in need. I refused forgiveness as well. Therefore, I must spend eternity like my comrades who have lived similarly. There is food enough for us and all around, yet we are either too heavy to get ourselves to it or too weak. We must live out eternity in constant hunger and are plagued by this insistent hunger and the attacks and stings of the wagnarts. I wish every day to be completely dead and at rest, but I will have to live this way for all eternity."

The man who had been John Carney had barely finished saying these words before his strength gave out and he collapsed. One of Apollyon's minions simply dragged him out of the way as he was still speaking. I wanted to ask him who sentenced him to this life in eternity, but it was too late. *How horribly sad,* I thought.

Without wasting a minute's time, another poor soul came out in front of me. I looked up again and saw there was another one. In the center of the circle stood what used to be a man and a woman. Neither of them had hair because it had been burned off of their heads. The remainder of each body was like leather, stretched over the bones in some parts and in other parts open and bleeding. This was the group who had been so wildly gesticulating at Apollyon. They had no mouths and a wild look in their eyes, as if they were in horrible pain. I could barely look at these two and said to Apollyon, "Please take them away. I don't want to even know this story. They are too pitiful for anyone to have to see. Can't you do something for them?"

He answered me, "I can do nothing for them, but you, my dear, will be able to relieve all their suffering when you become my queen. First you must know how and why they suffer. Do you not see that it is only logical?"

"How will I be able to do anything for them?" I retorted.

"When all it ready and the time is the time for you to eat from the tree, you will have all power. You must trust me, Louisanna. Do you really want to help them?"

"Go on with it. How will they tell me anything? The poor creatures have no mouths, for goodness sake. It is too sad!" I said, finally giving in.

Apollyon spoke to the two standing in the circle, "Remember what I have warned you of. Speak only of what is needed, or your pains will grow even worse." Both the man and the women shook their heads in understanding. As for me, I shook my head in disbelief!

Both the man and woman were trembling, and I could see that by some miracle, mouths were opening on their faces. They looked at one another, placing their hands over the mouths and touching them gently and with incredulity. Finally, in a voice that was as thin as a reed, the man began to speak.

"I had a good name in my former life. It was William Millstone. I was a representative for my government and sat on many councils and committees. I had a big happy family and was an honest and trustworthy citizen. I became tempted to rise in society and government by taking a little money here and there.. I succumbed and utterly misrepresented the honest people who had elected and trusted me. I grew rich and dishonest and was known as a scoundrel when I died. I am eternally burned alive and I am a fat man, eaten by the wagnarts, and must live in this pain and without a mouth never to lie, ask for help, or eat again."

Before this man's mouth closed, I asked him, "Mr. Millstone, can you tell me about the wagnarts? I mean, have they always been the way they are, or have they been mutated for some sort of punishment?"

Millstone looked quickly and sheepishly at Apollyon, who gave him a sharp, disgustedly approving nod to speak. The man said, "I hope you understand that I do not wish to speak badly about the wagnarts. They are creatures to be pitied as well as feared and are only surviving, as we all are. As I understand, they were a race of creature descended from many who were made mutant eons ago in the days when the Nephilim still had power in this world. They were originally bat-like creatures who lived in the Baneland Caves and had free range of the Elysian Fields. During the Great War between the Nephilim and the people of the Truthlands, the Nephilim used their dark powers to combine these bat-like creatures with wasps. The Nephilim trained them to attack and kill and used them as a part of their army to overthrow the people of Arielia, including our own mountain nymph army, when the war was won.

"The wagnarts are the descended from these creatures, and the propensity to kill is in their genes. They live for violence and killing and are very much to be feared. They attack and prey upon the extremely fat and thin because they cannot defend themselves and are an easy target."

"Thank you," I said. I had heard quite enough of a story like that!

Before I could recover from it, the woman began to tell her story. "Julianne Puette was my name before I died early in life from a fever. I was only twenty-one and was engaged to be married. My fiancé adored me and made me feel as if I was the most beautiful of all women in the world. He was a knight of the king's court. He gave me special gifts and dressed me in satin and silks, making me feel like a noblewoman. There was a meat cutter at the market who would talk a little sweet to me and I to him. It was only play.

"One day the meat cutter's wife gave me a jealous look and ugly words, and it made me angry—so angry that I never went to that cutter again. I told everyone I saw that his meats were often rancid and that he flirted with me and would put his hands on me and could not be trusted with women. The meat cutter lost all business because none of the women would go near him, and he was run out of town by husbands who feared for their wives. Some said he and his family starved; others said they caught the fever and died. I burn eternally for spreading lies against an honest person and have no mouth ever to tell another." As soon as she had finished her story, the woman's mouth disappeared, and the next thing I knew, she and the man were gone.

"Why do you continue with these shows? Why are you waiting?" I demanded from Apollyon. "I know there is a good reason you put this thing you want me to do off. What is it? Just tell me."

"And why are you concerned?" was his answer. "Are these stories not new and interesting enough to keep you entertained? What more could you desire while you wait?" he answered with his broad, toothy smile. I didn't say anything in response to him. I just gave him a half smile back and shrugged my shoulders.

"There now," he said and gave me a pat on my arm. "Let the presentations continue!" he commanded loudly.

As for me, I decided that he was waiting for his enemies who were my friends and rescuers to arrive. He was so sure of himself that he wanted the entire world to see what he would do. He took no precautions against it all blowing up in his face! He had ruled this upside down kingdom for so long he could not imagine anything else.

The person who came to the middle of the circle now was one who flew in from the sky so gracefully without wings, as if she was swimming in the air. This woman reminded me of Dulci or Elva, only of a normal size. She had very dainty features with a long, thin neck, a tiny, turned-up nose, and rosebud lips. Her chestnut hair was run through with golden lights, and she was dressed in flowing, fern green gossamer and silk. Her skin was as white as milk. Her eyes were green as green, and as rosy as her cheeks were, tears streamed down both of them. She stood before me with her hands out, as if she was begging something from me. I said to her, "What is it, and why are you crying? Are you in pain? Tell me, what is the matter?"

This woman explained her plight to me. "The others have told their names, but forgive me, I do not know mine. I have been this way so long that I cannot remember if I had a name at all. I do remember that I had a great love of all men and had many men friends. Some said too many. I was engaged to marry one of them but could not be faithful and so lost a husband and my good name. Now and for eternity I will never know love because of my lustfulness, but I am tempted every day. I and those like me can fly as if we are free, but we can never get close enough to touch one another. Never to be touched by another or to experience love again is our eternal fate."

I asked her, "Before you died, did you know your actions were wrong to God? And if so, did you ask for forgiveness?"

She said, "I did not know there was a god besides our master here, and forgiveness—I do not know what you mean."

"Thank you for telling your story and for being honest," I said to her.

Apollyon quickly piped up, "That is all, all! Get back to your place now!" He looked at me deviously and quickly looked away.

47

Never believe, my children, that the battle
is fought or even begun to be won in the field.
It is so in the hearts of each lover of the
One he goes in place of into the fight.
It is there, at that point, where all is lost or won.

I looked toward the woman who had just told her story of lustfulness and being tempted every day, and on the shoulder of one of the men not far from her, I saw what I thought was a giant monarch butterfly! *Could it be?* I thought.

I quietly touched Varta on his side and pointed in that direction. Varta saw and wiggled his ear meaning yes! *Yes!* I thought. *It won't be long now! Wormfly is the first sign.* I was so excited that I wanted to jump out of my seat and do a jig right there.

I was right. Wormfly, now Truluck, was the first of the company to arrive on the scene. Once he was sure Varta and I had seen him, he morphed into a centipede and began to crawl over toward us, hoping he would not be found out in the guise and could keep Varta at least apprised of the company's plans.

Apollyon still had me seated beside him in the strange tree-root chair thrones in front of the gigantic trees. The crowd had once again grown loud and chaotic. The entire assembled group was getting out of control, with the hogules shrieking and flying around those who had been burned, picking at their sores. These poor souls huddled together, wrapping their arms around their bodies for any possible protection.

The hoarders and wasters who were laying in their wagons, as well as the boars, were being fiercely attacked by the stinging and biting wagnarts at a nonstop pace. All control was lost, and Apollyon cried out in a thundering voice, "Enough and enough! This is your last chance to see the enactment! Knights, come forth!

Suddenly, out of nowhere Apollyon's knights in arms came flying. They stretched out their right arms to the wagnarts and the hogules. Nets of golden mesh drew them together tightly as they screamed and shrieked, but they could not get away. The two nets formed round balls, which hung in the air, one on each side of the circle. Apollyon's knights fired another substance into the mesh balls from their hands, paralyzing the belligerent creatures.

For one moment, all was quiet, and then a humming sound came from the mesh balls that grew louder until it became a dismal, melodic drone. This sound placated all the others in the circle so that control was restored and Apollyon's game could continue.

As for me, I was glad for the semblance of peace. I thought what the knights had done was pretty impressive! I wondered what it would be like to be inside one of the mesh balls.

As I was watching this take place, Truluck, now a centipede had crawled on his hundreds of legs over to us and was sitting on the arm of my tree throne. As a centipede, he blended into the chair itself. He was a handsome and quite large centipede, being dark green with orange spots in two rows down his back. I admired the navy blue lines going straight down between the orange spots and his bright red antennae. His hundreds of legs were black as black, as, of course, were his eyes.

As Apollyon was angrily scolding his minions and guests, as he called out to them, Truluck whispered to Varta and me, "The rescue party is on its way. The plan is to fly straight in. Louisa, you will be picked, or rather scooped up by a—"

"Louisanna, are you paying attention?" Apollyon cut Truluck off. "Your next group of guests is arriving. Use your manners and listen to them!"

I was so overwhelmed with all of the horror of these poor souls, what had happened to them, and the way they were forced to live that I didn't think I could take any more of it. In fact, I felt as if I might be sick if I had to see any more of them. I decided I would pretend to pay attention but tune it all out.

I really had to lie to Apollyon. "All right, I'm sorry. You know I will be nice and attentive. I'm ready." As this next group dragged themselves out, and one poor soul began to tell me his story of being a murderer and because of that, he now had no hands. I simply did the only thing I could do to survive. I completely tuned him out. I looked through him and not at him. I could not bear it.

Since I successfully tuned out the scene before me, and Apollyon continued to maintain control, Truluck, the master chameleon, crawled up my arm and was on my neck tickling me to death with his tiny legs. I was trying my best not to move or make a sound. Finally he stopped close to my ear and continued to tell me the company's plan to rescue me. He said that the dragon Fawshyvon would fly into the garden, swoop me up with his talons, and take me away. It would be as simple as that!

I hated to burst his big rescue plan, but I told him he had to think this through. Hadn't he just seen what those knights did to the hogules and wagnarts? Why should he not believe they could do the same to the fawshyvon or whatever dragon came their way?

"Truluck, you have been away from this master of yours too long. You no longer remember how powerful he is and how he controls all of his minions. They will fight to the death for him," I said desperately.

Truluck said to me in response, "Louisa, it is true that I have been away too long! You are absolutely right! I now know he is a liar. He lies to us and deceives us in everything he says and does. Louisa, he has had you in his grip and under his spell, so to speak, with no other influence. You have become blinded to the truth. I need to tell you what the one true Most High has done for—"

Apollyon grabbed my arm sharply and turned me to him. "You are not paying attention, Lousianna! What are you doing? Gazing dumbly into space? This is all for you, and here you are off in some dreamland! Tell me what that man has just said!" He commanded of me, and his eyes were red and burning. He was frightening me now. Loss of control made him very angry, and no one knew what he was capable of when he was angry.

I tried hard to give him an answer that would make sense and calm him down, "Apollyon, please forgive me. All of this is such a great honor to me, and it has been a very long performance. I am a little tired is all, really."

"What did the man say?" he asked again in an angry whisper as his grasp tightened on my arm.

"This man told us that he took another's life. He committed the offense of murder and therefore must go through eternity without hands," I said as he held his grip and pulled me up in my chair.

He continued to stare at me with his red eyes, and I dared not look away. "Good enough, and you had better be glad of it," he said and dropped me back down into my root-chair. He brushed himself off, as if he had been in contact with something filthy, took one more look at me, and said to himself, "Just in case."

At this, he waved his right hand toward me, and roots from the tree came looping up from the ground, twisting around my waist and chest and growing around me until I was a prisoner on my own throne. He never looked to see my response.

"Hey!" Truluck said to me in my right ear. "At least this is a good place for me to blend in!"

As for me, I said nothing to anyone. I was confused, hurt, angry, afraid, and crying. I would never let Apollyon know. The tears flowed down my cheeks from a stalwart face and eyes wide open. I could hear Truluck whispering to me in one ear and Apollyon threatening me in the other. The roots around my lap and chest were cutting into me and making it hard for me to breathe. There was yet another group of souls entering the circle, but I was unable to see what their condition was. Everything was getting blurry. All the voices, cries, and cheering sounded far away and blended together. Then there was darkness.

48

"Louisa? Louisa, can you hear me?" I heard a voice calling my name from a deep hole. I tried to open my eyes. "Louisanna, it is me, Eli. Can you hear me?"

Is that Eli? I thought. I tried again and opened my eyes. Everything was dimly lit, with candles all around. I was positive I was dreaming. I closed my eyes and began to doze off when Anna said, "Louisa, can you try to sit up, dear?" I recognized her voice right away. She was waving mild-smelling salts under my nose.

"Oh! Okay," I said and pushed myself up. "Where am I?"

Anna gave me a small hug, as if she was afraid she would frighten me, and then I saw Eli sitting next to me. I rubbed my eyes, grabbed his big neck, and hugged him as hard as I could.

"Whoa!" Eli said, laughing. "You have gotten a lot stronger, young lady. I am so glad to see you too. How are you feeling?"

"I feel fine—great, in fact. What happened? How did I get from the garden to here, and where are we?" I asked Eli a million questions, and he answered them all. I had fainted from lack of air from the tree roots binding me, and at that very minute, Eli, Sol, and Anna had flown in on the fawshyvon, led by Hogholke, and swooped me up, pulling my chair right out of the ground! Eli told me we were now inside the Tutor's Truth Passage in a dwelling space prepared for this purpose by Orla and her fairy magic.

I looked around to see beyond the candlelight. Anna smiled at me as she busily stirred a large pot of stew over the fire and worked with bread dough. Little Jepetto was doing his best to help her with kneading the loaves. The aroma of cooking was wonderful to my homesick nose.

I remembered that the Passage was all underground and inside mountains and had little to no natural light. This particular section of it must have had some light because there were mushrooms and moss on the ground and walls.

There was curious, lopsided furniture everywhere, including the bed I was on. All of it looked as if it had been through an earthquake, broken apart, and put back together with the wrong parts and colors. No one seemed to notice or care. I certainly didn't mind. It was funny looking and made me really smile for the first time since I could remember. The bed I was on and the chairs and tables didn't know there was gravity. Every now and then, one of them would just float up and then back down, taking you with it! The toads had an especially good time showing off the parlor tricks they had learned on the topsy-turvy furniture.

After we had finished our mushroom stew and bread, Eli went on to tell me that this place was a truth fortress, invisible and unknown to Satan and his minions. "Louisa, you are safe here," he told me when we were finally alone to talk. "My only concern is to get you home! Your safety is in my hands and—" I stopped him.

"Eli, do you know what Apollyon wants with me? Do you understand it completely?"

Eli looked at me, strangely worried, and said. "Louisa, I do not care what it is this evil being wants with you. It is beyond reason that you should even speak with him, let alone be in his presence! Stop thinking about whatever it is you have on your mind because you are going home!"

"Eli, do you trust me? I want to go home as much as you want to take me there, and I love you for coming to rescue me, but there is important work I have to do before I go."

Eli leaned back in his seat on the big sofa, took a long, deep breath, and said, "All right. You know I trust you. It is Apollyon I can never trust, and I know the deceit he has played with your heart and mind. What he wants is your soul. What is it that you believe he wants with you, and what is it you have to do?"

49

Dissention while waxing wild, Confusion
fuels the estranged who in common
Wait to torment and feed.

Back in the garden, everything was chaos. The fawshyvon had blown
fire at the mesh balls, partially burning up some of the wagnarts and
hogules. A large number of them who had escaped were hectically and
furiously flying, darting, shrieking, biting, and stinging each other and
tormenting Apollyon's guests.

Apollyon had suffered some severe injuries from being swooped up by
the fawshyvon, pummeled over the head and body by Hogholke's heavy
and well-sharpened mace, and dropped to the ground from a high altitude
into the top of a high and sharp mountain outside the garden.

Little Horn had seeing what was coming and in cowardice, slithered
deep into the brush, out of harm's way. He was lurking there for self-
preservation and had suffered no injuries, showing himself for the coward
he was. He saw Apollyon being taken away by the flying dragon but had
not seen or heard from him again.

Apollyon's knights had put up a good fight against the fawshyvon
and Hogholke and tried throwing their mesh balls on them and some
other tricks that failed as well. Injured from dragon stings, burns, and the
big hogules' plummeting, the knights were no match for Borneo and his
mate, Bella. The two of them tore three of the knights to bits and left three

others injured beyond the ability to fight any longer without Apollyon's evil magic to sustain them. The remaining knights flew after the dragon but were swept away in the wake of his wings as he disappeared above the clouds with me held tight in Eli's arms.

The remainder of Apollyon's injured comrades were left there to die. Those who were able fled in cowardice as Little Horn had done. Little Horn knew very well that in Apollyon's absence it was his responsibility to keep order and defend his master's regions and legions in his absence. In a situation such as this, it was his duty to go beyond defending. He should have called for more legions, and he knew this well. Instead, he had turned tail and run like a defeated dog.

Word spread rapidly of the absence of the master and the prey that lay undefended in the garden. Within hours, pests, wolves, bears, snakes, buzzards, giant lizards, hungry big cats, and all manner of mutated beasts and insects had descended upon all those gathered for Apollyon's plan for his queen that had failed to take place. The cries, screeches, howls, shrieks, and growls were heard for miles! It was truly every creature and man for himself. It was a defeat—not a good ending for the Star of the Morning.

50

I had fallen asleep in a great, huge, stuffed chair covered with patchworks of roses, rose buds, ivy, cantaloupes, and black olives. I had slept very well—so well, in fact, that I hardly remembered where I was when I woke up. Eli was stretched out on the sofa beside me, where we had talked long into the night. The air was damp, and there was a little chill about. Someone, probably Sol, had replaced the candles, and everything was glowing nicely. Across the way toward the kitchen area, Anna was near the roaring fire stirring her pot, as she always does. I could smell sausages and coffee and was immediately starving. It appeared that I was the only one awake besides Sol and Anna, so I drew a shawl around my shoulders and tiptoed over to Anna.

"Good morning," I whispered.

Anna turned from what she was doing and hugged me. It was then that we both noticed it—I in my voice and she when she saw my face. "Child, I know it is you! I saw this in a dream, Louisa!" Anna said stunned and smiling. "You are becoming a woman, my dear, and so quickly!"

"What is that, Anna? What's going on?" Anna stood there smiling with a good, steady look in her eyes that somehow made me feel secure. "Just take a deep breath, Louisa. This is to be. The Time is the Time. Think about it. You will know."

"Anna, I'm going over to that nook to think by myself for a while. I'll need—"

Anna said, "I will make sure you are not disturbed. You take all the time you need. Take this with you. It is the last one in existence and the only one you need." Anna handed me a leather-bound book that had been read so many times that it was dog-eared.

I read, I thought, I prayed, I listened, and the answer came at last. It took all day and all the next night. I knew I would need to return and face Apollyon. I knew that for some reason I had been chosen to do this—that it was no coincidence, that none of it had been.

Early that morning I rejoined the group who were all gathered around the large, round, blue-and-purple table having buns and coffee. Eli and Sol, being the gentleman they were, stood when they saw me walking toward them and pulled out a chair for me between them. Jepetto hopped over and hugged my neck, which triggered a ripple effect for the toads and everyone else in their turn. I stuffed myself with buns dripping with cinnamon and honey and downed two cups of Anna's steaming coffee before I could say a word.

There were playful jokes about my being all grown up from Churchill, which I took in good stride, but Tobias did scold him unmercifully. Everyone was in a good humor that I was back safely with them except for Eli, Sol, and Anna, who were aware that the danger was not over but had only begun.

After Anna and I, with the help of Jepetto and the toads, had cleaned things away after breakfast, Eli took us, along with Sol, to talk down into the nook where I had been. I took Eli's hand as we sat together on a rattan bench, as much to steady myself as to comfort him. Anna and Sol were sitting opposite us on a stuffed sofa covered in navy with white fish and circles. The candles flickered and gave a steady glow around us. It was with a heavy heart but a clear and certain mind that I told them what I had to do.

"You know we must go back to the garden and finish what was started. I am not ready. I must be prepared. To do that, I must go away on my own for a while to be with the Most High and gain the strength I need for what I will face. Apollyon, as I know him, is cunning and deceitful in all his ways, but the Most High is far more powerful. He created all things, including us in His image. He does not intend and never did intend this evil being to rule over all and run rampant as he has done in your kingdom. I know that it was no accident that I stumbled into your world. It was no accident whatsoever. Even if it was, the Most High wants to take that accident and use it for good. He has chosen me, and I don't know why. It doesn't matter. I must be faithful to that choosing. I will know where to go as the Tutor's Passage leads me and will stay as long as it takes. You should not worry about me because the Most High will be with me to guide and protect me, and he will lead me back to you. I hope you understand and will allow me to go freely." I looked from one face to another to see their reactions, almost afraid of what they might be.

Sol and Anna were holding hands and looking at each other. Eli, who had been on the edge of his seat, finally laid back against the back of the rattan sofa, smiled, and shook his head gently in approval. Sol looked to Eli, and Eli said, "She is wise beyond her years. She has grown in spirit as well. Those called for the most important work in history have always taken this path. I don't believe we have authority to oppose her. I certainly do not have the heart."

This made me so happy that I jumped up like a little girl and hugged Eli very tight. "Thank you, Eli. Not for permission—for that is not it—but for believing in me and supporting me in this, the most worthy thing I will do in my life."

I looked again at Sol and Anna. They were standing now with their arms outstretched to me. I knew their feelings by the look of the smiles on their faces and Anna's tears.

"We love you so much, child," Anna said. "Your safety and well-being have somehow been entrusted to us. That is our part—to watch and pray and to stand in the gap for you when you are doing your important work. You can count on us to always do that, for we are a faithful sort."

"I know," I sniffled. "I have come to look to you almost as grandparents and as much more than friends! Knowing you are at watch for me will allow me to rest and reflect."

Anna asked, "Do you men mind if Louisa and I have a moment alone?"

"Not in the least," Eli said.

"Let's go find our pipes, Eli," said Sol as they ventured out of the nook toward the others.

Anna and I sat down on the sofa that had now changed its cover to green and pink carnations with intertwined ivy and purple irises. "What is it, Anna? Are you still worried?" I asked her.

"It is not that, child. There is One in this kingdom whose name is unspoken, for it is said to speak his name is to turn to stone. It is said that the one you call Apollyon commanded the curse. Before the evil one took total control, this One was like a priest to all our people. In his presence there was truth and goodness. I could not see his face, but I know he is able and he is good. I also know he is powerful against his enemies and is to be feared."

"Is this being a man, Anna, and why are you telling me about him now?" I asked, curious about this One she named, but not understanding Anna's concern.

She continued, "In my visions, he is there with you where you are going. That is all I know because I could not see his body; I could only sense his presence. It is said that he is a man but much more. Be watchful and aware. I also know that if Sol knew this, he would tell it all to Eli and they would have second thoughts about letting you go alone."

"Thank you, Anna," I said. "I have been blessed with many helpers, including you. I am grateful for you and your gifts, which have guided me along my way. I am not afraid. Please be sure of that. Besides, I don't know this One's name so I have no chance of turning to stone."

Anna looked at me, smiled her lovely smile, and said, "Well put. Come, we must get a few simple things together for your pack. Not much, but I know what you will need." I knew she spoke the truth and followed her to her rooms.

Epilogue

First comes the physical and then the spiritual.
This is the way it has always been.
The Most High knows that is how we come to understand His ways.

The Powers and Principalities in the Heavens had been watching this game Apollyon played with me and their forces were at work. I was correct in believing that it was no accident that I had made my way into the Lopsided Kingdom-it had been ordained. Act I was over and there were songs of thanksgiving being sung in Heaven for my safe escape.

The forces of Darkness were gathering as well. Apollyon had many friends who were planning with him for Act II for he knew it would come. Accomplices of his ruled any and every region into which it was feasible I might venture. The dark forces were angry. Each one was waiting for me to set foot upon his or her soil, only to capture and torment me into submission. Not one of them would honor the promise to return me to Apollyon.

I had said goodbye to my friends with misgivings I dared not share. The first door that opened for me in the passage took me to a bright sunshiny day facing a large lawn. Straight ahead of me was a round green hill.

End